IDLE GOSSIP

Also by Renee Patrick

Lillian Frost and Edith Head mysteries

DESIGN FOR DYING
DANGEROUS TO KNOW
SCRIPT FOR SCANDAL *
THE SHARPEST NEEDLE *

* *available from Severn House*

IDLE GOSSIP

Renee Patrick

**SEVERN
HOUSE**

First world edition published in Great Britain and the USA in 2022
by Severn House, an imprint of Canongate Books Ltd,
14 High Street, Edinburgh EH1 1TE.

Trade paperback edition first published in Great Britain and the USA in 2022
by Severn House, an imprint of Canongate Books Ltd.

severnhouse.com

British Library Cataloguing-in-Publication Data
A CIP catalogue record for this title is available from the British Library.

ISBN-13: 978-0-7278-5049-2 (cased)
ISBN-13: 978-1-4483-0893-4 (trade paper)
ISBN-13: 978-1-4483-0894-1 (e-book)

This is a work of fiction. Names, characters, places and incidents
are either the product of the author's imagination or are used fictitiously.
Except where actual historical events and characters are being described
for the storyline of this novel, all situations in this publication are
fictitious and any resemblance to actual persons, living or dead,
business establishments, events or locales is purely coincidental.

All Severn House titles are printed on acid-free paper.

Typeset by Palimpsest Book Production Ltd.,
Falkirk, Stirlingshire, Scotland.
Printed and bound in Great Britain by
TJ Books, Padstow, Cornwall.

When you get hold of a stunt that sells papers, you don't drop it like a hot potato.

Barbara Stanwyck, *Meet John Doe*, 1940

CAST OF CHARACTERS

Lillian Frost – All it took to bring her from a cloistered life in Flushing, New York to a coveted social secretary post in Los Angeles was a beauty contest victory, a single terrible screen test, and solving a murder

Edith Head – Her many years at the Paramount Pictures Wardrobe Department have yielded another skill: spotting the loose threads that might unravel a crime

Lorna Whitcomb – Once called 'the nicest of all the Hollywood gossip columnists,' the faintest praise in the history of Southern California

Doctor Jerry Whitcomb – Lorna's faithful physician husband

Sam Simcoe – Lorna's leg man, who has lately stumbled into trouble

Glenn Hoyle – Deceased; the trouble into which Sam has stumbled

Vernon Reynolds – A force to be reckoned with in the days before talking pictures, forced to trade in his director's chair for the maître d' stand at Arturo's Ristorante

Delia Carson – America's singing and dancing sweetheart, determined to grow up whether America wants it or not

Rhoda Carson – Delia's domineering mother, who is beginning to regret taking her little girl to that first tap-dancing lesson

Arthur Davis – A background player in pictures who has stepped into the spotlight of Delia Carson's love life

Earl Lymangood – An aspiring producer, although exactly what he aspires to produce is an open question

Frederick 'Freddy' Sewell – Presently a gentleman of leisure and eternally a namedropper, as his former employer Alexander Korda would tell you

Count Oleg Cassini – Debonair man of the world whose flair for fashion and talent for tennis have netted him a position at Paramount Pictures, much to Edith's regret

Detective Gene Morrow – The man who released Lillian's heart on its own recognizance

Addison Rice – Lillian's employer; richer than Croesus and mad about the movies

Katherine 'Kay' Dambach – A columnist on the rise who has let her friendship with Lillian fall

Hank 'Ready' Blaylock – Western stunt rider extraordinaire, and Kay's exclusive escort to events of import

Violet 'Vi' Webb – Skilled songstress always ready to sing her pal Lillian's praises

Detective Roy Hansen – Gene Morrow's partner; a man of few words and fewer scruples

Florabel Muir – A canny newspaperwoman who brings New York brio to her coverage of Los Angeles

Barney Groff – Paramount's problem solver supreme; trouble is, he regards Lillian as a problem

Wiard 'Bill' Ihnen – An accomplished art director and Edith's most trusted confidante

Mrs Quigley – Lillian's landlady, when the poor dear remembers to collect the rent

Brenda Baines – One of Paramount's prized starlets, and a good friend to Lillian

Plus assorted cameos, walk-ons, and special guest appearances not to be spoiled here.

NET TIGHTENS IN HOYLE MURDER CASE

Focus Remains on Gossip Column 'Leg Man'

Los Angeles, Aug. 13 (AP) While no arrest has been made in the August 9 murder of Glenn Hoyle, sources within the Los Angeles Police Department indicate that the investigation continues to center on Samuel Simcoe, 'leg man' for renowned columnist Lorna Whitcomb.

Simcoe, age 32, was seen leaving the Hollywood home of the 26-year-old Hoyle on the night in question. Officers entered Hoyle's residence to find him dead of a blow to the head. Questioned extensively by LAPD homicide detectives, Simcoe has claimed he discovered the body and was on his way to inform the police.

Throughout the investigation Mrs Whitcomb, whose 'Eyes on Hollywood' column is syndicated in newspapers coast to coast, has vigorously defended her employee in print.

ONE

C ary Grant gave me the eye from my right, but I leaned toward William Powell. Not because of the actor's considerable charms, but the sag in the sofa. The springs had shuffled off their mortal coils, the couch pulling in unsuspecting victims like quicksand. Edith Head and I both had the misfortune of sitting on it, and we were forced to prop each other up like orphans in a storm.

The shabby settee was in keeping with the rest of the room's décor. A radiator molting paint sizzled and sighed but mercifully didn't give off any heat. The lamp next to it hung its head in shame. A desk – so large it should have been surrounded by generals pushing toy soldiers around with sticks – occupied most of the remaining space, its surface littered with scrapbooks, newspapers, stacks of correspondence, three tubes of lipstick, and a brown pump with a broken heel.

On the back of the office door hung a black silk gown, a gold-fringed belt draping from waist to knee serving as an elegant grace note. The woman who would later be wearing the dress stood behind the desk, currently clad in a light gray suit and red blouse. The shell frames of her signature spectacles matched the blouse's shade exactly. She undoubtedly had a second pair of eyeglasses on hand, coordinated to complement her evening attire.

Lorna Whitcomb nodded at the gown. 'Feel free to weigh in on my wardrobe, Edith. Expert advice always welcome. It's been ages since I've seen you. Why aren't you ever out and about?'

'That's what I always ask her,' I said, shoehorning my way into the conversation. I hadn't uttered a word since my 'Good morning' to Lorna five minutes earlier. I'd met the gossip columnist before, thanks to my position as social secretary to retired industrialist and movie maven Addison Rice. Lorna was a fixture at his many parties, where my duties included making sure her drinks were always topped off while any drunks were steered away. Our exchanges at these functions were perfunctory and professional, Lorna casting her eyes over me as if I were one of the dilapidated pieces of furniture in her office.

Edith smiled thinly. 'Running a costume department isn't a job that allows for much of a social life.'

Cary Grant raised an eyebrow. Or perhaps I'd imagined it. The room was stuffy, the single window looking down on the intersection of Hollywood and Vine painted shut. Every other square inch of wall had been papered over with photographs of silver screen stars. Not just Cary and Bill, but any luminary I could care to name. Robert Taylor, Tyrone Power. What's more, every last photo had been personally inscribed to Lorna. *Thanks for being in my corner*, Clark Gable had scribbled.

'You're not doing yourself any favors, shackled to your sketch pad. You're an executive. Toot your horn, make your presence felt.' Lorna peered down at us as she prowled behind her desk. The angle wasn't flattering, exposing the fleshiness of her nose, the incipient jowls at her jawline. But it allowed her to flaunt her trim shape and particularly the chorus girl gams she'd managed to preserve during her near-decade as a chronicler of Hollywood happenings; only her face and her thinning black hair, most of it tucked under a Tyrolean-style hat festooned with feathers, hinted at her age, in the vicinity of Edith's forty-something years.

'Learn to delegate. That's what successful types do,' she continued imperiously. 'After all, you're running the show over there now. Must have been a relief to have Travis Banton out of the way at last.'

'Travis was never in the way,' Edith said. 'I learned so much from him. I was sorry to see him go.'

'Point being he's gone. You made an impression back when I was at Paramount, deluding myself that I could be an actress. Quiet, industrious, always making plans. Banton may have been the bigwig, but you were the power behind the throne. And now you're sitting on it.' Lorna's distant smile sharpened into a smirk. 'The trick will be keeping it.'

With a start, I realized my leg had fallen asleep. I hoisted myself from the sofa in as gainly a fashion as I could. Lorna glared at me. The down-at-heel davenport, I now understood, was a ploy, a means of placing visitors immediately in her thrall. My standing up had thrown her off her game, especially because I had a few inches on her.

'Paramount had no clue what to do with me,' she said. 'I don't even like mentioning the few pictures you dressed me in. As if anyone could ever spot me in them. Lounging in the background of *Gentlemen Prefer Blondes*.'

'You lounged very well, as I recall.' Edith spoke with the enthusiasm of a teacher awarding a medal for perfect attendance.

'Never be purely decorative. At least I had the honor of appearing in one of your first credits. *Ladies of the Mob*.'

'Clara Bow was wonderful in that. Her best performance.'

'You and Clara were thick as thieves then. Poor Crisis-a-Day Clara. Says she's happy being a farmer's wife now, but who can believe that? And I remember Pola Negri in the commissary, asking for scrambled eggs and no one understanding that accent of hers. She's back, you know. Ended her European sojourn and is making noise about returning to pictures here.'

In the outer office, a telephone trilled, followed by a second one at a more insistent pitch. Phones had been ringing the entire time we'd been sequestered with Lorna, a never-ending chorus of bells. Charles Boyer eyed me seductively from the wall. Every face on display was male, save for Lorna's own. I spied a photo of her on the arm of Fred Astaire, and a caricature highlighting her eyeglasses and her dancer's legs. No Hepburn, no Lombard, nary an actress in sight. Only the most famous men in the world could join Lorna in her private chamber.

I turned to find her glowering at me, as if she'd sensed my thoughts. I shivered in my short-sleeved dress of marine blue. The two embroidered daisies on the buckle of the belt cinching it looked fresher than I felt in the stagnant air.

Edith, crisp as usual in a black-and-white striped shirtwaist dress buttoned down the front, seized the opportunity to stand up. She winced briefly in discomfort. 'Much as I'd love to reminisce, Lorna, I can't help wondering why you summoned us here today.'

Lorna gazed balefully at the sofa, her secret weapon having failed her. 'Summoned? Hardly. It was a friendly invitation.'

The kind sent by firing squads, I thought.

'And you know perfectly well why,' Lorna continued. 'You've seen the papers. I'm in the soup. Or my leg man Sam is, so I'm drowning, too. Did you see Hedda's column this morning? The second time this week she's needled me. And Jimmie Fidler has been positively murderous.'

Hardly a felicitous word choice. 'What is a leg man, exactly?' I asked.

'Just what you think it is, dearie. He legs out what I need. Tips, information, confirmation. Ideally, you want people to come to you. Sometimes, you go to them. On occasion, you send someone else. Someone you can trust. That's Sam. He's the best in the business, with me for five years. The column wouldn't be what it is without him. But now he's in trouble. He's the primary – hell, the *only* suspect in the murder of that Hoyle fellow. The whole town smells the blood in the water. Mine.'

Sam's blood didn't count for as much, I supposed, and glanced at Edith. She wore a pained expression. She didn't want to be here, and neither did I. 'I've been following the story. It's most unfortunate. But what do you want us to do about it?'

'I should think that was obvious. I want you two to clear Sam.'

It was indeed obvious, and Edith and I had acknowledged as much when we met outside the building housing Lorna's office.

'I'm afraid we don't know what you mean,' Edith said.

'Don't play coy, Edith. If you could act, Paramount would have signed you to do that.' Lorna stared down through her eyeglasses at Edith, who gazed placidly back through hers, each woman utilizing her spectacles to a different strategic end: Edith to appear enigmatic, Lorna to accentuate her most fearsome feature. I turned toward Groucho Marx, who naturally was sporting cheaters, too. *Dear Louella*, he'd scrawled on his photograph, *I like you a lot more than that Lorna Whitcomb. Love and kisses, Groucho*. Lorna apparently possessed a sense of humor about herself, even if it wasn't in evidence at the moment.

'The pair of you have worked up quite the double act. I've heard the stories. Even told a few, only not in my column. Some details are better kept hidden.' She winked. 'Looking at it that way, you both owe me a favor. I'm calling in the marker. I want you to get Sam off the hook and spare me a lot of heartache.'

'We're not about to interfere in an active police investigation,' Edith said.

Lorna flapped her hand. 'Active, nonsense. They've made up their minds. They're railroading Sam.'

'Railroading?' I snapped. 'That's hard to believe.'

'Why, sweetie? Because your boyfriend is on the force? I'll have my girl fetch some java to wake you up. The fix is in. They're dragging this out to keep my name in the papers, spatter it with mud. They want to lay me low.'

Little surprise Lorna had done her homework. She'd unearthed that Edith and I had found ourselves embroiled in the odd homicide case, and that Detective Gene Morrow and I had kept steady company for a time. What's more, she'd intended to blindside us with her wealth of knowledge.

I wasn't having any of it.

'Who's they?' I asked, coating each syllable in disdain.

'The powers that be in this city. You can't do this job without making enemies. Mine intend to make an example of me.' A full stop followed; clearly, these dastardly foes were to remain nameless.

Edith charged into the dramatic pause. 'Surely the police are interested in your associate Mr Simcoe because he was at the crime scene.'

'For good reason. Sam and this Hoyle fellow— talk to Sam, he'll explain it. The LAPD is using poor Sam to make life difficult for me. Somebody has to concentrate on the truth and help him.'

Edith set her jaw, decision made. 'There are agencies for hire, reputable ones—'

'Of course I've thought of that. Even the best of them don't understand the Hollywood balancing act. Who to talk to, what to keep quiet. But you, Edith, know it instinctively.'

I, apparently, had been relegated to the status of chopped liver. I remedied that by asking a hard question as simply as I could. 'Why should we help you? What's in it for us?'

Lorna whipped around to face me, red eyeglasses flashing like flames. 'An innocent man victimized solely because he works for me, and you don't want to help?'

'It's not our responsibility. All the police have done is question him, according to the newspapers. If they arrest him—'

'It will be too late then. "Lorna's Leg Man Lands in Clink".' Her hands laid out the damning headline in midair. 'The stain will be permanent. Every untrue word against Sam is a dig at me. Two lives ruined, while a third person lies dead. A tragedy, that's what this is. David O. Selznick would snap up a story like this. Meanwhile, you debate whether to lift a finger.'

Edith folded her arms. I knew what that meant. 'I'm sure the scenario you fear won't come to pass.'

'I guarantee it won't,' I added.

'I hope you ladies are right. I couldn't live with myself if it did.' Lorna removed her glasses and inspected the lenses carefully. 'I'd have to continue to work, even without Sam. There's always a column to write. My judgment would likely be impaired under the circumstances. I would hate for that to happen while I was jotting down my impressions of every Paramount picture, right down to their costumes. Or my thoughts on Addison Rice's parties.' She shook her head sadly, shoulders sagging. Aside from that, she maintained her perfect posture.

I understood why Paramount Pictures had cut Lorna loose all those years ago. Careers could not be built on performances so clumsy. She would use her position to strike back at us if we didn't rally to her aid, issuing the threat in the most obvious manner. Although to be fair, Lorna probably didn't have much practice when it came to making demands. A nationwide column usually provided all the persuasion that was necessary.

Still shaking her head, Lorna stepped out from behind her desk. I, in turn, swung behind it to keep my distance, a celestial object on a parallel orbit. From this new vantage point, I twigged what other aspect of the office had struck me as wrong. Lorna's desk was not set up for writing. A pad of paper had been tossed amidst the newspapers and lipsticks, but there was nowhere to spread out and tackle the task at hand. Thanks to an upbringing at the hands of relatives affiliated with show business, I had arrived in Hollywood five years earlier aware of the effort required to sustain the illusion of glamour. Making movies, I knew, took toil and strain. I looked around this seedy space, stunned that a column I read religiously could emanate from within these walls. But then I wasn't in Lorna's office. This was her dressing room, where she prepared for her performance. I was backstage, the curtain yet to go up.

The telephones in the outer office rang. They had never stopped.

Edith cleared her throat. 'The young man is here, you said. I suppose it wouldn't hurt to have a word with him.'

TWO

E very desk in Lorna's office suite bore at least two telephones, so many ringing simultaneously that they seemed to be playing an arrangement of 'Frenesi' by Artie Shaw. Many of the calls were fielded by a secretary who sat perpetually hunched over, snatching up one receiver after another. 'She'll get a hump on her back, the poor creature,' I could hear my uncle Danny saying with sympathy.

Lorna escorted us to two desks facing away from each other, as if their occupants weren't on speaking terms. In truth, the duo gleefully swapped gibes over their shoulders.

The man seated on the left had a boyish countenance and a

slight stature; those elements, combined with his dark suit and bowtie, gave him the appearance of an overgrown ventriloquist's dummy – Charlie McCarthy with a day job. He'd styled his dark hair in a wave that gave him an extra inch of height, and bolstered his presence with a pronounced sense of flair. His tie was a jaunty scarlet, the color picked up by his cufflinks.

'Meet Sam Simcoe,' Lorna announced. He barked 'Gotta go' into a phone and swung toward us in his chair, dragging a matchstick as he moved. He had affixed a striker strip to his desktop so, as he faced us, he brought a bloom of flame to the tip of his waiting cigarette.

Lorna gestured at the woman with her back to his, her fingers flying across a typewriter keyboard. I feared her hair would become snarled in the type hammers, but she flicked her head back with practiced ease. 'Mildred and I have to tidy up the column,' Lorna said, 'so take over my office.'

'No thank you,' Sam said. 'One, you're going to need my help and I don't want you yelling in at me every five minutes. Two, I hate spending time amidst your relics.' To Edith and me, he said, 'Make yourselves uncomfortable on that sofa of hers?'

'It's the first piece of furniture I bought when I came out here. That lamp I brought all the way from Indiana. Your ride in this business could end any time, kids, and when mine finishes I'm at least going to leave with what I started with.' Sam and Mildred mouthed the final words of this litany along with Lorna, having heard it many times before. 'All right, Mildred, where were we?'

Sam gestured to a pair of chairs as he puffed away furiously. 'Did Lorna do me justice? Introduce me as nature's true innocent man? Bringing you in was my brainwave, you know.'

'Yours?' Edith said.

'I need all the help I can get. I've heard about your antics. It's an open secret, what you two get up to.'

'For what it's worth,' I said, 'I thought you were a fictional character.'

Sam occasionally cameoed in Lorna's column – 'Friend Simcoe says critics may carp, but the laffs are long and loud in *At the Circus*' – alongside her medico husband, referred to affectionately as Dr Jerry, and Hildy the Hairdresser, who proffered her opinion on every picture.

'My claim to fame. If only the boys back at Warners could see me now. Of course, they do. I pester them every damn day.'

'Is that where you worked before?' Edith asked.

'Publicity flack. I got tired of inventing stories about Joe E. Brown and pitched my tent here in '35. Became instantly indispensable to the organization. Isn't that so, Lorna?'

'Lies, all of it.' Lorna tapped a notepad on Mildred's desk. 'Scrap this Orson Welles item. We've had our fill of him this week.'

'Bad idea, boss.' Sam didn't turn around, firing his words into the ether. 'Welles makes good copy. And he's taken a shine to you, for some reason.'

'It's because I went to that ghastly party at RKO the day he finally started work on his picture. Everyone else gave him the brush in favor of the Gable premiere. Golden boy damn near talked my ear off.'

Mildred weighed in. 'I'm with Sam. I say keep it.'

Edith, growing flustered, leaned toward Sam. 'Might we speak about the incident that has you concerned? The young man who was killed—'

'Two Ns.'

Edith blinked several times. 'I beg your pardon?'

'Glenn Hoyle. That's how he'd introduce himself. "Glenn, two Ns." Always spelled his name because he said people would want to remember it.'

'How did you know him, exactly?'

'He was a tipster. One of my best. He kicked around town, working various jobs. Whenever he heard something juicy, he'd pass it along. It often proved out, so we stayed in touch. I cultivated him, you could say.'

'Sure you could,' Mildred cracked. 'Sam spit nails whenever anyone else took his calls.'

'Did Mr Hoyle ever come to the office?'

Sam reared back in mock surprise. 'We can't have our reliable sources seen here. That'd be bad for business. Lorna never clapped eyes on the kid.'

'It's true,' Lorna called.

'It got so we became sort of close.' For the first time, Sam's bravado buckled. He cast his eyes down at his two-tone brown wingtips. 'Two Ns had aspirations. Wanted to be a leg man himself.'

'Which the police have made hay with,' Lorna said. 'They say it goes to motive. Say Sam saw the boy as a threat.'

'Did you?' I asked.

'Like hell. Glenn was still wet behind the ears. But I could always count on him for a lead or two when we had to fill out Lorna's column. Truth is, the kid was a sponge, always picking my brain. I found it a little flattering, having a protégé. I miss the squirt.'

'Even though he was after your job,' Lorna said.

'He wasn't about to stop there. He was gunning for your spot, too, sweetheart. Had the name for his own column ready to go. "According to Hoyle".'

'Like the card games expert,' Mildred said. 'Not bad.'

Edith took the reins of the conversation again. 'How did Mr Hoyle acquire the information he gave to you?'

'He came from a show-business family. His old man had been a magician in vaudeville. Glenn was even part of the act for a spell. So he had connections that way. But mainly . . .' Sam flashed a cockeyed grin. 'He picked up a few bucks working as a bookie. He had ins at some of the studios and heard a lot of scuttlebutt that way. Bookies are like bartenders and priests. Everyone shares their troubles with them.'

'And he shared them with you,' I said.

The receptionist leaned around the scrollwork divider separating her desk from the others. 'Your man at Columbia's on the horn, Sam. He says Harry Cohn's on the warpath again.'

'When is Cohn *not* on the warpath? That would be newsworthy. Tell him I'll call back. I'm fighting for my life here.'

'About the night in question,' Edith pressed.

'Right. I—'

'You'd better call your man back,' Lorna interrupted. 'I could use an item on Columbia. We've been light on them lately.'

'Coming, Mother.' Sam rolled his eyes. 'If I was in Glenn's neighborhood when I was doing the rounds, I'd drop by. That's what I did last week, even though it was late. His door was ajar. Figured he'd ducked out for a minute, so I stepped inside. I'd about made it to his couch when I saw him. Poor Two Ns, lying on the floor. At that point, I beat a hasty retreat.'

'You didn't call the police,' I said.

Sam flushed, his face almost as red as his bowtie. 'I was going to. At the appropriate time.'

Edith sat back primly in her chair. Or perhaps her spine still ached from Lorna's treacherous sofa. 'And what time would be appropriate, Mr Simcoe?'

Sam shrank to an even smaller size. 'After I called Lorna to see if Two Ns's passing rated a tumble in the column.'

'It didn't, incidentally,' Lorna added.

'Last I heard, it wasn't against the law for a fellow to know on what side his bread is buttered. I know it looks bad, but I swear I was going to call them. From a safe distance.' He took a long, deliberate drag on his cigarette, as if it had been prescribed by his physician. 'Truth was, after finding Glenn like that I needed to get out of there.'

Having been in a similar situation myself once or twice, I wasn't about to pass judgment on him.

'Trouble was the neighbor,' Sam continued. 'Glenn lived in one of those bungalow courts. Fellow along the way popped out and asked the back of me if Glenn was home. I made like I hadn't heard him and continued to the street. I've seen enough of those *Crime Does Not Pay* shorts that MGM cranks out to know you don't want to monkey with any potential evidence, so I left Glenn's door open, the way I'd found it. Which meant the neighbor was about to find Glenn himself. I reached my car, and lo and behold there's a harness bull ambling up the block. So much for my quick getaway. I hotfooted it back to Glenn's in time to see the neighbor barreling out.'

'At which point he summoned the police officer?' Edith asked.

'We both did. The neighbor starts in about how I tore out of there like I'd done something. I said I was in shock, wanted to find a pay telephone. Both statements true, by the by, but now I'm in a bad light from the outset. The cop herds me back into Glenn's place. Exactly where I wanted to be.' He shuddered. 'Fortunately, a squad car came along and delivered me to a detective for the first of several far-ranging interviews. They've been hounding me ever since. Tying up the phone lines here at the office. Which doesn't help, considering the LAPD knows next to nothing about the doings of the Bennett sisters. It's imminent.'

Edith peered at him. 'I'm sorry? What is imminent?'

Sam spun in his chair toward Lorna and Mildred. 'Read that last item again.'

Mildred scanned the paper in her typewriter. '"Speaking of comebacks, expect the eminent arrival of longhorn congressman Martin Dies, on the trail of fifth columnists in our airplane factories. Here's wishing him better luck than his last trip west, when his committee heard testimony branding little Shirley Temple a raging radical."'

'I was right,' Sam crowed. 'You mean imminent, not eminent.'

Lorna squinted at the sheet through her specs. 'That doesn't sound right.'

'Nevertheless, it is. The eminent man is expected imminently.'

'He's not eminent if he thought Shirley was a Red. I wouldn't believe she had a wagon that color. It still sounds wrong to me.'

'Word of advice, boss. If you have to check with someone else, maybe don't use the word.'

Mildred began throwing out alternatives, which Sam summarily rejected. Edith glanced at me, her exasperation mounting. I nodded, and we both rose to our feet.

'I think we'll take our leave,' Edith announced. 'You're clearly busy and, at this stage, there's little Lillian and I can do for your cause.'

'But you can't.' Sam's voice cracked on the last syllable. Despite the cigarette, he looked like a frightened boy. He made eye contact with Lorna.

'Tell them, Sam. The whole story. It's why we asked them here, after all.'

He fidgeted and eyed the striker strip on his desk with longing, already craving another smoke. 'I told you the cop sent me back into Glenn's place. I was nervous, as you might expect, and I didn't want to look at Glenn. I lit a cigarette and walked around, keeping my eyes elsewhere. I happened to glance in the wastebasket and I . . . I found something.'

He paused, and the phone rang. But then the phone was always ringing. The secretary looked in at us, read the atmosphere, and took a message.

'It was a sheet of paper.' Sam kept his voice low. 'Glenn always carried these notebooks around. He kept track of his tips for us in them. He'd shown them to me plenty of times. The paper was torn out of one of those notebooks. He'd folded it in half, dropped it in the trash. It had started to unfold in the wastebasket. I'm nosy. It's what I'm paid for. I tossed my match in next to it as an excuse to open it completely and recognized Glenn's handwriting. I'd seen it enough to know. By now the bull's fed up with me, tells me to sit down. But I'd seen all I needed to see.'

Edith asked the question. 'What was written on this paper?'

'A list. Of three names.' He pulled a sheet of paper out of his desk drawer and handed it to me. 'You'll want to jot these down yourself. Number one, Delia Carson.'

'The actress?' I asked.

'I wouldn't go that far,' Sam said.

'Songbird, maybe,' Mildred suggested.

'Canary's better. But yes, Lodestar Pictures's lovely little ingenue, their spick-and-span answer to Deanna Durbin. Only how spick and how span? Number two, Earl Lymangood. I don't expect you to recognize him. A Poverty Row producer so obscure I had to telephone a pal at the *Hollywood Reporter* to dig through the files and tell me who he was. Last, and who knows if he's least, Vernon Reynolds.'

'I know that name,' Edith said. 'He's a director.'

'Not to correct you, but he *was* a director. Made his last picture before sound came in. These days you can find him maître d'ing at Arturo's, a spaghetti joint off Sunset. A little truffle of information he doesn't exactly advertise, so believe you me it took some digging to unearth it.'

'I had no idea,' Edith said. 'As I recall, he was a talented craftsman.'

'You're one of the few who do recall him.' Lorna tapped something that Mildred had typed and shook her head wearily.

'And this list means what, exactly?' A practiced ear could detect the doubt in Edith's voice.

'Glenn had dirt on these people.' Sam stated this as if it were incontrovertible fact. 'He'd never breathed a word about any of them to me before. But he'd hinted about a big story he was cooking up for me. It's why I'd stopped by. We needed material for the column.'

'The column was solid that day,' Lorna snapped.

I didn't wait for Edith to speak up. My resentment boiled over. We'd been here long enough. 'That seems awfully thin.'

'I know, but hear me out. Glenn tried to hide this information.'

'How do you know that?'

'Because there was no notebook in Glenn's place.' Sam jabbed a finger conclusively down on his desk. I wondered if he'd also picked up that move from a *Crime Does Not Pay* film. 'Not that I could see before the bull ordered me to sit down, anyway. And Glenn was never without one. So where did it go? His killer took it. That's what his killer came there for. Glenn figured that out, tore out the telltale page, and dropped it in the trash. But that didn't save him. He had something on one of those people and, whatever it was, it got him killed.'

I must have looked dubious, because Sam began pleading. 'You weren't there. That piece of paper was on top of the garbage. It was the last thing Glenn had thrown out. And that may have been the last thing he ever did. I don't want to tell you how to do your job, but that seems significant to me.'

Before I could point out that this actually *wasn't* our job, Edith spoke up. 'Surely the police have this information.'

'Yes, because I told them. I pointed it out to the cop who pushed me around. Then to the detective who questioned me, name of Horvath. Could mean something, I said. I asked my contacts at the department. They found no notebook on Glenn's person. But Horvath doesn't care. Instead he keeps calling here or hauling me downtown, asking how well I knew Glenn. Did he angle for my job, did he feed tips to Lorna regularly? We had a nickname for him! Of course he was a regular!' He stabbed out his cigarette in a frenzy of frustration.

I gave him a moment to settle down. 'Then the police are investigating these names.'

'Far from it.' Lorna launched herself out of her seat and began to stride around the room, fueled by indignation. 'If the police had questioned Delia Carson, I would have heard about it. Sam hands them a choice lead – the final act of a dead man, possibly even the name of his killer – and their response is to badger him. I won't stand for it. If they won't look into these names, you two can. I can't do it. If any of these people catch wind of me snooping around their histories, they'll think I'm after material for the column. But you two are in a position to ask around quietly. Find out what Glenn had learned about these three, and I'll take it from there.'

Unbelievable, I thought. She wanted us not only to exonerate her leg man, but to provide grist for her gossip mill. All by digging up the secrets of – I consulted my notes – a starlet on the rise, a producer with a paucity of credits, and a director the world had forgotten.

Edith tried to smooth the skepticism out of her tone, but it was like ironing a shirt collar. It kept popping up. 'Then you don't want us to visit the crime scene or consider Mr Hoyle's past—'

'Heavens, no! The police can find out about Glenn's enemies, if he had any. A bookie usually does. And the crime scene's unimportant. Give it a wide berth.' Lorna added an earnest reasonableness to her voice. 'I'd never ask you to put yourselves in jeopardy. I'd simply appreciate it if you did what the police have neither the time nor the inclination to do. Research three people connected to the picture business. People already in your circle. Then tell me what you find.' Lorna pointed a finger directly at me. The diamond ring on her digit dazzled. 'And don't share it with your old friend Katherine Dambach. Who happens to be my competitor.'

I was impressed that Lorna knew I'd once lived under the same roof as Kay, who penned a syndicated column of her own, even if she hadn't found out Kay and I were on distant terms these days. The sly expression on Sam's face informed me that he'd legged out that connection, and I began to appreciate his importance to Lorna's empire.

'May I tell Kay you regard her as a competitor?' I asked sweetly. 'That would put her over the moon.'

'Tell her whatever you like once you've helped me. Now what do you say?'

After brooding a moment, Edith said unhappily, 'It seems like an effort we'd be able to undertake.'

'Splendid. I don't suppose you could also provide a kicker for today's column? I'm not wild about this item on George Raft hitting the New York nightspots in his bedroom slippers.'

'It's funny,' Mildred insisted. 'He's a dancer. He probably has terrible corns.'

'I danced with him once,' I offered out of desperation.

'How fantastic for you, Lillian, but it's not the sort of story that will captivate my readers. Sam? Care to throw a drowning woman a line?'

Sam licked his fingertip and paged through a notebook with diabolical speed. He stopped and grinned. 'Bingo. Madeleine Carroll is making eyes at her co-star in *The Southerner*. Did some hair tonic ads. Strapping kid named Sterling Hayden.'

'Really?' Edith gasped. 'I did the costumes on that.'

'What happened to that French flyer Madeleine was involved with?' Mildred sounded wounded by this bulletin.

'Word is Pierre ran out of gas.'

Lorna clapped her hands. 'Perfection. Feed me the details and we'll hash it out.'

Edith and I stood up to leave. Edith stepped closer to Lorna to share a few words, so I turned to Mildred. 'It was nice almost meeting you,' I said. 'Next time, you'll have to tell me how you got this job.'

'I arrived in Los Angeles, full of hopes and dreams. Then I told somebody I could type.' Mildred turned back to her keyboard. 'Never make that mistake.'

THREE

After the ratatat of repartee, the relative calm of the elevator came as blessed relief. Edith and I kept mum on the trip to the lobby in case the elevator operator was on Lorna's payroll. When I cleared my throat halfway down, he went up on the balls of his feet, poised to absorb anything I might say.

We stepped outside into the sunlight. Somewhere nearby a bird chirped, and I mistook it for a telephone ringing.

'Must you rush right to work, or do you have a moment to stop by the studio?' Edith asked. I told her the morning was mine. I knew enough to set aside additional time for us to analyze our assignation.

'Would you mind terribly if we rode in silence and simply enjoyed the day? I've had enough chatter for a while.'

'You've already said too much.'

The short trip proved a balm to my jangled nerves. I breathed easy the entire way, except when Edith took corners too fast.

As we strolled through the studio's Bronson Gate, Edith asked if I'd mind accompanying her while she stopped in to see someone. Before I could ask who, Barney Groff planted himself on the pathway ahead of us and crooked a finger toward the Wardrobe building.

'Never mind,' Edith said. 'The mountain would appear to have come to Mohammed. Again.' She began walking faster. Groff had already vanished into the building.

By the time we reached Edith's outer office, Groff looked peevish, as if he'd been waiting for hours. 'Let's have the damage report,' he said, throwing open the doors to Edith's salon and striding in ahead of her.

Barney Groff's title at Paramount, chief of security, could be interpreted broadly. He protected peace of mind, of the studio as an entity and its various potentates, a function he performed by tending to Paramount's property, namely the stars and technicians under contract to it. He acted as an all-purpose fixer, riding to the rescue whenever a prized asset was in peril. Because he valued directness in his dealings, even when that route took him across unsavory terrain, a hint of menace clung to him like the woodsy Dunhill cologne he favored. He was dressed as usual in a sober black suit, cut loosely enough for him to frog-march a felon off his lot without spoiling the drape of the fabric. The only color came from his regimental stripe tie in maroon and gold. I wondered what regiment would claim Groff when his allegiance lay with Paramount alone.

As usual, he paid me no mind. He looked at Edith and said, 'Well?'

'It went much as we anticipated, Mr Groff.'

'She wants you to get her leg man off the hook, then.'

Edith admirably encapsulated our confab with Lorna Whitcomb, Groff nodding at every pertinent fact as he stowed it in his mental filing cabinet. He made particular note of the three names on Glenn Hoyle's list. When Edith finished her recitation, he sat behind steepled fingers and plotted.

It occurred to me as I waited that in all the years I'd been visiting Paramount, I had never been to Barney Groff's office. Surely he had one, a place where he could hang upside down in silent slumber, eyes snapping open when one of his charges went astray.

'Fine,' he said abruptly.

A pause, then Edith said, 'Fine in what way, Mr Groff?'

'Fine as in play along. Do what she wants. Provided it doesn't interfere with your work schedule.'

'You'd like me to assist Mrs Whitcomb by attempting to clear Mr Simcoe.' Edith's tone made it clear she would have preferred another outcome.

'I wouldn't *like* you to do it, but there's no sense making an enemy out of her.' Groff's fingers brushed the knot of his tie. 'Lorna's a tough bird. She's the type who'd knock our pictures out of spite – and I guarantee she'll come out swinging for you if you don't do this. Why rile her when she's asking so little? Would it kill you to make her happy?' His voice rose on this final query, as if Edith were putting up a protest.

'I agree, Mr Groff. It's the simplest solution. I would be happy to undertake an investigation of these names. And, of course, to visit the crime scene, which would have to be arranged.'

I was still attempting to parse Edith's comment when Groff thrust his chin at me, finally acknowledging my existence with the least amount of effort necessary. 'Can't she call her friend?'

'I'd rather not,' I said, my tongue nearly snapping off at the root as I prevented myself from adding 'sir'.

'So, once again, I have to do everything.' Groff released a mighty sigh, Atlas shifting the globe to his bum shoulder. 'All right. I know some people. I'll get in touch with them and let you know. In the meantime, do as Lorna asks. Anything you learn, you report it to me first. Then her.' He stood up and brushed his hands together. 'Wrap this business up quick and keep all our friends happy.'

He left without another word. Edith waited a moment. 'I don't want to keep you any longer, but I could certainly use a cup of coffee after that morning.'

'Can it be Irish coffee?'

Edith laughed, not grasping that I'd meant it as a serious question.

*   *   *

We made our way toward the commissary. 'We're actually going to do this, then?' I asked. 'Put our shoulders to the wheel for Lorna Whitcomb?'

'I'm doing it, Lillian. You don't need to. My efforts should be enough to spare Mr Rice any aggravation.'

'If you're in, I'm in. When did you tell Mr Groff?'

'As soon as Lorna's girl telephoned yesterday, asking to see us both. You won't be surprised to learn Mr Groff already knew she'd contacted me and surmised what was in store.'

'What's the plan? What exactly are we going to do for the team of Simcoe and Whitcomb?'

'As little as possible. I'm not risking injury to person or time-table on some wild-goose chase. Additionally, we are going to keep the authorities apprised of anything we discover. I won't do anything extra-legal. Not for that woman.'

'She certainly has us over a barrel. She could have asked us for our help nicely. We might have said yes.'

'We wouldn't have.' Edith smiled grimly. 'Besides, Lorna's incapable of asking nicely. She believes it's a sign of weakness. She's grown so accustomed to people currying favor, she's lost the ability to make a simple request.'

'She wouldn't really use her column to get even with us?' I spoke in the hushed tones of a child inquiring about the monster in a bedtime story.

'I wouldn't put it past her.'

A mid-morning lull had settled over the commissary, the quiet seeming to put Edith on edge. As we sat with our coffees, she looked around nervously, her eyes darting to the doors every time they opened. A glumness lurked beneath her usual lively demeanor, an unknown burden weighing her down. Was it the devil's bargain we'd made to assist Lorna? Or something more?

When in doubt, I thought, babble. 'That was some show Lorna put on. What was she like when she was under contract here?'

'The fledgling version of what you saw this morning. She fussed at every fitting. Always groused that the costumes we put her in were insufficiently glamorous. Insisted that the advent of talking pictures would make her a star. I didn't exactly mourn when her option was dropped.' Edith stirred her coffee thoughtfully. 'But it must be said I remembered her, even before she became a

columnist. She made an impression, when so many girls who come
through here do not.'

'I have to ask. If we're going to do as little as possible, why
did you tell Mr Groff you wanted to go to the crime scene?'

'Because Lorna was so adamant about our *not* visiting it.
Whatever she says we shouldn't do, we should make an immediate
priority.'

I made a note of the thought, and decided to put it into practice
myself a little later.

'My turn to ask a question,' Edith said. 'Is there any reason
you didn't want to involve Detective Morrow?'

The query didn't catch me off guard. Gene Morrow and I had
been an item for a number of years – and then we weren't. We
kept in touch, although as I formulated my response, I realized it
had been well over a month since he and I had spoken. Edith
maintained a hope we'd come to our senses and get back together.
She carried more of a torch for our relationship than I did.

'We're on good terms,' I began slowly. 'I don't want to queer
that for Lorna.'

'A wise move. Again, let's not upset any apple carts on her behalf.
Mr Groff's contacts on the police department should be sufficient.'

I proposed that we compile some basic background on the three
names on Glenn Hoyle's alleged list, and Edith agreed. Her gloom
hadn't lifted. I was about to ask what pictures she was working
on when a chaos of color ambled toward our table. With a few
more steps, it resolved into a figure garbed in a clashing array of
garments. An 'outboard' shirt with a garish Polynesian pattern
of green and yellow, worn untucked over rust-colored slacks. A
porkpie hat completed the ensemble, and a pipe dangled easily
from the man's hand like a golf club.

'Why, Edith Head, I do declare,' Bing Crosby announced in the
voice that drifted out of my radio every week on *The Kraft Music
Hall* like so much beguiling smoke. 'I thought I saw you perambu-
lating this fine morning. And this other face seems familiar as well.'

He means you, said the far less mellifluous voice in my head.
My brain spasmed trying to think how the entertainer knew me,
and landed on the wholly illogical notion that Crosby had intuited
I'd gone to see *Road to Singapore* multiple times. I wasn't the only
one; the comedy in which Crosby cut capers alongside Bob Hope

and Dorothy Lamour had been a surprise smash, a much-needed hit for Paramount. Then Edith introduced me, mentioning my job with Addison Rice, and reality reasserted itself. Crosby occasionally attended Addison's parties. At these soirées he projected an unforced calm that could be mistaken for diffidence; he was so at ease in the spotlight he never felt the need to seek it out. Crosby and his wife Dixie were always among the first to leave, offering heartfelt thanks and excuses of early calls or tee times. In these brief exchanges, I felt I hadn't made much of an impression.

Clearly, I was in error. 'Addison's right hand. How could I have forgotten? I shall never forgive myself.' Crosby lowered his gaze in mock shame. My eyes instinctively followed his, and I noticed he wore one red sock and one brown one.

'Just reminding you about Friday,' Crosby said. 'I'm hosting that preview of *Rhythm on the River* at Del Mar. Even running a special race in honor of the occasion, with a nag owned by Louis B. Mayer himself vying for honors. We'll set up a big screen in front of the clubhouse for the picture. You can take in your handi-work under the stars, admire those togs you assembled for Mary Martin. And I tried not to slouch in what you put me in.'

'If I make it, I'll take any wagering tips you care to offer.'

'Then I shall put you onto my patented system, designed for the lady and gentleman of leisure. Allows you to lose at a steady pace over the course of the afternoon instead of all in one go. Better for the digestion, you know.'

'I look forward to it. Almost as much as I look forward to the fittings for your next picture with Bob. My research on Zanzibar has begun in earnest. It will be great fun having you two in front of a camera again.'

'Bob's already lining up his ad libs. You're sure I have to come in for fittings? You can't describe my stylish attire over the blower?'

'You know how I work. Like a painless dentist.' Edith patted his arm reassuringly. 'Is there anything you'd like me to bear in mind for your wardrobe?'

'Keep the pot belly under wraps and make me look a third as good as Dottie, that's all. Oh, and let's minimize my hijinks. Funny hats and wild costumes are Bob's department. Now if you'll excuse me, I've got to brush up on my ad libs, too.' Crosby doffed the porkpie, exposing a largely bald pate.

Once he'd sauntered off, Edith said, 'You weren't taken aback by his lack of a hairpiece, I see.'

'He never wears one when he comes to Addison's parties. I was hoping you could explain the socks.'

'Mr Crosby is color blind. Which also accounts for his penchant for . . . flamboyance. If you pointed out the socks, he'd simply observe that both of them fit.'

'He's got a point. You'd better be going to Del Mar on Friday. When the owner – well, part-owner – of a racetrack invites you down, and for a movie premiere no less, I'm pretty sure you're obligated.'

'I hadn't planned on it. Too much work to do.'

I started to protest, but Edith raised a hand. 'I said I *hadn't* planned on it. That may have changed, thanks to Lorna's advice. Perhaps I will put in an appearance. See what the hue and cry is about. Learn to delegate and trust that benevolent elves will complete my work in my absence. No doubt that's what any man in my position would do.' The chuckle that followed bore a tinge of bitterness, but as it was Edith's first laugh of the day, I accepted it.

FOUR

M y kindly employer Addison Rice had a full afternoon slate of appointments – I'd scheduled them myself – leaving me to my own devices in his home. Not that this occasioned any 'cat's away, mice will play' frolics; being largely alone at his palatial residence always felt like I was in a museum after hours. I beavered away at his mountain of correspondence. I arranged supplies for his home workshop – Addison had acquired his wealth manufacturing electronics, and remained an inveterate tinkerer – and for his liquor cabinets in preparation for the weekend's guests. I tracked down copies of obscure textbooks and back issues missing from Addison's extensive collection of movie magazines. I took a break for a stroll through the garden. Drinking in its full late-summer riot of colors, I built my resolve to make a single telephone call.

If Edith and I were to do the bare minimum to investigate Sam Simcoe's protestations of innocence, and thus avoid Lorna Whitcomb's wrath, we needed information on the people named on the list Sam claimed to have found in the late Glenn Hoyle's home. At my desk, I reviewed the notes I'd taken in Lorna's office. Already I had come to think of this trio in shorthand: the actress, the producer, the has-been. How to gather intelligence on all three, and quickly?

By following Edith's example. Whatever Lorna instructed us not to do, we should do at once. I picked up the receiver.

Astoundingly, I managed to catch Kay Dambach at her desk. Halfway through my honeyed pitch for us two old friends to get together, she cut me off.

'If you mean tonight, you're in luck. Meet me at the Brown Derby around six. On Vine, not the original. Better make it the Bamboo Room. I'll be the one at the bar alone.'

Kay had the right idea. Autograph hounds thronged the entrance to the Brown Derby, jockeying one another in hope of a glimpse of some notable. Meanwhile, the adjacent door leading to the Derby's cocktail lounge, the Bamboo Room, was uncluttered. I stepped inside cautiously, searching for Lorna Whitcomb or any member of her staff; this outpost of the Derby was close enough to her office to be their local.

The Brown Derby on Wilshire Boulevard had cornered the kitsch market, the building itself shaped like the hat, the booths nestled against curved walls. The Vine Street iteration was housed in a sedate Spanish-style structure, but each table featured a light fixture resembling the signature skimmer.

Seeing no sign of Lorna or Sam, I elbowed my way to the Bamboo Room's bar. Kay anchored the far end. She had managed to secure two seats, thanks to the extra space taken up by her midnight-blue gown. She shifted the skirt to allow me to sit down, grunting the entire time.

'And I didn't get fancied up for you,' I said.

'I'm invited to a mystery party for Bonita Granville's birthday,' she said to her Manhattan. 'For a story on teenage stars. We meet outside the Derby at seven to pile into a bus that takes us on an evening of adventures who knows where.'

'That sounds like fun.'

'I knew you'd say that. I already know where we're going. I slipped a few bucks to a kid at the bus outfit. First it's hot dogs, then bowling, then off to the fun house on the Venice pier. I can't face that kind of tomfoolery sober.' She sipped her cocktail. 'I already filed the story and said I had a wonderful time.'

Kay and I had met soon after I'd arrived in Los Angeles from New York in 1936, the beauty contest victory under my belt stirring the half-baked notion of becoming a star. I'd abandoned that dream but found a life. Kay had come west determined to make it as a writer. Through luck and tenacity, she'd landed a column with a small syndicate, and her constant quest for fodder had put a crimp in our camaraderie. But I required use of her encyclopedic knowledge of Hollywood, and Lorna expressly forbidding me to speak to her only made the prospect more enticing.

I ordered a Manhattan to accompany Kay's. As we clinked glasses, Kay said, 'So what do you want?'

'What do you mean? It's been a while since we've seen each other, and I thought—'

'Save the sob story. What's it about?'

Kay's honesty, though inspired by ruthlessness, was as reliable as the tides. Not that I planned to respond in kind. I mentally made the sign of the cross before telling my little white lie. 'Addison recently met the actress Delia Carson, and I wondered what you know about her.'

Kay reached into her glass and plucked out the cherry. She chewed it thoroughly, taking in her reflection in the mirror behind the bar as she thought.

Then she turned to me. 'What's the deal with Orson Welles?'

'I'm sorry?'

'You know him, right?'

'A little. He's been to Addison's a few—'

'The boy genius is making a big case for himself all over town now that he's finally gotten off his duff and started directing his picture. Wining and dining Louella Parsons, sweet-talking Hedda Hopper. Why hasn't he pitched any woo my way?'

Kay turned to me, expecting an answer. I cast aside my first – *Because he's never heard of you* – and opted for a more pragmatic one. 'Did you go to the party RKO threw when production started?'

'No, damn it, I had to see *Boom Town* because MGM promised

me a Gable story. Which they reneged on, naturally. I knew skipping that bash would come back to haunt me.' Kay polished off her Manhattan and signaled for another. 'Here's the deal. Mention my name to Welles. Give me a real build-up, convince him he should talk to me, too.'

Having no inkling when or if I'd see Orson Welles again, I shrugged. 'I can but try. Now spill on Delia Carson.'

'She almost made my teenage stars story. A few months too old. Delia's squeaky clean. Irritatingly so. Much like her pictures, which I suppose you enjoy.'

'Some of them. *My Spring Romance* was sweet.'

'They're *all* sweet, in that saccharine way only dentists and young girls love. But they make piles of money for Lodestar, so what do I know? Actually, I do know there's trouble at home. Her momma – name's Rhoda – is the stage mother to end stage mothers. Rhoda makes Ginger Rogers's mother Lela look like she's working bankers' hours. Rhoda controls every facet of poor Delia's life. Which is why she got so upset when her little girl ran off and tied the knot last year. No guest list. Not even Rhoda.'

A spark flared in one of the deeper recesses of my brain. 'I remember something about this.'

'The nuptials didn't get the play they normally would. Lodestar hushed it up at first. They hoped Delia would come to her senses. They did a fair business in "My Dream Lover" stories about her with the fan magazines, always sending her out on dates with their new young contract players. But apparently Cupid's aim was true. The deadeye little bastard. The husband's an older fellow and, if you can believe it, an *extra* to boot. Arthur something. Can you imagine? Young girl with a bright future, basically carrying a studio on her back, and she gets hitched to a guy who looks like a racetrack tout and earns his few measly shekels a year standing around in the background. Davis, that's his name. Arthur Davis.'

'And Rhoda's none too happy about this union.'

'Nor should she be. Lady Svengali loses control of her Trilby? She doesn't care for Arthur *at all*, one hears. Did Addison meet him, too?'

I stared at her for an instant, blanking on what fib I'd told. 'I think he was standing around in the background. You don't happen to have a photo of the happy couple on file, do you? I'd hate to reintroduce him to Addison.'

'That kind of faux pas can get you fired. If I have one, I'll send over a copy. In return for the promised favor with your buddy Orson, natch. Let's see, anything else? Delia's very active with Bundles for Britain, that war relief group for the English. You must have heard of them. They knit things and send them overseas. Battleship cozies and such.'

'That's nice of her.'

'Is it? Rhoda doesn't think so, and neither do I.'

'You have a problem with war relief?'

'When it isn't our war, I do. Let her knit things for Americans down on their luck if she has time on her hands.' Kay, in her role as Hollywood's plainspoken conscience, had assumed an isolationist approach to the war in Europe, along with a narrow, show-business-centric interpretation of every other subject under the sun.

When she ran out of steam on geopolitics, our talk drifted to friends we had in common from our days living in Mrs Lindros's boarding house. I asked after Hank 'Ready' Blaylock, the gentlemanly stunt rider who served as her steadfast steady. Their partnership was for appearances only; Ready preferred to spend his nights in the bunkhouse with the boys, while Kay's true love was her column.

'He's his usual stoic self. Broke some bone or other on a picture last week and never said a word about it. Came home, put a godawful poultice of his own concoction on it, and is good as new. He's disappointed he couldn't come to this silliness tonight. He'd have a better time than I will.'

I waited for Kay to inquire about my love life. When she didn't, I moved on to the next name on the list. 'Addison also encountered another fellow, Earl Lymangood.'

'Who's he?'

'I was hoping you could tell me. Apparently, he's a movie producer.'

'Apparently not, because I've never heard of him.' So emphatic was her response that I abandoned the subject at once.

A fellow in a seersucker suit and pinwheel bowtie jostled us both. Kay's steely stare sent him scampering. 'Things can get a little chummy in this room,' she said sniffily. 'I'd rather have met you in the Derby, but the bar there is so much smaller.'

'I love the caricatures of the stars they have hanging next door. Though I can't always tell who they're supposed to be.'

'Did you know the poor maître d' has to ride herd over that gallery? When a couple breaks up, he has to separate their sketches. Needs to keep track of who's on the rise, who's on the outs. It's like my job.'

Thus did Kay provide the perfect segue to the final name on my list. 'That reminds me, I heard a sad story the other day. Vernon Reynolds, who used to direct silent pictures, is working as a maître d'. At a place called Arturo's off Sunset.'

'You've got a soft spot for ancient history, don't you? Always bringing up these names from the dusty past. Plenty of people from silent pictures have other jobs now. It's the way of the world. Whoever this Reynolds fellow is, he's luckier than most. I've heard Arturo's has fair grub. Maybe I'll stop by some evening if I need a "whatever happened to" item. Never hurts to jerk the odd tear.'

The hour approached seven o'clock. Kay fumbled in her purse, already half off her bamboo-legged stool. I should have wished her and Bonita Granville a lovely evening. But the Manhattan and my lingering resentment toward Lorna had gotten the better of me. 'So how much trouble is Lorna Whitcomb in?'

Kay slammed her backside back down; red meat had been dished up. She issued her dire prognosis with barely restrained glee. 'This business with her leg man could be the end of her. Timing couldn't be worse. Some of the studio brass think dear old Louella has spent too long at the fair. Believes she's every bit as important as the people she writes about. Hopper's getting support as a potential challenger to the throne. Lorna should be ideally positioned – she's younger than both of them, she's been in the business, she's savvy. And Simcoe chooses now to make her look bad.'

'Do you think he killed that other fellow?'

'Everyone says he did.'

'But why would he?'

'It doesn't matter why. It matters that everyone says he did. Word's out the other fellow, Hoyle, used to provide Sam with tips. Maybe Sam took credit for them, or Hoyle got ambitious. Who knows? Those relationships are always seamy. Take it from me.'

'What's the word on Sam Simcoe?'

'Lorna's column wouldn't be what it is without him. Has a

reputation for being fast, clean, and accurate with his copy. If he tells you something, it's not the bunk. And when he cuts your throat, he'll do it from the front with a smile on his face and walk you through every step of the procedure.'

'That's a ringing endorsement around these parts.' I paused. 'And the book on Lorna?'

'Several volumes long. The abridged version is she's mean but fair. Even when she's angry, which is often, you can bargain with her. She's got Dr Jerry to keep her fat and happy. He's getting on in years, but still rakes in enough at his practice to keep her in ermine and caviar. She was sitting pretty before Sam Simcoe slipped on the banana peel.'

I noted the time and idly suggested I'd head next door for dinner. 'Wish I could join you,' Kay said. 'Chicken livers sauteed in butter sounds better than the hot dogs I have in store. I thought of your pal Edith before. I remember a story about her old boss, Travis Banton. He was in the Derby when inspiration struck and he started sketching a gown on the tablecloth. Took it with him when he left. They didn't even charge him.' She extracted the cherry from her second cocktail and popped it into her mouth. 'Did Lorna turn to you and Edith for help? Because it's what I'd do.'

I had a denial poised on my tongue – *What? No, never* – but I choked on the last of my drink, the bourbon washing my rebuttal away. Kay had timed her question perfectly.

'I knew it,' she said, gloating. 'When did you talk to her? Today? You don't happen to know what she's got for tomorrow's column, do you?'

I almost told all about Madeleine Carroll and her new hair tonic consort, but as much as I smarted at Lorna's manipulation, I maintained that confidence. 'Couldn't say. Anyway, Edith and I aren't planning on doing anything for her.'

'Good. Keep the skids greased under her. The less competition for me, the better.'

Over the Bamboo Room's din came a scream from the street – the unmistakable sound of a gaggle of teenage girls assembling. Kay shuddered and rummaged in her purse, relaxing only when she confirmed the presence of a few cotton balls.

'They're for later,' she explained. 'Our final scheduled stop on tonight's voyage of the damned is a jitterbug contest. Although if the girls are already carrying on like this, maybe I should pack my ears with them now.'

Los Angeles Register   August 15, 1940

LORNA WHITCOMB'S
EYES ON HOLLYWOOD

The Great McGinty premiered in New York this week to such raves that Paramount bosses can't wait to get Preston Sturges behind the camera again. It's about time they realized their hottest screenwriter is also their hottest director. Not only that, his new script, *The Lady Eve*, is a doozy, with actresses all over town itching to play the lead . . . One would have to be deaf not to hear those little birds chirping about the dire straits our office is in. While we mourn the loss of young Glenn Hoyle, we're not losing sleep over the fate of Friend Simcoe. We know for a fact he wouldn't hurt a fly. If you don't believe me, you haven't seen what's buzzing around his wastebasket . . . A tour of the nightspots finds midriff-baring gowns on gals from fifteen to fifty-five. Take my advice, ladies: if you're older than the first Model T, it's time to cover your chassis.

FIVE

Addison Rice ambled into my office in casual attire and a state of consternation. He wore lightweight gray slacks and an open-necked shirt an arresting shade of sky blue; my adipose employer was not a man averse to color. He clucked at the newspaper in his hand. 'Lillian, have you read this story? What are we to make of this?'

I had left my copy of the *Los Angeles Times* on my desk, knowing he would want to discuss it. 'I wouldn't make much of it myself.'

'But it's on page one! Grand jury testimony from a big wheel in the Los Angeles Communist party, identifying dozens of show people as fellow members.'

'What interested me was how the testimony was related to a murder case. A poor sailor in San Pedro. The article forgets about him entirely and focuses on the names this supposed bigwig dropped.'

'Point taken. But still, can you blame them? Look at the names he dropped! James Cagney, Fredric March, Humphrey Bogart, Franchot Tone.'

'All of whom deny the allegations. Of course, that's buried on the inside of the paper.'

'Well, yes. I stand firmly in favor of people believing whatever they want in this country. But I can still hope for this not to be true, can't I? Communists think I don't deserve the money I worked hard for.'

I exhaled softly, balanced myself, and set out to walk the tightrope. 'I don't know if the people named in that testimony are Communists, but I do know they've all been to your house. Clearly, they don't have an issue with your money.'

Addison brightened. 'Say, that's true!'

Politics apparently dispensed with for the morning, I lobbed him a curveball. 'I heard a fascinating story yesterday. About Vernon Reynolds, who used to direct pictures. Although I couldn't think of one.'

Addison drew up a chair. '*The Wayward Path* is maybe my favorite of his. And *Storm Cloud*, with Madge Granger. A thin imitation of *Sadie Thompson*, but it ends with a mighty hurricane that I can still picture all these years later.'

'So can I. I lifted my feet off the floor because I was sure they'd get soaked.'

'He was a talented man, Reynolds. His pictures always had a certain sophistication. Maybe too much. Whatever happened to him?' As I recounted Reynolds's present circumstances, editing out how and why I'd learned of them, Addison tutted mournfully. 'Such a shame. I remember when he was mentioned in the same breath as D.W. Griffith.'

Griffith's name isn't on many lips these days, either, I thought.

Addison drummed his thumb against his chin, thinking. 'I

wonder if it would be possible to talk to the man.' Over the past year, he'd become passionate about preserving the history of motion pictures, which he loved like nothing else. I knew he could never pass up a chance to speak directly to an industry pioneer. 'We should have dinner at the restaurant where he's working as soon as possible.'

He had fallen into my carefully laid trap. 'How about tonight?' I asked sweetly, well aware that he had no prior commitments. Addison instantly agreed, and I told him I'd make the arrangements. He toddled off to the library to read up on Vernon Reynolds. I had spent the morning researching him, and had taken the liberty of laying out a few articles about his career in advance.

Progress made on the director front. An advance on the actress thread of the investigation arrived via messenger mid-morning. The envelope contained a note from Kay – *Make sure Orson calls me Katherine!* – clipped to a photograph. The familiar face of Delia Carson appeared at the far left, her blonde ringlets perfect. Her prominent cheekbones tricked the eyes, creating shadows that made her always appear to be smiling, even in this photo, where if you studied her face you'd see she looked somewhat lost. That random quirk of anatomy accounted for the sunshiny presence that rendered her beloved by millions of young girls. The photo appeared to have been snapped at the premiere of *Father's Found a Friend*, in which Delia played the daughter of widower Eugene Pallette, saving him from financial and romantic ruin with her usual arsenal of spunk and a song. Even I didn't care much for that one.

Behind her, helpfully circled by Kay, was the man I took to be her partner in wedded bliss. Kay hadn't been kidding when she'd described Arthur Davis's features. He had a big-city pallor evident even in a black-and-white photograph. He'd combed his dark mane tightly back, giving his sizeable forehead more prominence. I could see why he toiled as a background player. His visage, from lantern jaw to dense eyebrows, would appear right at home at ringside, or passed out on a bar's counter, or gazing down pitilessly from a policeman's uniform. He might have been an extra in this photograph were it not for the vigilance with which he studied his bride, poised to leap to her defense.

At the right edge of the frame, Kay had scribbled *Momma!*. Rhoda Carson stared resolutely forward, as if counting every flashbulb aimed at her daughter. She resembled a rough draft for Delia, each line and curve not only echoed but improved in her progeny. Rhoda wore a gay embroidered organza dress that didn't suit her marcelled hair or her age, and an expression that dared anyone to inform her of that fact.

I tucked the photograph – *The starlet, Exhibit A* – into a file with the notes I'd already accumulated. As I replaced the folder, my telephone rang.

'I bear news,' Edith said. 'Mr Groff has arranged for us to visit the unfortunate Mr Hoyle's residence today. A police representative of his acquaintance will meet us. It was impressed upon me more than once that this expedition is meant to be low-key.'

'Right,' I said. 'Nix the cowgirl chaps and the feather boa.'

'If you would. To minimize disruption to our schedules, I've set the trip for the lunch hour. I hope that doesn't pose a problem.'

I glanced down at my outfit. A cotton pique skirt with green and yellow vertical stripes, and a matching jacket. Not my preferred wardrobe to wear to a crime scene, but what choice did I have? 'It's dinner tonight I don't want to miss. I'll explain when I see you.'

Glenn 'Two Ns' Hoyle had lived in a bungalow court like countless others in Los Angeles. Two rows of low-slung buildings bleached white by the sun stared each other down across a pathway that widened in the middle to accommodate a bone-dry fountain. At the rear of the lot stood a long building split into three residences, with barely enough red Spanish tile to go around. These complexes, which sprouted up across Southern California like mushrooms after a rainstorm, were meant to be snug and inviting but never seemed that way to me. I stubbornly remained a New York girl, favoring boarding houses and apartment buildings. I had come west seeking sunshine, not space.

I took in Hoyle's abode from the back seat of Addison's Cadillac. I'd borrowed it and his chauffeur. Rogers had largely stopped speaking to me after my sole driving lesson resulted in both of our lives flashing before our eyes. What few words he did say, he

spat out of the corner of his mouth. Bearing in mind Edith's
instructions, I asked him to park a few blocks away.

By the time I walked back, Edith had pulled up outside the
bungalow court. I slid into the passenger seat of her roadster.

'You didn't come here on foot, surely,' she said.

'A chauffeur-driven Cadillac idling out front seemed a mite
ostentatious under the circumstances.'

'Good thinking. I asked around the lot and learned a few things
about the producer on Mr Hoyle's list, Earl Lymangood. And I do
mean a few.' She ticked them off on gloved fingers. 'He's from
New York. He has a handful of credits at Monogram, one of the
smaller studios. And he doesn't need money from the pictures
because he's independently wealthy. I'll continue to make inquiries.'

'I haven't been dozing, either. Addison and I are dining at
Arturo's tonight so I can size up Vernon Reynolds in the flesh.
Here's the brief on the life and times of Delia Carson, her mother,
and her husband.' I closed with the tidbit about Delia's involvement with the war relief effort through Bundles for Britain.

Edith rapped the dashboard. 'That's our entrée to talking to her.
They knit and sew clothes. I'll send over a token of my apprecia-
tion this afternoon.'

'If she's anything like her characters, she'll respond with an
immediate thank you and some freshly baked cookies. Probably
learned her manners from her mother, who looks like quite the
stern taskmistress. Take a gander.' The photograph of the extended
Carson clan slipped out of its folder as I went to show it to her.
Edith surveyed it and clucked.

'Shall I take it you consulted your friend Miss Dambach despite
Lorna's warning?'

'Correct. Speaking of Lorna, she certainly promoted Preston's
new script in her column this morning. Is that one of your next
projects?'

'Indeed, one that has me champing at the bit. He says the lead
role is a true clothes horse. I can't tell you how I'd relish the
opportunity to indulge myself.'

'What lucky actress is playing the lead?'

'That's to be determined. I've heard tell it may be Paulette
Goddard.' Disquiet edged into her voice. Goddard, fresh off a pair
of hit comedies co-starring Bob Hope and with a film directed by

her husband Charlie Chaplin on the way, had talent. She also possessed a brittle nature that had provoked clashes with Edith in the past. Clashes Edith was reliving now.

She shook off her woe. 'Whoever it is, I will welcome the opportunity. Adrian over at MGM isn't the only one who can pull out all the stops. Provided I can remember where all the stops are.'

A sedan nosed into the space opposite us. I immediately sank to the floor of Edith's car. 'What's wrong?' she asked.

'Our escort has arrived,' I whispered. 'I know him. So do you. Maybe you could drive away?'

But it was too late. Detective Roy Hansen quickstepped over, the brim of his hat pulled low over his gaunt face. He had a build so lean it looked like a stiff breeze could send him tumbling, but history taught that a switch could effect its share of damage. Hansen was Gene Morrow's disagreeable partner. Moreover, he occasionally played cards with one Barney Groff. How could I have overlooked this essential piece of information?

'Awright, ladies,' he said in his prairie-wind voice, high and harsh. 'Let's get this over with. This is unofficial, you understand? This place is no longer a crime scene, but it ain't exactly a tourist attraction, either.'

'We understand and we thank you, Detective Hansen,' Edith said. 'It's been some time since I last saw you. How is your wife?'

'She's fine, ma'am. Still loves the pictures. Always perks up when she sees your name.' Now somewhat chastened, he opened the door of the car for her.

As I clambered onto the sidewalk, I begged, 'You can't tell Gene I was here.'

'Are you kidding?' Hansen spoke with agitation. 'You can't let on *I* was here. This is strictly a favor for Mr Groff. I'm not assigned to this case, but I talked to the fellers who are. I can answer any questions you got – but try not to have any. Take a look around, then scram. We clear?'

'Absolutely,' Edith said cheerfully. 'Lead on, Detective.'

SIX

It should have been a sunlit room. But architecture conspired against the left corner unit of the building that stretched across the rear of the bungalow court. Shadows from the adjacent structure spilled across the doorstep, and the high wooden fence marking the edge of the property poached most of the light from the side windows. Isolated, gloomy, and small, it felt like a home the occupant would return to each day with resentment.

Hansen had to turn on a lamp despite the noon hour. Once he did, I revised my opinion slightly. Glenn Hoyle had selected the sparse appointments with an eye toward making his den more habitable. Vintage vaudeville playbills, carefully preserved, hung on the walls, along with two simple landscapes likely purchased direct from the artist on the beach in Santa Monica. The sprightly green shade of the davenport lightened the room's oppression further. The weathered bar cabinet alongside it looked scavenged from a second-class hotel.

Then I noticed the faded bloodstains on the davenport, and the broader swath of discoloration on the floor beneath it. And I understood that the darkness was doing the room one final favor.

'Be it ever so humble.' Hansen slumped against the door.

'It's strange,' I said. 'Being here when I have no idea what Glenn Hoyle looked like.'

'Good thing I come prepared.' Hansen extracted a photograph from his jacket pocket. It showed a young man in a suit too big for him, the shirt collar gapping at his neck. He wore his sandy hair in a style that spilled into his dark eyes, which stared down the camera with cocksure confidence. It was an expression encountered frequently in Southern California, the look of a person who might not know exactly what he had to say, but by God he was ready to say it. I handed the photo to Edith, thinking it could have run over the column he was certain he would one day have. *According to Hoyle.*

Edith made a faint sympathetic sound, then returned the photograph to Hansen. He pointed it at the nearest playbill. 'Only family we could track down is the father. Magician, performed under the name The Great Horatio. Disappeared while on tour in Saskatchewan a few years ago. His last trick. Got tired of pulling penguins out of his hat for Nanook of the North, maybe. Hoyle tried following in his footsteps, but gave it up.'

The few bottles atop the bar cabinet bore trace amounts of dust, Glenn taking his cleaning duties seriously. I'd started calling him Glenn, I noticed, now that I had seen his face.

'Don't bother looking for the good stuff,' Hansen said of the liquor. 'The best he had was used to brain him. Nearly full bottle of Irish. Rolled under the sofa. No prints.'

'Is this how the place was found, Detective?' Edith asked.

'Aside from Hoyle's body, yeah. There weren't any glasses out, if that's what you mean. Whoever killed him wasn't expected.'

'But likely known to Mr Hoyle.'

Hansen pushed himself off the door. 'Sez who?'

'Mr Hoyle was seated when he was struck. He had allowed whoever killed him into his home. Perhaps his visitor went to the bar to pour a drink and instead seized a weapon.' Edith moved around the room as she spoke. In so doing, she drew closer to the wastebasket that loomed so large in Sam Simcoe's story. The bin was set where the front room widened out into the tiny kitchen. Edith adjusted her spectacles, using the motion to cover her peering into it.

Hansen wasn't fooled. He closed the distance between them in two gangly strides. By the time he reached the wastebasket, Edith had moved off to inspect the equally compact washroom. 'Maybe so,' he said, casting his own eyes into the receptacle. 'But we don't do guesswork. We haven't figured this as spur-of-the-moment yet.'

'Of course. As you say, I can indulge in speculation where you can't. What time was Mr Hoyle killed?'

Grumbling, Hansen pulled out a notebook and made a show of flipping the pages. 'Doc estimates between seven and ten p.m.'

'And when was Mr Simcoe seen leaving?'

'A little after eleven thirty.'

'A difference of ninety minutes, if not more. And yet Mr Simcoe remains the focus of the department's investigation?'

'Can't discuss that. Sorry.' Not a scintilla of sorrow registered in Hansen's voice.

I decided to get involved. 'Mr Simcoe was seen leaving by a neighbor, is that right? And that neighbor saw Glenn – Mr Hoyle – dead, because the door was open?' I pointed to the door in question, striving to be helpful. 'If Mr Simcoe had committed a murder, why didn't he shut the door behind him?'

Hansen grinned. 'That's how these affairs typically go. Details don't make sense until you get the whole picture.' *And you're not getting that picture from me* went unsaid.

'Naturally,' Edith said. 'We understand the information you can provide is limited under the circumstances, Detective. We appreciate what you've been able to share.'

Which so far, I thought, *amounts to bubkes.*

'But surely you can indicate whether your colleagues have looked into the matter of Mr Simcoe's whereabouts that evening. We have no wish to waste your time or ours.'

The reasonable nature of the request won Hansen over, though he turned the pages of his notebook sullenly. 'They did, and it's part of your pal Simcoe's problem. He was all over town that night. Seen by lots of people. Trouble is, he's jawing at them while they're on the go, fetching cars outside restaurants or pouring drinks at Ciro's. That's the nature of his business. There's a whole line of people saw Simcoe that night, and not one of them can say exactly when. It's one of those alibis that's no alibi at all.'

While he spoke, I drifted toward the wastebasket nonchalantly, yet conscious of every move I made. When I reached it, I glanced away – *throw Hansen off the scent*, I thought cagily – before bending down to re-buckle the strap of my shoe. I don't know what I expected to see when I glanced into the bin. The note on which Simcoe had pegged his hopes wasn't there. Just some clumps of dust and a few stray brown hairs. Glenn had tidied the room not long before his death, the duster he'd used having shed feathers when he shook it over the trash. They lay atop the refuse – two a drab gray, another a jaunty flash of brown – next to a spent match, conceivably the one Sam had tossed in there when he spotted the paper.

As I rose, Hansen barreled toward me. A few words from Edith cut him off. 'About this neighbor.'

Hansen stopped short. 'What neighbor?'

'The one who saw Mr Simcoe leaving.'

'Don't talk to him. Do *not* talk to him. I told Barney I'd let you have a look around, but I'm not gonna—'

Edith raised both hands, showing she was unarmed. 'We won't talk to him, Detective. I assure you. We'd simply like a sense of his statement to the authorities.'

'What he saw,' I added eagerly. 'What he heard.'

Hansen pinched the bridge of his nose so tightly I thought I heard it pop. Once more into his notebook he went, reciting the words like a bored child repeating catechism. 'The neighbor had a few friends in that night at approximately nine p.m. and saw them off shortly after eleven thirty. He was going to ask Hoyle to join him for a drink when a man later identified as Sam Simcoe passed him. The neighbor asked if Hoyle was home. Simcoe did not respond. The neighbor went to Hoyle's door, found it open' – here a sarcastic bow in my direction – 'and saw Hoyle dead on the floor. He had started back to his place when he saw Simcoe on the path. Simcoe claimed he'd gone to find a telephone. He then added a police officer was coming up the street, and they should get him.' He shut the notebook with a snap.

'I don't understand,' I said.

Hansen glowered at me. 'A patrolman was outside—'

'No, the neighbor's story. He's having a party and—'

'I didn't say a party. I said he had a few friends in.' He flipped back through his notebook, prepared to quote scripture again.

'The point is he had guests, and he's friendly enough with Glenn – Mr Hoyle – to invite him over as well. Why wait until *after* the others have left?'

Edith raised an eyebrow at the question. Even Hansen looked thrown by it. He flipped ahead one page in his book. 'I didn't talk to the man. But maybe he wasn't ready to turn in and didn't want to have a nightcap alone. Is there anything else? Because lunch hour's almost over and I ain't had a bite yet.'

Edith and I exchanged a look. The excursion had come a cropper so far, and we hadn't eaten yet either.

'Well, yes,' I said. 'We were wondering about the list.'

Hansen smirked triumphantly. 'The famous list. I knew it. I knew you were after it the second I caught you bird-dogging the trash. It was fished outta there after Simcoe apparently wouldn't shut up about it. Told you about it, did he?'

'Yes,' Edith said. 'He placed considerable emphasis on it.'

'We were hoping we could see it,' I added.

'*See* it? You pulling my leg? We don't make a habit of showing evidence to anybody who asks. Especially when they're aiding and abetting a gossip columnist. One who's wrong half the time anyway. Never read her myself.' He rocked back on his heels with the swagger of a carny in on the gaff, sizing up a sucker. '*I've* seen this fabled list, of course.'

'That's as good as our seeing it, Detective.' Edith's voice brimmed with confidence. 'If you can let us know what it said.'

Sufficiently buttered up, he riffled through the notebook. 'Figured you'd want that. Just a few monikers.' Hansen reeled off the same three names Sam Simcoe had given us, in the same order. The starlet, the producer, the has-been.

'The boys say it's Hoyle's handwriting,' Hansen continued. 'Matched it with a few samples.'

'Mr Simcoe said the page was torn out of a notebook,' Edith said. 'Is that correct? And was the notebook found here?'

'The page looks like it was torn out of something. But a search did not find a notebook with missing pages.'

His deliberate phrasing sounded ready-made for a courtroom, I thought. So did Edith; her eyes narrowed. 'Did your colleagues find a notebook *without* missing pages?'

Hansen thumbed his hat back, exposing his abashed expression. 'That's a question Perry Mason would ask. Who played him again?'

'Warren William was the best one.' I answered quickly, to keep him talking.

'They did turn up a notebook. Full of drawings. Diagrams for magic act equipment. Hoyle used to build it for people. Must've learned from the old man. It's funny, once you know how they saw a woman in half, it's kinda obvious.' Hansen looked disappointed by this newly acquired knowledge. 'The paper was the same kind they found in the trash.'

'Then Mr Hoyle could have had another notebook of that style, one that is now missing, from which that sheet of paper could have been torn,' Edith said. 'Meaning Mr Simcoe's story could be valid.'

Hansen came as close to snorting as he dared. 'Could be.'

'Is the department investigating those names, Detective?'

'They were on a piece of paper fished out of the garbage.'

'At a crime scene. Are the detectives looking into them?'

'They know what the paper says.'

'If they're taking Sam's story seriously, there's no need for us to be in their hair.' I made the prospect sound as appealing as possible.

'They know what the paper says.' Hansen's second take of the line didn't improve on his first. He walked to the door. 'And now this expedition comes to a close. I gotta eat.'

Edith followed him. I trailed petulantly behind. 'Then they're considering other suspects.'

'Sure. But they keep circling back to your pal Simcoe.'

'Why? What's his motive supposed to be?'

'He's in a cutthroat racket. Hoyle was part of it. Who knows the particulars yet? But when a feller leaves somebody he claims is a friend dead on the floor and doesn't call us straight away, you start with him and don't stray too far.'

A whirl of colors – reddish-orange, flecks of green – hovered above the courtyard fountain: a hummingbird, pausing to slake its thirst. Finding nothing but dust, it fluttered off in a fit of pique.

Edith was thanking Hansen again for his assistance when he loped alongside her. 'What's Lorna Whitcomb like in person?'

'Exactly like you think. Only more so.'

'Yeah, like I said, I don't read her myself. I'll take Jimmie Fidler over Lorna and that lot any day of the week. You know why? He's *mean*. Doesn't pull his punches.'

Hansen chuckled and waved broadly toward the street, as if we were unaware of its existence. But this pantomime, every bit as flashy as the hummingbird's plumage, hadn't done the job. I'd spied the motion of the shade in the window we were passing an instant before Hansen had interrupted Edith. He'd intended to distract us from that sight. The neighbor who had identified Sam Simcoe, I suspected.

At the curb, I bid farewell to Edith. She vowed to dispatch a token of her esteem to Delia Carson upon her return to Paramount, and I promised to spare no detail about my dinner at the restaurant that employed Vernon Reynolds. As she motored off, I gave Hansen my best ingenue smile, dewy and trusting. 'My ride is around the corner.'

'I'll walk you.'

'That's not necessary.'

'It's not the best neighborhood. Didn't ya hear? Guy got killed here last week.'

He didn't show me to the door. When we were close enough to see our reflections in the gleaming fender of Addison's Cadillac, he tugged his hat and spun back toward his own car. I piled into the backseat. Rogers didn't bother to set aside his newspaper.

'There may be a car following us for a little while.' Why I was whispering, I had no idea. But a touch of drama never hurt. 'As soon as it's not, I'd like to come back here. You can park in front this time.'

Rogers turned the Caddy's engine over. He seemed somewhat pleased by these instructions.

Sure enough, I spotted Hansen tooling along behind us. Once it became obvious that Rogers was navigating his way back toward Addison's house, Hansen peeled off, no doubt in pursuit of a defenseless ham steak. Rogers drove on another block, then word-lessly began looping back to the bungalow court.

This time, the window shade didn't budge. I mounted the steps to the door. A worn scrap of paper alongside the jamb identified the resident as Pincus. With a handkerchief at the ready, I knocked on the door.

I had worked up to a fusillade before getting a response. The man who wrenched the door open blinked furiously at me, tugging his suspenders over a grubby undershirt. He stood several inches over six feet in height. He had a head shaped like the last potato at the greengrocer's, enormous and dented. He shoved his fingers through the tuft of jet-black hair that crowned it, the motion unleashing a tangy musk. Every shade behind him was drawn, cloaking the room in a coffee-colored light. From what I could see, his place was the masculine cave I had expected Glenn's to be.

'Yeah?' he said in a soft voice, a bear not yet completely roused.

'I'm sorry to disturb you, Mr Pincus. But I believe you saw us leaving with the officer just now. He told us you were the one who found . . . Glenn.' I almost flushed with pride at the hitch in my voice before I said the name.

He squinted at me. 'You family?'

Time to deploy the handkerchief. I raised it to my eyes without a word or a nod. Pincus, as I'd hoped, glanced away at this show of emotion. Technically, I hadn't lied. I hoped at least one of the saints observing this encounter had sufficient legal training to argue this point when the time came.

'That was a rough night,' he said.

Pincus took me for Glenn's kith and kin. I probably shouldn't have felt a strange thrill at that. To ignore it, I kept talking. 'We're trying to make sense of what happened. If there's anything you can share . . .'

He slouched against the doorjamb and relayed a story much like the one Hansen had told us. He described Sam Simcoe as 'squirrelly' and referred to him more than once as 'the little fellow.' Picturing the two men standing next to each other in Glenn Hoyle's doorway, Pincus dwarfing Simcoe, did smack of a Mack Sennett sight gag. At least until I remembered that Glenn Hoyle was laid out on the floor mere feet away from the mismatched twosome.

'Always felt bad for Glenn, living in the corner back there.' Pincus spoke easily now, relishing his expert status. 'He was a good neighbor. Except when he'd leave his car in the alley so he could use his garage as a workshop. Hammering away on different contraptions, mixing up chemicals. All for these magician friends of his, he said. Figured he knew that stuff and those people on account of his father.'

'The Great Horatio,' I said, nodding. 'You two must have been good friends, then.'

Pincus came off the jamb, frowning. 'Why would you say that?'

'You were looking for him at almost midnight, the detective said. To invite him to your party.'

'Oh. Yeah. That.' Each sentence fell like a drop of water into a full bucket. Pincus mussed his hair. 'It wasn't really a party.'

'I see.' Actually, I didn't, but I had an idea and decided to run it up the flagpole. 'May I ask, did you want to see Glenn regarding his . . . his other business?'

Pincus crossed his arms. The acrid smell hit me again. I didn't want to upset him. 'We know how Glenn kept the wolf from the door,' I continued. 'It's an open secret. He'd handle bets. Is that why you wanted to see him?'

After a glance around the courtyard, Pincus relaxed a little. 'Considering you know, yeah. I'd hit a good one at Del Mar the day before. Guy at work gave me the tip and it panned out for once. I wanted my winnings before I went out that night, it being a Friday. Thought I'd be able to live high for a while. Then I ran my mouth about it and asked some friends back, picking up a few bottles on the way. Why not, seeing as I had money due me? Guess I'm not getting any of it now. Leave it to me to pick a winner and wind up in the hole.'

I mustered my most sympathetic look. If Pincus blamed Sam Simcoe for the loss of his windfall, it might account for his animus toward the squirrelly little fellow.

Pincus was still grieving his fate. 'My own fault. Shoulda gotten the cash earlier, but—' The enormous head rocked back, as if he'd been literally struck by a thought. He scanned the courtyard again, this time fearfully.

'Is everything all right?' I asked.

'Yeah. Sure. It's nothing.' He gnawed on his lower lip like it was a porterhouse.

I had to push him. 'What's nothing?'

'No, I just realized I forgot. I did try to see Glenn earlier. To get my money before I went out. Around four that afternoon.'

'And he wasn't home?'

'No, he was home. But he had company. I didn't bother to knock. Just figured I'd come back later. Then, like I said, I ran into some friends, and I was feeling flush even though I wasn't yet, and I—'

'You didn't tell the police this?' I cut in.

'Only because I forgot, like I said. They were asking about how I found him, and the last time I saw him. Not the last time I *didn't* see him.'

'Or his guest.'

Pincus shook his head. 'Nah. I didn't see her, either.'

'Her? It was a woman?'

'Yeah. Not like I thought about it when it happened, but yeah. I didn't hear her voice.'

'Then how do you know it was a woman?'

He pointed at my shoes. 'I could hear her walking around while

Glenn talked. Glenn liked to talk. Couldn't get a word in edgewise with him. She stretched her legs while he chattered away. Heard her shoes clicking against the floor.'

'And that was unusual, Glenn having a woman visit him?'

'I suppose it must be. Glenn had company before, but they were usually fellows looking for their money.' Pincus was poised to say more when his colossal cranium again reared and he stared at me. It was slowly dawning on him that *I* was a woman, one who knew – or claimed to know – Glenn Hoyle, and theoretically could have been his guest, and thus his killer. Moving in an exaggerated casual fashion, he put the door to his bungalow between us. He pushed it and the pungent aroma toward me.

'This could be important information,' I fairly shouted at him. 'You should let the police know.'

'I will.' He shut the door. Before I could step off the low porch, he edged it open again. My eyes watered. 'Sorry for your loss.'

I walked around to the garage, which stood on the opposite side of a dusty alley. It was in more dilapidated condition than the bungalows. I peered in a succession of cracked windows until I spotted a car parked underneath a faded poster trumpeting the lineup at Kansas City's Orpheum Theater two decades ago. The Great Horatio rode high on the bill, listed third. Aside from a few bottles and jars on a high shelf, I couldn't see anything else.

Rogers broke his vow of silence when I returned to the car. 'We actually going to Mr Rice's this time?'

'Yes. But keep your eyes peeled.'

He regularly checked the rear-view and side mirrors on the drive back. Maybe he was warming to me at last.

SEVEN

The boy stared at me every time he pedaled past Arturo's Ristorante. Bigger than one of the *Our Gang* rascals, not quite the size of a Dead End Kid, he sported a shiner and a whoopee cap festooned with pins. He'd take long laps around

the neighborhood, disappearing for minutes at a time. Then the
sound of his rickety bicycle would herald his return long before
he hove into view. I was alone on the sidewalk, so I tried ignoring
the little scrapper. But he kept circling back, swinging closer with
each pass. I fixed my gaze toward Sunset Boulevard, willing
Addison's Cadillac to appear.

I had arrived early, my uncle Danny's watchword ringing in my
ears: 'Anyone worth waiting for, pet, wouldn't make people wait.'
I'd rushed home to change for the evening, donning a dinner dress
in black rayon with a print of moons and stars. Loitering outside
Arturo's, though, I feared I'd overdone it. None of the other women
entering the restaurant looked quite so formal, all of them eyeing
me up and down before heading inside. The restaurant itself didn't
exactly dazzle, the exterior painted a white so stark it resembled
the stubby end of some root vegetable discarded by the kitchen
staff.

The kid made his latest circuit at his slowest speed yet, his
expression boldly inquisitive. He swung the bicycle to a halt before
me and spat on the road.

'You haven't eaten there, have you?' he said sadly. 'It's not
worth getting dolled up for.' With that, he rode off into the fading
light.

A horn tootled behind me. I turned to find Addison's Cadillac
at the curb. Behind the wheel, Rogers looked mortified; he didn't
strike me as an innate tootler. I happily clambered into the car,
overheated after my wait in the sun.

'Don't you look lovely?' Addison had opted for a lightweight
summer suit, accented with a cool green tie and matching pocket
square. 'I assume we're sticking with the plan.'

We had spent the afternoon studying movie-magazine photographs of Vernon Reynolds, the director who once had the
Hollywood tiger by the tail. Reynolds had struck a dynamic pose
in every shot, forever pointing or peering into a camera. Together,
Addison and I had committed Reynolds's broad features to
memory. Once inside the restaurant, I would pretend to recognize
him and Addison would broach the subject of his late, lamented
directorial career. Granted, I would be keeping Addison somewhat
in the dark, not telling him about the mission Edith and I had
reluctantly accepted on Lorna Whitcomb's behalf. But his delight

at the prospect of meeting the man responsible for *The Wayward Path* assuaged whatever guilt I felt. Which, as usual, was considerable.

Our success was ordained when Reynolds himself swept over to greet us as we stepped into Arturo's, a dim grotto that smelled of candle wax and basil. Reynolds's hair had thinned and grayed, and he wore a serviceable if shiny black jacket that didn't quite match the shade of his trousers. Still, his tie was immaculately knotted, and his mantle of authority – over the front of a restaurant if not an entire film set – completed the ensemble beautifully. He ushered us to a booth, chatting amiably about the weather as he pulled out the table so we could sit. He then presented us with impossibly long menus on which cartoon gondoliers navigated from the hors d'oeuvres to the hot dishes.

'That's definitely him,' Addison whispered as Reynolds retreated. 'Let's order some food and figure out the timing.'

We nibbled on jumbo ripe olives and caviar canapés – 'Maude would never let me eat these, so I'm going to indulge' – as we watched our quarry. Reynolds darted to-and-fro with the poise of a ship's captain, tamping out fires before they erupted into infernos. Some of his aplomb was pure artifice; he pumped his arms as he flitted about the restaurant, creating the illusion of speed without moving any faster. At other times, he carried himself like a man with an ear cocked for a telephone call that would never come. He had commanded larger stages than Arturo's, and some part of him clearly longed to return there.

While we decorously demolished our appetizers, I noticed that one of Reynolds's duties was to proffer an arm to any woman seeking the restroom. Addison agreed that it provided the perfect opportunity to initiate conversation. I rose from the table and set my course.

Only to be intercepted by a busboy, who bolted over and seized my arm as if he were drowning. He looked terrified as he asked, in a pronounced Italian accent, if I was having a nice evening. Assuming that all of Arturo's staff had been instructed to provide this service to the fairer sex, I allowed that I was and double-timed to my destination. I powdered my nose, counted to sixty, and returned to the table.

Where I found Addison chuckling. 'He came at you like a pirate ship!'

Reynolds emerged from the kitchen, flicking at his lapel. 'Second time better be the charm,' I muttered, sallying forth again.

As I feigned hunting for the facilities, Reynolds angled toward me and extended an elbow. 'May I?'

I accepted. 'Forgive me for intruding,' I said, 'but we were wondering. Aren't you Vernon Reynolds?'

The question scarcely sullied his sangfroid. He merely inclined his head toward me and smiled. 'It's not often I'm recognized. I'm not surprised it should be by Mr Rice.'

'You recognized him?'

'Of course. He's a leading light of our city.'

'And a great admirer of motion pictures and their history.'

The busboy who'd escorted me on my first trip stared at me with deep concern, undoubtedly thinking I'd fallen victim to some kidney ailment.

As we neared the ladies' room door, I told Reynolds, 'Mr Rice would very much like to say hello in person.'

'It would be my honor.'

He arrived at our table minutes after I returned, bearing a gift. 'With my compliments, Mr Rice.' Reynolds placed a dish of fragrant, lightly breaded sardines before us. 'The specialty of the house, prepared in traditional style.'

Addison praised the offering extravagantly, along with Reynolds's filmography. 'Would you care to join us for a moment?'

Reynolds's bow managed to be both discreet and full of regret. 'If only I could, but duty calls.'

'I would love to talk to you about your trailblazing days in Hollywood. What this town must have been like then! When would be convenient to get together for a drink?'

A tremor briefly rumbled through Reynolds's composure. He seemed genuinely moved by Addison's interest. 'I'm here almost every night. I occasionally stop in at Club Bali around the corner after work.'

'How about tonight?'

'I won't finish until ten. I couldn't ask you—'

'Nonsense! I have no problem making an evening of it. Do you, Lillian?'

'Not if you put in a good word with my boss.'

'Then it's set. We'll take in a picture and meet you at the Bali at ten.'

Reynolds left, and Addison and I set upon the sardines like seagulls. They were delicious, prepared simply but well. The rest of the meal didn't equal them, but we didn't mind. Not when Vernon Reynolds was bounding about the restaurant like a man reborn, a newfound spring in his step.

I gushed about *Pride and Prejudice* all the way back to Sunset Boulevard. Having been wowed by Laurence Olivier in *Wuthering Heights* and *Rebecca*, I was rounding into form on his turn as Mr Darcy as Addison and I strolled under a sign blinking *Bali* and up to a small white turret, its roof covered in Spanish tile.

The second I saw the interior's ruby red walls, I commended myself on my wardrobe change. I might have been overdressed for Arturo's, but I fit right in at Club Bali. Japanese lanterns and bamboo decorations conjured an exotic atmosphere, augmented by the beguiling scent of spices from the kitchen; already I was wishing we'd dined here instead of Arturo's. The waiters ferried out platters of curried food with cautious steps. Once my eyes adjusted to the darkness, I saw that they were clad in sarongs and sandals. Murals on several walls depicted doe-eyed island maidens who looked strangely familiar.

When the headwaiter heard we would be joined by Mr Reynolds shortly, he smiled with easy familiarity and led us to a coral-red booth with a view of the evening's entertainment. The pale man in the tuxedo seated at the piano didn't sing as he tickled the ivories so much as speak in a style suited to his thin but precise voice. His current number described a 'Nympho-Dipso-Ego Maniac' in a dizzying cascade of words, double entendres flying. The audience, studded with fans, hooted even before he'd reached the risqué lyrics. I didn't need to read the sign by the door identifying him as Bruz Fletcher. His name had been a staple in gossip columns, including Lorna Whitcomb's, for years.

'I've always wanted to see him,' Addison said over the applause. 'Even thought about having him entertain at one of my parties. But Maude isn't partial to bawdy songs, I'm afraid.'

Fletcher sounded utterly exhausted as he introduced his next song, 'My Doctor'. As he boasted about the size of his physician's practice to gales of laughter, a waiter led Vernon Reynolds to our booth. Reynolds whispered a few words to the man, who good-naturedly slapped his arm. As Reynolds sat next to me, a second server dropped off an unordered tumbler of brown liquid with a wink.

'You *are* a regular,' I said.

'I'd work here if I could. But alas, sarongs are a younger man's game.' Reynolds looked spent at the end of his shift. But he hadn't loosened his tie or removed his jacket, in deference, I thought, to Addison.

'Is it your first time hearing Bruz?' Reynolds asked as Fletcher took his bows, saying the name so it rhymed with *buzz*. 'A wonderful talent. Just back from performing in New York. He'll close this set with a favorite of mine.'

'Drunk with Love' made for a change of pace, a melancholy tune about a tempestuous romance. Real pain resounded in Fletcher's delivery. I alone gasped when he worked 'Goddammit' into the lyrics, but only Addison and Reynolds heard me. Or so I hoped.

As Fletcher rose from the piano, I took in the adoring crowd. A figure at the bar resembled Ready Blaylock, Kay's sham sweet-heart, down to the natty brown suit I'd seen him wear on multiple occasions, but the man now stood with his back to me. I persuaded myself it wasn't on purpose.

Our awkward settling-in chat with Reynolds focused on the room. I mentioned the oddly familiar paintings on the walls and he explained that they were the work of one of Walt Disney's animators.

Addison brought up the subject of Reynolds's former career tactfully. 'You don't have to discuss it. But I love hearing about the early days of the picture business.'

'That's so long ago. It might as well have happened to a different person.' He gazed at the stage even though it stood bare. 'In some ways, it did. Most of the staff at the restaurant don't know I used to make pictures. I'm convinced half of them think I'm Arturo.'

'Do you see anyone from those days?' I asked.

'Yes, but not socially. They come in to eat sometimes, and the same routine plays out. They see me, have a moment of recognition, then panic over the tip. Usually, they leave nothing. Which means either they've always been tight-fisted and I never knew it, or they think I'd be embarrassed to accept their money.'

'My uncle Danny always says shame and work don't belong in the same sentence.'

'A wise man. It's strange, I must admit, showing people I once directed to their table. So I act like I'm still directing them.' A practiced chuckle, a sip of his drink. 'But I take pride in what I do. I help people enjoy themselves. I like to think I'm making a little movie every night. The food's certainly better than it was on set. No more bread-and-butter sandwiches with a hard-boiled egg.'

'Still, it would be marvelous if you could share your memories for posterity,' Addison said. 'So future generations would have them along with your films.'

'Do you think future generations will care for the pictures we made? I can't see it.' A second glass of whiskey had miraculously appeared before Reynolds, and he drained half of it in one pull. 'As for my memories, Lord knows I have enough. From the days when this place was nothing but orange trees and you were five minutes from brushland. Staying at the Hollywood Hotel on Highland, the rocking chairs lined up on the porch. Cribbing my best ideas from C.B. DeMille, who cared about the business more than I ever did. And scandals, so many scandals. Most of the people involved in them have been forgotten . . . but quite a few haven't.'

I felt a charge at those words, like a hound hearing the horn at the start of the hunt. 'Anyone you'd care to name?' I asked, aiming for a sufficiently blasé tone.

'Those stories go with me to the grave.' He sounded as if he expected to be making that trip shortly.

Before I could say anything more, Bruz Fletcher sauntered over to the table. Reynolds embraced him. Fletcher had handsome Midwestern features, at first glance looking like a small-town druggist recently elected alderman. But his deathly pallid complexion and the indolent droop of his cigarette gave him an amiably louche quality.

Addison asked him to stay. 'Only for a moment,' Fletcher said wearily. 'The slave driver calls.'

As we sat down, I looked back across the room. Yes, it was definitely Ready at the bar, talking to a strapping blond man while peering over at me. I waved, and Ready turned away. I wondered how I'd wronged him, or likely Kay.

We made nice with Fletcher, Addison and I both praising his songs. 'No doubt you're asked this all the time,' I said, 'but where did you get the name "Bruz"?'

'A childhood mispronunciation of "brother". Tragic, isn't it, how one mistake can haunt you the rest of your life?' Fletcher pressed a single finger to his forehead, as if forestalling agony. 'Still, better that than to be stuck with my Christian name. Stoughton. Stoughton Fletcher the Fourth, to add insult to injury. How could four generations be so cursed? Every one of them bankers into the bargain.'

'How's your menagerie these days, Bruz?' Reynolds asked.

'Calm for the moment, but the lull will never last.'

Reynolds turned to us. 'Bruz keeps monkeys.'

'You mean they keep me. Up at night, for weeks on end. Patsy escaped last year. Do you know where we found her? On a ranch owned by Edgar Rice Burroughs. When a monkey goes looking for the creator of Tarzan, there are ancient scores to be settled. *Ancient*.' This time, two fingers to the forehead. 'Patsy developed a taste for life on the road, because she seduced Peter – my other brute – into going along on her next crash-out. They killed my goldfish, smashed all my preserves, and stole pennies from the wishing well. Who does that?'

'Monkeys,' Reynolds said sagely.

'Then they should tell you that when you acquire them. Ah, well. At least the new goldfish suit the décor better.' Fletcher signaled someone across the room. 'So many people to see before the salt mine beckons. Excuse me, won't you?'

Conversation continued, a third whiskey allowing Reynolds's mask of hospitality to slip. 'Pictures are, at their core, a thuggish business. Do your job competently and you'll amass enemies, people plotting your ruin.' He rambled in that vein until he sensed Addison's disappointment. His survival instinct spurred him to tell a story about working with Mary Pickford to win our host's favor again. Talk drifted, as it always did, to the news from Europe. I steered the topic toward another item on the front page.

'That was a terrible story about that young man who was killed. The one tied to Lorna Whitcomb.'

'Yes,' Reynolds said. 'I saw him a few times.'

'Where? Would he come to the restaurant?'

'He may have, but I saw him here. Little wonder, given the crowd Bruz attracts. He's in the columns constantly. Keeps a scrapbook, but he'd never dare admit it, poor darling. Speaking of . . .' He made eye contact with someone by the bar. 'There's someone I should say hello to before Bruz takes the stage again. Would you mind?'

He left, and Addison scooted closer. 'Can't say I blame him for feeling bitter, but I'd hoped he'd open up about his career. But then I'm no professional. I can't coax answers out of people.'

'You're doing fine so far. One more round and he'll be putty in your hands.'

'Do you think? Then perhaps I'd better excuse myself as well.' Addison left me in the booth with the din of the club for company.

As I waited, I wondered. Was Vernon Reynolds a homosexual? It seemed a possibility. And if so, could that be the scandal that Glenn Hoyle had discovered? The prospect struck me as unlikely. Reynolds hadn't been a household name at his height. His descent to the status of head waiter would make for a bigger story. Perhaps Hoyle had induced him to divulge some of those rumors from days of yore.

I was pondering the menu's island-style desserts when Ready slid into the booth. 'Evening, Lillian. Everything all right?'

'I'm fine, except for you high-hatting me.'

'My hat's plenty high, but I'd never give you the brush. I had to come over, make sure you're OK.'

'Why wouldn't I be?'

'It's that feller you're with. I was fixing to say howdy to you and Mr Rice when he joined you, and I figured I'd keep an eye on you.'

'Whatever for?'

'You know me. I don't care to spread rumors.'

'I dearly wish you would.'

Ready leaned closer. He smelled of woodsmoke and rye. 'I don't know him by name. Only by reputation. Which in this stretch of Sunset is if you're after a little pick-me-up, well, he's your man.' His inflection and the deftly timed scratch of his nose left no doubt as to his meaning. 'Not everybody comes here to see Bruz, entertaining as he is.'

A former top-drawer director reduced to peddling drugs? Now
that was a scandal, one Lorna Whitcomb could have made hay
with for weeks. A rush surged through me. I had dug up dirt, and
felt the petty power that came with it. For the first time I could
fathom the allure of the job for Sam Simcoe, and his benevolent
attitude toward Glenn Hoyle, supplier of scuttlebutt.

'Is that all you've heard?' I asked Ready.

'It's enough, isn't it? What's his name? Arturo?' Ready made
it sound like a town in Mexico.

'Vernon Reynolds. He directed pictures once upon a time.'

'He did?' Ready sat back. 'Now that you mention it, he does
strut around like he's cock of the walk. Used to folks listening to
him. Do you need any help?'

'You've already done more than enough.'

'Give me a sign if there's trouble.' He leant in to kiss my cheek.
As he did, he whispered, 'If you could not tell Kay you saw me,
I'd be much obliged.'

Ready stopped to exchange greetings with Addison. Reynolds
bounded energetically back to our table, the spring in his step now
suspicious. Perhaps he partook of his own product. A smattering
of applause greeted Bruz as he returned to the piano. 'The late
show is where the blue material is,' Reynolds said.

Addison laughed. 'I thought it was plenty blue already.'

'I hate to spoil a party,' I said, 'but it's a work night.'

'Of course. It's been a pleasure, Addison, truly. Don't worry
about your drinks. I've taken care of them.'

'No! But I invited you.'

'If it eases your conscience, I didn't pay very much. Friend of
the establishment. One of the benefits this business has over
pictures. We support one another.'

We said our goodbyes and beat a path to the exit. Ready winked
at me. I glanced back to see that Reynolds had moved closer to
the stage. He laughed at Fletcher's patter and signaled to a waiter
to set up a round for friends seated nearby. He seemed confident
and at ease, even if he didn't make it to Pickfair much anymore.

Los Angeles Register   August 16, 1940

LORNA WHITCOMB'S
EYES ON HOLLYWOOD

Paulette Goddard was on the town this week blinding dinner companions with the flash of her new diamond bracelet. A gift from hubby Charlie Chaplin, she told everyone who asked – and some who hadn't . . . Yes, we've read all about the explosive grand jury testimony branding some of our solid citizens as Communists. Just remember that plenty of bombshells turn out to be duds . . . Idle questions: when's the last time an Addison Rice affair set the town ablaze? Has he ceded his title as our most prominent party-thrower? . . . Someone should stop Edgar Bergen from throwing his voice at waitresses. Last night a poor girl at the Hollywood Tropics, thinking she heard Charlie McCarthy sassing her from under a table, sent her tray crashing to the floor. Restaurant owners say Bergen is responsible for more broken dishes than a third-rate juggling act . . . There's a new face at Paramount's wardrobe department. Count Oleg Cassini has been hired to bring authentic Continental style to the studio's glamour gals. We hear the dashing count is as clever with costumes as he is with the ladies. Could this mean the days of the studio's diminutive lead costume designer, Edith Head, are numbered?

EIGHT

I paced the portico of Addison's home, too anxious to enter. What I wanted to do was track down Lorna Whitcomb, knock the feathered hat from her head, and remove her hair one clump at a time. But first I had to ensure her barb hadn't wounded my employer too grievously. A faithful reader of the major columnists, he'd have seen her potshot.

No sense delaying the inevitable. I drew a deep breath and threw open the doors in my best Joan Crawford fashion.

I found Addison in the library, gazing forlornly out at the lush lawn. A cup of coffee cooled next to the open newspapers.

When I got my hands on Lorna, I vowed, I would make every column in the country. Maybe some in Europe.

'I'm so sorry,' I said by way of greeting.

A startled Addison twitched in his seat. 'Good heavens, Lillian! You're sorry for what?'

I gestured helplessly at the newsprint. 'Lorna Whitcomb's hateful column.'

'I don't care about that. Besides, it's hardly your fault.'

But it is, I thought, prepared to confess my sin.

'And she's right,' Addison continued. 'Parties aren't as important to me anymore. Not with all that's happening overseas. All of us acting like the war won't affect us when it already is. But to be honest, I'm still thinking about last night.'

'You mean Mr Reynolds?'

'It's a crime, seeing him reduced to that status. Working in a restaurant. The man who directed Norma Talmadge in *Hearts Ablaze*, who called down the fury of heaven in *Fury of Heaven*! Why isn't he still making pictures? At the very least he should be a mentor to other young directors, a teacher. He should have some other means of keeping body and soul together.'

I decided not to enlighten my employer about Reynolds's alleged sideline.

Addison hoisted himself out of his chair. 'And why aren't we paying attention to the history of the picture business all around us? I've been up half the night stewing about this.'

'This is what happens when Mrs Rice is away,' I cautioned.

'I know, I know. I fixed myself some warm milk, not that it did any good. Pictures are the definitive art form of this century, and they need to be preserved and celebrated as such. They're off to a good start at the Museum of Modern Art, this project of Jock Whitney's. A national film library is essential. But that's in New York. We're smack dab in the middle of where pictures are made! I'm cooking up a plan to address the problem. Something I can do here, in Los Angeles, to further the cause of film history. It has the feel of a grand project. A legacy.'

'Tell me what I can do.'

'It will start with a few phone calls that won't make much sense. And you'll have to listen to me ramble.'

'I'd do that anyway.'

'Are you at work?' Edith asked the instant I identified myself on the telephone. 'How is Mr Rice?'

'Surprisingly sanguine, considering. While I feel terrible. I haven't told him I'm to blame for Lorna's nasty little dig. Why would she attack us like this when we're working for her?'

'Come to the studio this afternoon.' A hardness I'd never heard before slipped into Edith's voice. 'You and I are going to find out.'

Nearly a full day's toil had pushed Lorna's treachery out of my mind, but by the time I reached Edith's office I was steamed anew. I stormed in at full boil, ready to shriek like a tea kettle, when I saw that Edith wasn't alone.

Barbara Stanwyck had thrown a leg over the arm of a chair in Edith's salon. She wore tan slacks with a pale yellow blouse, a blue-and-yellow neckerchief amplifying the color. A jacket matching the slacks had been tossed cavalierly over the chair's other arm. The actress looked effortlessly comfortable, save for the sunglasses she hadn't removed.

'Hey there, Flushing. How's tricks?' She waved casually, not rising from her chair. 'I'll tell you up front I'm not a barrel of laughs today. I'm in one of my black shanty Irish moods.'

'So am I,' I said. 'We'll keep each other company.'

'I'll apologize for the glasses. I got some kind of damned infection on this Capra picture.' She lowered the shades, exposing a vividly pink eye. 'Can't have anybody claiming I'm hiding a shiner, can I? My doctor gave me some drops that don't seem to be making a bit of difference. You wouldn't think a thing like this would matter much, but my world's topsy-turvy because of it. Had to drop out of a Bill Wellman picture I was set to do.'

'Which leaves you free to be in Preston's.' Edith stood to adjust the blinds. She had accented her taupe dress with a lavender scarf, cinched around her waist as a belt. 'As I've been saying.'

'I don't know.' Barbara swung a leather loafer back and forth, all nervous energy. 'The character's a real glamour-puss. Very refined. Gloves and gowns and everything just so.' She said the last in a cod highbrow accent that sounded like the McCoy to me. 'But I don't do clothes.'

'Yes, you do.' Edith snapped the blinds shut with such force that Barbara's foot stopped moving at once. 'You just don't know it.'

'I appreciate the cheering section, but I've been working with this body a long time. Everything I put on ends up looking like a burlap sack.'

'That's because I didn't design it for you. Preston wants you for this picture. He's written a glamorous role. Therefore, he sees you as glamorous. As do I. All that remains is for *you* to see yourself as glamorous. With me designing your wardrobe, you will.'

Barbara sat up straight and raised her eyebrows at me. *Get her.* 'I'll say this for you, Jughead. You're no shrinking violet when you're after something. You may want this more than me.' She started to lower her sunglasses, then thought better of it. 'You really think you can pull off those get-ups on me?'

Edith picked up several sketches on her desk and held them aloft. 'Without a doubt. And I'll make them so much like a second skin that you can pull them off, too.'

'That's reason enough to do the picture right there. You weigh in, Flushing. What do you think?'

'One, I think you're glamorous. Two, a wise woman once told me whatever Edith's advice is on clothes, take it.'

'That was me, wasn't it? Serves me right, boxing myself into a corner.' Barbara shrugged into her jacket. 'Preston did tell me he'd write me a whale of a comedy someday. Maybe *The Lady Eve* is it. Even if Madeleine Carroll and Paulette Goddard got their mitts on it first.'

Barbara's leave-taking included a plug for the Hollywood Stars, the baseball team she and her husband Robert Taylor partly owned – 'Go to a game while the weather's perfect.' As Edith shut the salon door behind her, she said, 'I cancelled my outing to Del Mar for Mr Crosby's premiere. Lorna is next door at RKO, interviewing Orson Welles. I propose we ambush her.'

As we readied ourselves for the assault, I raised a thorny subject.

'What's the story with this Oleg Cassini fellow she mentioned in her column? Is that true or the bunk? Is this why you've been out of sorts lately?'

'Have I been out of sorts? You've seen through me.' She half-smiled, which, considering she never bared her teeth, was more of a quarter-smile. 'Yes, the studio has hired Mr Cassini as a designer. Noise has been made about me being spread too thin, kind souls saying I can't be expected to do every picture. But I know he's viewed in some quarters as a potential replacement for me. Mr Groff said as much when he "encouraged" me to assist Lorna. But I will only assist her so much.'

Again, I was reminded that whenever Edith spoke of anyone other than a close friend using their Christian name, she had consigned them to the lowest circles of damnation.

We started at a brisk pace over to the RKO lot, just on the other side of the studio wall. As we walked, I told Edith what I'd learned since we last spoke: that a woman had visited Glenn Hoyle shortly before his death, and that I'd determined what our director's scandal likely was.

Edith seemed particularly struck by the former note. 'We will not tell Lorna any of that. Or that we've made an overture to the actress on the list, Miss Carson. We shall play our cards close to the vest.'

I strode on, confident that if anyone knew how to conceal items in a vest, it would be a costume designer.

Edith was welcomed onto the RKO lot without question, on what I presumed was a good neighbor policy; Mr RKO never knew when he might have to drop by to borrow a cup of sugar or a Klieg light. She steered us toward a soundstage, its elephant doors open. I couldn't make sense of the set. Erected in pieces, it seemed to coalesce into some kind of theater, but I couldn't be certain.

Lorna stood looming over a seated Orson Welles. I saw the back of her pale green suit; she hadn't spotted us yet. Welles gazed up at her like an angelic schoolboy with a peashooter in his pocket. He'd shaved off the beard that had been an object of scorn in Hollywood since his arrival the year before, his newly exposed cheeks making him look even more boyish.

Only as we drew closer did I realize that Welles was sitting in a wheelchair, one leg bandaged and elevated.

He greeted us like the cavalry riding to his rescue. 'Ladies!' he roared, voice echoing. With a fork he speared a chunk of pineapple from a platter by his side. 'I'd rise and embrace you, but as you can see, I'm in a state of extreme relaxation. Nothing serious, just a slight disagreement with a flight of stairs. Fortunately, I only use that ankle when I stand. Or walk. May I present to you Lorna Whitcomb?'

Lorna turned to us. The smirk may not have been on her lips, but it had settled into her eyes, behind glasses a deeper green than her suit. She wore the same hat she'd had on the other day.

'We've met,' Edith said.

'That's right,' Welles purred. 'That was rather a nasty shot at Edith in this morning's column, Lorna. And another at Lillian's boss! His parties are delightful. He's one of the few people in this hamlet aware that we're living in a wider world. What accounts for this enmity between my friends? I demand to know!'

'Then you do read the columns, Orson.' Lorna shifted her stance away from us, making him the exclusive focus of her attention again. 'I thought you thought you were above that.'

'I have to look at something while I'm waiting for the butler to bring my kippers, don't I?'

'The columns can be your friend. We all managed to keep that dust-up between you and Big Boy Williams at the Brown Derby quiet.'

'Tempest in a teacup.'

'That's not how I heard it. The blow-by-blow says Big Boy called you queer and you traded punches in the parking lot after he cut off your necktie with a knife.'

'I never liked that tie. Made my neck look heavy.'

'I know you don't want advice, but I'll give you mine anyway. Free of charge. Use the columns to your advantage. Win audiences over now, before opinions on you are set. And above all, stop dancing around the truth about this picture of yours being about Hearst. You're nimble enough, but you're no Fred Astaire.'

'Say, is Fred around here?' Welles scanned the area. 'I'm meant to dance in this picture. I could use some pointers.'

'This is what I'm talking about.' Lorna whipped off her glasses and pointed them at Welles. 'You're always joking and you're seldom funny. Lay it out for the public. "I'm making a picture about William Randolph Hearst." Because there *should* be a picture about Hearst, damn it. It's like they say, a cat may look on a king. People know Hearst is a king. You've got to tell them you're the cat.'

Welles stared at her in open astonishment. 'Why, Lorna. I believe you care.'

'I do, and I wish to hell you'd realize it. I'm on your side. Hedda's out for herself, Louella's out of her element, and the rest are mere pikers. I like you, Orson. More importantly, I know what you're doing with this picture, and I like that, too. Listen to your aunt Lorna. Stop playing the boy genius and act like a man with a job. Which is making a picture people will pay to see.' She replaced her spectacles, the better to glare at Welles. 'A good first step would be to stop giving lectures where you say Americans only go to movies because it's better than drink. I don't know what pictures you're seeing or what cocktails you're having, but if you came to my house, I'd set you straight on both fronts.'

Welles pressed a hand to his chest. 'Are you propositioning me? What would Dr Jerry say?'

Lorna tossed up her hands. 'I give up. You're incorrigible. And throwing away the chance of a lifetime.'

A young man, jittery and prematurely balding, darted over to whisper in Welles's ear. After two words, Welles waved him off. 'I'm afraid I must bring this colloquy to a close. And I never had a chance to talk to you, Edith. And you, Lillian.'

'It's quite all right.' Edith looked at Lorna as she spoke. 'We only came over to wish you well after your accident.'

'To tell you the truth, ladies, I welcomed my misfortune. From calamity comes greatness. When we did *Caesar*, the whole cast groused about the five open traps on the stage. "Nonsense," said I, "get used to them!" At the first dress rehearsal, who falls through one?' He howled. 'Old muggins himself. They found me unconscious twenty feet down. Sprained my ankle then, too. The resulting show? An unalloyed triumph. Whenever my confidence flags, I slam my hand in a door.' A haunted look passed over his face. 'I actually stabbed Caesar in that production, too. But that was his fault. All right, children!' He bellowed this last to the company as he aimed his wheelchair at the set. The young man moved to push him, but Welles slapped his hands away. It didn't seem the time to bring up Kay's interest in interviewing him.

'I don't know what on earth that boy's doing,' Lorna said as Welles rolled off. 'He's put ceilings on all of his sets. I suppose we'd better finish our chat outside.'

We emerged from Welles's incomplete world into the sunlight. Sam Simcoe, perched on a staircase, looked surprised to see us. 'Edith! You didn't jump ship to RKO, did you? This is news!'

'No, they're here to castigate me,' Lorna said, suppressing a sigh.

'You're damn right we are,' I snapped.

'You visited Hoyle's place. After I told you not to waste your time.' Lorna's tone made it plain she felt she was wasting her time addressing me. 'Did you think I wouldn't find out? I have eyes and ears everywhere. Let that serve as a reminder. Do as I ask and it will never happen again.'

'I don't trust you to keep your word. And how dare you say anything against my boss.'

Lorna studied me through her eyeglasses. 'What I said is true, isn't it?'

It was, which only made my frustration mount. I felt angry. That made tears spring to my eyes, and I felt angry about that.

'Don't cry.' Lorna offered the words as counsel. 'It's seen as weakness.'

'She's right,' Edith said. 'I never cry. Not at work.'

'I heard you had your tear ducts soldered shut. One of those exotic surgeries down in Mexico.' Lorna checked the time on her wristwatch. 'Very well. Let's get this over with. Say your piece. Sam and I have places to be.'

Edith glanced at me to gauge my status. When I nodded, she faced Lorna. 'Our arrangement is at an end. Lillian and I won't be dealing with you again. My apologies, Mr Simcoe.'

'Because of the column?' Lorna cackled. 'You understand I can do so much worse.'

'It's not only the column, Lorna. I know you're lying.'

'Edith, dear, I'm *always* lying. It's part of my job.'

'You knew Glenn Hoyle. You visited him, at his home, the day he was murdered. We have witnesses. And evidence. There's no sense lying about it now, because I've already informed the police.'

Edith never raised her voice. She might as well have been ordering
bolts of fabric.

Sam needed the handrail to pull himself to his feet. He gaped
at Lorna, stunned.

Lorna, to my surprise, looked utterly delighted. She clapped
her gloved hands. 'Sam, you were right. It was a good idea to
enlist these two.' She turned to him. 'I think we can afford to be
late for this silly cocktail function, don't you?'

NINE

We convoyed to Lorna's car, parked in a shaded spot
alongside less impressive vehicles owned by RKO
executives. Lorna caressed the front fender. 'Paid for
by Dr Jerry. I gave Orson my unsolicited advice. Here's some
for you ladies. Find yourselves wealthy husbands. You didn't the
first time around as I recall, Edith.'

Edith climbed silently into the sedan's backseat. I followed suit.
Lorna and Sam settled in front. There was enough room left over
for a full tea service.

Lorna finally broke the silence. 'I let Sam drive sometimes.
When I remember to bring the telephone books for him to sit on.'

'That line grows funnier with each passing year.' Sam looked at
her directly. 'What is going on? Were you really at Glenn's place?'

'Let's have Edith tell it.'

Edith obliged without preamble. 'The wastebasket in Mr Hoyle's
residence was as Mr Simcoe described, save for the note, which
had been removed as evidence. It was clear that shortly before his
death Mr Hoyle had cleaned his home. Perhaps in anticipation of
a special guest. Someone worth impressing.'

'Naturally, you assume that was me.' Lorna suppressed a yawn.
I suppressed the urge to sink my teeth into her neck.

'Lillian did discover that Mr Hoyle had a female guest the
afternoon he died, a fact the police had overlooked. But what
convinced me was the contents of the wastebasket. The strata of
the debris, as it were. Dust at the bottom. The note Mr Simcoe

discovered presumably atop that, along with the match discarded as part of his ruse. Several turkey feathers.'

'Turkey feathers?' Simcoe said.

'Common in dusters. Like the one Mr Hoyle used to tidy his home. Then a second variety of bird feather. A more decorative one. Exotic, almost. Identical to the ones on the hat you wore the day we met, Lorna. The very hat you're wearing now. Mr Hoyle disposed of it after you left.'

I pivoted toward Lorna as I pictured the feather I'd also seen in the wastebasket. Sure enough, the plumage peeking out from the band in Lorna's hat matched it. I then turned toward Edith and gawped.

'The sort of detail only a costume designer would notice,' Lorna said with grudging admiration. 'You're telling me Hedda Hopper would have gotten away unnoticed, then? Because she changes her hat every damn day. I went with glasses as my signature, once they foisted the title "Eyes on Hollywood" on my column.' She removed her green-framed spectacles and waved them around, as if to demonstrate that they wouldn't bite. 'They're only a gimmick, you know. The lenses are clear glass. Just for appearances. Might as well confess to that, too, if you're exposing my other secrets.'

'Really?' I said. 'You don't need glasses?'

'Wait a minute!' Simcoe sputtered. 'You *were* at Glenn's place?'

'Yes, sweetheart, but you heard Edith. I left, and Hoyle disposed of any trace of me.'

'You could have returned later,' I said.

'But I didn't. Why would I?'

'Why would you go there in the first place?' Simcoe rubbed his temples. 'You swore up and down you didn't know him.'

'I didn't, Sam. I knew *of* him, as you are well aware.' Lorna shifted in her seat to face Edith and me. 'I don't want this commonly known, but I like to place a wager on the horses now and again. Picked up the habit when I was on stage in New York. I have people I use. Discreet people. Sometimes I can't reach them. Sam mentioned that Hoyle kept book, so in a pinch I'd lay a bet with him. Through Sam, of course.'

'Of course,' I said.

'Always using proxies,' Sam said. 'It's the Whitcomb way. But Glenn never knew those were your bets. Is that why you were there? To place another one?'

'No!' Lorna sounded insulted. 'He called the office that morning and insisted on speaking to me directly. He said we had to meet in person. That day. I tried fobbing him off on you, Sam, but he said he didn't trust you anymore. Said you sometimes took credit for his stories.'

'Sure, I did.' Simcoe didn't show a trace of guilt. 'A practice I learned from you.'

'Then who am I to cast blame? Hoyle said he had a lulu of a story, but he'd only tell me in the flesh. I agreed, because he'd caught me in a good mood.'

'And the column was light that day,' Simcoe muttered.

'Like hell it was. I drove out there. Let me tell you, if he'd tidied up that squalid little pit, it's news to me. I asked what this honey of a story was, and he answered with a question of his own. He wanted to know if he brought me the particulars of a white-hot scandal, a *huge* one, would I give him a job. I got the distinct impression he aimed to leapfrog you, Friend Simcoe.'

He grunted. 'You told him yes.'

'No, as it happens. I did not.'

I wasn't sure why I spoke up. 'You told him it depended on how big the story was.'

Lorna peered at me with detached interest, the way a zoologist would reappraise a previously uninteresting specimen that had abruptly sprouted wings or grown a horn. 'That's right. Almost my very words. He said he'd have to settle for that. Once he confirmed the details, he'd present the entire bundle to me with a bow on it. I gave him an earful about wasting my time. He said he wasn't going to do the last licks of work unless he had a guarantee from me, which I had to admit was a smartish play. He promised once I heard what he'd discovered, I'd want to move fast. I told him he'd better come across and went on about my night. The next thing I know, Sam's calling me from the police station asking do I know any lawyers.'

Simcoe stared out at the RKO lot beyond the windshield. 'Well, sports fans, isn't this a turn-up for the books?'

'Yes,' Edith agreed. 'And all because of a feather in a wastebasket.'

'That tears it,' Lorna said. 'Henceforth I exclusively wear turbans.'

'You could have told the police you'd seen him the day he died.' Sam sounded understandably petulant.

'They didn't ask me, dearie. I'll be telling them now, apparently.'

'When you spoke with Mr Hoyle,' Edith said, 'did he happen to have a notebook with him?'

'Did he ever. Peered over the damn thing at me the entire time we talked. Kept consulting it, trying to whet my appetite. Created a very theatrical mood. "If only you knew what treasure these pages contain." Rather effective.'

'That notebook now appears to be missing,' Edith said.

'Unless it's the one the police recovered, and Hoyle used it as a prop,' I countered. 'Or it could have been full of bets he'd taken, and that's why someone swiped it.'

'No, no, no.' Simcoe thumped his fingers on the dashboard, to Lorna's irritation. 'I saw Glenn write the bets down when I placed them for Lorna. He used a completely different kind of paper. Said he did it deliberately, so he wouldn't confuse them. Tips in the notebook, bets on paper.'

'And that notebook was no prop,' Lorna said. 'Hoyle had gotten hold of dynamite. I know the look. He was so sure of what he had he wanted my word I'd hire him at once. That's why I told you to concentrate on the names on that list. The police are fixated on Sam as a suspect – although they'll probably give me the eye now, thanks to you. But Sam's right. That list is the key. Hoyle's actions prove it.'

'You genuinely believe one of those three people murdered Glenn Hoyle?' I heard the incredulity in my voice.

'If not one of them, someone close to one of them. I'm certain of it. I feel it in my bones. And these bones never lie.' Her expression dared us to say otherwise. 'Now tell me what you've found out.'

I deferred to Edith.

'Nothing,' she said. 'Yet.'

Lorna considered her through her useless eyeglasses. 'I don't believe you.'

'Good. You shouldn't. Lillian and I will share what we've learned when we're ready, and after you've informed the police about your visit to Mr Hoyle. I told you I won't conceal any facts from the authorities.'

'You drive a hard bargain,' Lorna said, poised to say more.

Edith spoke over her. 'Also, if you speak ill of Addison Rice again, we will never tell you our findings.'

I wanted to clench Edith's hand at that statement. Instead, I squeezed my own palms together.

Lorna drummed the car's steering wheel. The words came out of her like air from a punctured tire. 'I was perhaps too hasty in my comments in the column today. I'll exercise better judgment in the future.'

'That's as close to an apology as you're going to get,' Simcoe told us. 'If I were you, I'd take it.'

'Oh, hush, Sam. I suppose I'd better make my peace with the police instead of attending this cocktail party. Just as well. Lips never get loose enough at these studio affairs to divulge anything useful. Can I drop you two at Paramount?'

'We're close enough to walk,' Edith said, opening the door.

Simcoe also bailed out of the car and trotted over to us. 'I have to tell you both how much I appreciate your help. What you're doing means more to me than you can ever know.'

'Don't be so quick to thank us, Mr Simcoe. We haven't accomplished anything yet.'

'You put Lorna in her place. That's an achievement.' He grinned. 'I know she didn't exactly charm you into lending a hand. I'm sorry about that. Lorna can be a pain, it's true. But what you have to understand is she—'

Lorna interrupted his defense of her by leaning on the sedan's horn. Simcoe shrugged and scampered again to her side.

We started back. I told myself I only imagined that our footsteps sounded hollow as we made the return leg to Paramount.

'Did you really call the police?' I asked Edith.

'Indeed I did. I telephoned Detective Hansen and had him inform his colleagues. He appreciated that we're making him look resourceful.' She paused. 'At least I think he appreciated it.'

'Lorna's a suspect now.'

'Yes, considering she admits to being the last person to see Mr Hoyle alive.'

'And if Glenn was looking to buck Sam, that makes Sam an even bigger suspect.'

'Agreed. On the other hand, the apparent theft of Mr Hoyle's notebook lends credibility to Mr Simcoe's story.'

Upon returning to the sanctuary of Paramount, we encountered the lot's signature Mutt and Jeff duo. The screenwriting team of Billy Wilder and Charles Brackett looked like a gremlin and his agent, Wilder compact and roguish, the lankier Brackett projecting the unease of a man suffering through a long-winded after-dinner speaker at the Rotary Club. Wilder had nudged his trilby back to make a point, prompting Brackett to signal us frantically.

'What are you ladies up to this afternoon?' he cried.

'Visiting a friend next door at RKO,' Edith said.

Wilder screwed up his face. 'Don't tell me. Was it Orson Welles? They let him direct a picture. Preston is in New York for the premiere of his picture. While I wander the lot polishing lead for Charles Boyer to say.'

'Be fair,' Brackett said. 'I'm polishing, too.'

Wilder removed his hat and pressed his shirtsleeve to his forehead. 'It's Friday, at least. Any plans for the weekend?'

I mentioned that I'd seen Bruz Fletcher the night before.

Brackett laughed, the sound more like a cough. 'Is he back in town? At that tawdry little spot on Sunset? He's my wife's cousin.' To Wilder, he said, 'I told you about him. Fragile creature, too touching to think about. Once the crown prince of Indianapolis.'

'A kingdom I too would forsake,' Wilder said.

'Do you know what I'm looking forward to?' Edith looked squarely at me. 'A quiet few days of doing nothing at all.'

I knew what that meant. Lorna was on her own.

San Bernardino Lamplighter   *August 19, 1940*

KATHERINE DAMBACH'S
SLIVERS OF THE SILVER SCREEN

Seen sharing a chocolate mousse at the Florentine Gardens, Madge Granger and Lloyd Michaels, her co-star in *Delicate Hearts*, now lensing at Lodestar. But isn't Madge playing Lloyd's aunt in the picture? That's no May–December romance, it's a sapling facing down a blizzard . . . There are so few paragons to look up to in this racket, it's a disappointment to encounter one with feet of clay. Imagine my shock to learn one of the exemplars of my trade has found herself in Dutch thanks to the rash actions of a trusted ally. Someone with her many, many years of experience should have known this town is full of people who never show their true faces while they climb the ladder. Note to self: One must choose one's 'friends' wisely . . . Imagine that studio boss's embarrassment when the string on his wife's pearls broke during a dinner party at their home. Guests who helped rescue the baubles quickly realized they weren't the McCoy. No one uttered a peep, but word does get around, doesn't it?

TEN

The weekend passed like the bottom half of a double bill, a B picture I sat through while waiting for the main attraction to start. Addison didn't require my services, with only an intimate dinner party and an evening at the Hollywood Bowl planned. I didn't hear from Edith, or Lorna, or the police. Instead, I made do with oblique, catty asides regarding Lorna's current woes in other columns, like Kay's. If Lorna had been called to account by the authorities, it had been kept quiet.

I read the rest of the papers as well, the tidal wave of news threatening to overwhelm. Further details on the German bombing of England, Wendell Willkie accepting the Republican nomination to run against President Roosevelt, Congressman Dies's return to Los Angeles on the prowl for saboteurs. A recognizable face eyed me from Saturday's front page. Benjamin 'Bugsy' Siegel had been hauled out of a hiding place in the attic of his Holmby Hills mansion and charged with the murder of an associate. I had made the acquaintance of Siegel, the 'sportsman' now identified as one of the most dangerous gangsters in the United States, and while I could readily picture him gunning down a confederate, I couldn't see him cowering in a crawlspace. Siegel, as usual, looked natty in his photograph, wearing a houndstooth jacket and a necktie with a pattern of fanned playing cards.

At Sunday mass, Father Nugent thundered from the pulpit about the indignities of war. He larded his homily with references to *The Fighting 69th*, starring his personal holy duo of James Cagney and Pat O'Brien, but they didn't make his strong medicine go down easier. As the ladies around me fidgeted uncomfortably, I conducted a detailed survey of the feathers in their hats for possible future reference. I spent the rest of the morning cleaning gummy jacaranda petals from my best white shoes. It felt like my only accomplishment of the weekend.

Mainly, I went to the movies, finally catching up with Clark Gable and Spencer Tracy in *Boom Town*. I also treated myself with a return trip to see *Irene*, silly fluff about an Irish lass working in a department store – as I once did – mistakenly plunged into a world of glamour. Maybe I identified with it. Maybe I wanted to see the signature Alice blue gown, which warranted its own Technicolor sequence, again. After the movie, I rushed home and wrote a long letter to my uncle Danny and aunt Joyce in New York. I didn't feel homesick. Simply at a loose end.

I chased away the Monday blues with a red dress in lightweight crepe garlanded with white polka dots. It helped me bound into work with confidence, or at least a facsimile of same.

I greeted Addison by asking about the weekend's concert. 'I trust maestro Georg Szell was equal to the build-up.'

'Honestly, I don't recall the performance. I had too good a time chatting with the fellow I invited to join me. In fact, he's here now.'

'At nine in the morning?'

As Addison led the way to the library, I had visions of him entertaining a vagabond who'd freeloaded the entire weekend. I didn't expect to encounter a slender man with angular features, his brown hair worn unusually long. His dark blue suit of tropical wool advertised its fine Savile Row tailoring. A yellow and white tie provided an excessive note of flash, a foreigner's idea of California attire. I could hear his cultivated English tones before he opened his mouth.

'Mr Frederick Sewell, Freddy to his friends.' Addison, clearly

cowed by his guest, had lapsed into a mid-Atlantic accent remi-
niscent of the narrator of the 'March of Time' newsreels. 'This is
the indispensable Lillian Frost.'

The ends of Sewell's mouth twisted up in what I took to be
his rendition of a smile. 'Addison has been singing your praises
since the last strains of Tchaikovsky died away.' I had been correct
about the accent. Sewell made Leslie Howard sound like a
Cockney costermonger.

'Freddy used to work for Alexander Korda.' Addison swelled
with such pride you'd think he'd landed Sewell the job.

'Plied my trade as a pressman before that,' Sewell said modestly.
'I've taken up the ink-stained mantle again. Something of a jour-
nalist without portfolio these days.'

'You'll find no greater admirer of Alexander Korda than
Addison,' I said. 'I couldn't tell you how many times he watched
The Four Feathers.'

'Is that so?' Sewell lofted an eyebrow at my use of Addison's
first name, finding my familiarity amusing. 'Mr Korda only
produced that particular film. But I'll certainly pass along that
endorsement the next time I see him.'

'Are you trying your fortunes in Hollywood?' Considering
Sewell was trying my patience, I thought I posed the question
with great politeness.

'In only the vaguest sense.'

'Freddy's planning to pen a history of motion pictures,' Addison
bragged. 'He's an authority on American films.'

'Are you?'

'You sound surprised, Miss Frost.' Another of Sewell's simulated
smiles. 'You thought I would find American films déclassé? Or
be unable to acknowledge superior work being made in our former
colonies?'

My uncle Danny had an almost rabid dislike of all things English.
'Stiff lips, weak knees, the lot of them,' he'd bark when he got in
his cups. I sensed a similar sentiment building in me.

'I'm using Freddy as a sounding board for my idea about creating
an archive of movie history,' Addison said. 'What was that term
you used, Freddy?'

'A living museum.' He stepped forward into some imagined
spotlight and began addressing an appreciative if non-existent

audience. 'Drawing on the experiences of the people who make motion pictures. Showcasing the tools they use.'

'Like costumes,' I heard myself saying.

Sewell faltered in his speech. 'Come again?'

'Lillian is good friends with Edith Head, Paramount's costume designer,' Addison explained.

'Forgive me, I was just thinking out loud. About how costumes are important, but also overlooked.' *Stop talking*, I told myself, then ignored my own advice. 'But I've always thought costumes are where we collaborate with the actors. We the audience, I mean. The actors wear them, and we see them. It's something we both share. But then to save money, the costumes are broken down, turned into other costumes. That seems wrong to me. I understand why it's done, but it would be nice to keep one or two. As a physical record of that moment in time.' I paused. 'I'm doing a terrible job of explaining this.'

'Not at all. I quite understand.' Sewell eyed Addison. 'That would require a physical plant of considerable space.'

'Then we'll have one.' Addison struck a nearby table as if the matter had been decided – but lightly, indicating there would still be a vote. 'Another subject for our conversation.'

'I'll leave you gentlemen to it, then.' I retreated before another of my utterances led to Addison acquiring real estate.

'I can tell you this,' Edith proclaimed down the telephone wire. 'Delia Carson's mother raised her right. This morning I received a lovely acknowledgment of the gift I sent, a beautiful handwritten card.'

'What *did* you send her, anyway?'

'A number of hanks of yarn along with a complete set of knitting needles, so she can outfit everyone from the burliest seaman to the scrawniest ensign for Bundles for Britain. Miss Carson offered her thanks and invited me to see the work the organization is doing firsthand. As it happens, she'll be at their headquarters this afternoon. I thought I'd stop in during the lunch hour, if you'd care to join me.'

'Make it after my standing lunch date, and I'll be there.' After Edith provided the particulars, I said, 'That probably answers my other question. Are we still helping Lorna?'

'We might as well. Until the next time she deceives us.'

'Or snipes us in print again. See you after lunch.'

I went to inform Addison of my afternoon plans. Frederick Sewell still dawdled on the premises, stretched out on a sofa in the library, paging through one of Addison's reference books. His socks had yellow clocks to complement his necktie, and I decided that I hated them.

'Have you gentlemen had any refreshments?' I asked. 'I could have some tea sent in.'

'Heavens, no.' Sewell idly fanned pages.

'An Englishman who doesn't drink tea?' Addison said.

'On the contrary. It's simply that it's made horribly here.'

Addison chuckled, which only made me bristle on his behalf. 'By "here", I take it you mean the United States and not Addison's house. You'll be surprised by what his kitchen can produce.'

'Thank you, but no. I've learned it's better not to set myself up for disappointment.' Sewell glanced up from his book. 'I trust I don't offend, Miss Frost. Americans pride themselves on their plainspokenness, but when someone else follows their lead, they're taken aback.'

'Not at all. In your best plainspoken style, Mr Sewell, is there anything you would care for?'

'I've become partial to your orange juice.'

'Make it two, Lillian,' Addison said. 'I was telling Freddy about our visit with Vernon Reynolds.'

'Again, Addison, he'd be an ideal person for us to talk to as part of this project of yours. A great many open questions about his career.'

'Such as?' I asked.

'It's rumored he directed part or all of several films on which he isn't credited. It would be helpful to settle that matter for the historical record.'

'Just the sort of thing I'd like to do,' Addison said.

'And then there's the scandal surrounding *Storm Cloud*.'

My ears perked up. 'Do tell.'

Sewell smoothed the perfect crease in his trousers. 'A bit of Hollywood lore, spoken of in the wee hours after strong drink. The story goes that Reynolds called "Action" on the *Storm Cloud* flood sequence before the stuntmen were informed. Two of them died, they say, with others injured to the extent that they never worked again. The whole wretched business hushed up from on high, apparently. Claims of skulduggery abound. It's said that the tragedy accounts for Reynolds's subsequent descent into narcotics addiction, which ended his career.' To Addison, he said, 'Surely not the kind of tattle you have in mind for this enterprise.'

'If we tell the story of Hollywood,' Addison declared as if on the Temple Mount, 'we tell it warts and all.'

While Sewell nodded thoughtfully, I wondered if *this* was the scandal that Glenn Hoyle had discovered. Had he acquired incontestable proof of a conspiracy and unknowingly stirred the slumber of some studio potentate? I began to hope that Glenn had stumbled onto Reynolds's sideline selling drugs, a far more preferable option.

Thoughts of Arturo's Ristorante reminded me of why I'd come into the library in the first place. I told Addison I'd be back from lunch somewhat later than usual.

'I must say, this is quite the democratic workplace. You decide when you return from lunch?' Sewell marveled. 'If Mr Korda had run his shop that way, I might have stuck it out a while longer. Perhaps I should seek a position in the States.'

'Why not? Employees aren't treated like Bob Cratchit here.' I regretted the words the instant I said them. Addison peered at me in concern. Sewell, mercifully, opted to disregard my comment. 'I'll get that orange juice,' I said.

'You're crazy.' Vi looked me dead in the eye across the diner table. 'Addison would never fire you. Never.'

Violet Webb, another single girl who'd washed up at Mrs Lindros's boarding house, became one of my first friends when I'd relocated to Los Angeles. The pint-sized blonde had a heart of gold and a set of silver pipes. She had caught on with a dance band that had developed a local following, complete with regular radio appearances. She demonstrated her peerless breath control at lunch, inhaling Turkey à la King while recounting the group's internecine struggles. As she talked, I brooded over what Edith and I were doing for Lorna. We had leads on our has-been and were about to meet our starlet. On our producer, though, we had drawn a goose egg.

'My every word has gone in one ear and out the other,' Vi said. 'Why so glum?'

'I'm trying to help Edith, but I'm getting nowhere. At least on one part of it. And for the record, I heard everything you said, about Gregory the new drummer and how he doesn't get along with half the horn section and . . . wait a minute.'

I pulled out the file containing all we'd learned about our three names. Papers scattered as I searched for, and found, an address. 'I can't get anywhere on this business with Edith. But maybe you can.'

'Me? How?'

'There's this fellow Earl Lymangood. He's a producer. You're an actress.'

'I'm a singer.'

'But you want to be an actress.'

'No, I don't.'

'Sure you do. You don't want to be Ginny Simms? She was just in a picture with the Kay Kyser Orchestra, and she started like you.'

Vi's eyes grew wide. Not wider than her stomach, though. She gathered another forkful of lunch while she pondered my proposal.

'His office isn't far. After lunch, go over and say you want to see him. Don't take no for an answer.'

'But what if I do get in to see him?'

'Promote yourself. Ask him to come see you and the band. Just clap your eyes on Lymangood so you can describe him to me. If you come out of there with a job, that'll be gravy.'

Speaking of gravy, Vi sopped up the last of hers with a roll. 'OK,' she said. 'Why not? But lunch is on you.'

ELEVEN

Bundles for Britain had established its headquarters on the lively stretch of Sunset Boulevard known as the Strip. Bruz Fletcher held court at Club Bali a few blocks away, with Ciro's and the recently shuttered Trocadero even closer. But during the day the neighborhood had the feel of a resort town, lined by homey buildings, some in a faux-French design, others in Tudor revival style. I waited in the entrance of a sleek, low-slung white structure with glass-brick walls as I pondered a politic way to pose a question. *Miss Carson, are you implicated in any hidden scandals that might drive someone – possibly you – to kill?*

I had yet to home in on a satisfactory tactic when I heard the metronomic clicking of Edith's heels on the pavement. Short strides charged with purpose.

'I parked by Preston's restaurant, near the Chateau Marmont. Have you eaten there?'

I told her I hadn't yet dined at The Players, the eatery owned by Paramount's newly minted director Preston Sturges.

'You should go before it bankrupts him. Although I've often thought that's the key to Preston's genius. His extravagance spurs him to greater creative heights. Spend money like mad and you're forced to make more of it. Behave cautiously, and you live cautiously.'

What Edith suggested contradicted decades of Catholic instruction, so I blocked it out. 'Do you have any thoughts on how we approach Delia Carson? Because I have no ideas.'

'Yes. I intend to ask about her war relief efforts, and offer what assistance I can. Then I'm going back to work. As are you.' With that, she opened the door.

Bundles for Britain's base camp had the makeshift feel of a film set. The sunlight filtering in through the glass brick exposed fresh white paint and secondhand furniture. From the back wall came the hum of sewing machines, tended by well-tended women too sharply dressed to be seamstresses. All the accoutrements of Edith's domain were present, with little of the industry. Still, she visibly relaxed, instantly at home.

I didn't recognize anyone except Delia Carson. She was compact but projected tremendous energy. She possessed a heartland beauty, her face like a sunflower, open and bright, with a scattering of freckles typically concealed from the camera. She wore a coat-dress in green-and-navy cotton gingham with low-heeled shoes, the look giving her a wholesome air in keeping with her image. As she moved toward us, though, I noticed an earthy, womanly confidence I'd never seen onscreen. She glided like a jungle cat. Delia Carson was clearly no longer a teenager.

'Howdy there. Are you Miss Head?'

Scratch that. Maybe Delia still had some growing up to do.

After the introductions, Delia proceeded to gush. 'I can't thank you enough for your interest in what we're doing here. And for your thoughtful gifts! That sure was grand of you. We've already put them to work. Let me show you. Sorry about the mess, we only moved in last week. I think this used to be a travel agency. Or a dentist's office. Anyway, we've adopted the crew of a destroyer. We're outfitting the hundred men on it as best we can. Knitting socks, gloves, sweaters. Every piece according to British navy regulations. Why, the Queen herself couldn't turn them down.' All of this exclaimed in a single breathless rush. She complimented the work of two women who had the air of studio executives' wives. They chatted about their gardeners as they knitted furiously.

'Our organization was started by Mrs Ernst Lubitsch.' Delia gave the name the careful pronunciation of an entrée read off the menu in an ethnic restaurant.

Like Arturo's, I thought, reminding myself why Edith and I were here.

Delia led us around the bare but busy room, relentlessly praising the efforts of others. She said 'Golly' several times, and I counted at least one 'Shucks'. Beneath the dewy demeanor lay an undeniable sincerity. I couldn't for the life of me fathom what scandal might have befallen this all-American paragon, now blossoming to womanhood.

Delia acknowledged this transition herself. 'What I wouldn't give to be dressed by you, Miss Head, like Dorothy Lamour and Paulette Goddard are.'

'I'm sure Lodestar's designers can't wait to let you expand your palette.'

'Expand my palette.' Delia repeated the phrase dreamily, then grabbed a pad of paper and scribbled it down.

'It's difficult, navigating a career,' Edith said. 'I trust you have people providing you sound advice.'

'Oh, yes. My husband's been a huge help.'

'That's right. Congratulations,' I said. 'Isn't your husband an actor, too?'

'He'd be right thrilled to hear you say that, then he'd dig his toe in the dirt and say he's just a bit player. Still, he notices a lot. Artie says it's when people ignore you that you really learn things.'

I agreed with Artie on that score.

Delia led the way to a small but amply stocked kitchen, particularly when it came to china cups and saucers; several sets were
in evidence. 'I'm so excited about this,' Delia crowed. 'We're
going to have bandage-making classes, then afterwards a traditional
English tea.'

I made a note to pass that fact along to Freddy Sewell if I ever
set eyes on him again.

A woman bustled in, wearing a green-and-white lily-of-the-
valley print on black jersey and a dyspeptic expression. I would
have made Rhoda Carson as Delia's mother even if I hadn't seen
her photograph. 'I don't know what those women are doing,' she
said. 'I'd never pick up those sweaters in Tremayne's.'

'You're not on a drafty destroyer in the North Atlantic. I thought
you weren't coming today, Mother.'

'I wasn't about to miss meeting Edith Head.' Rhoda nodded
through the introductions, interpreting 'Edith's friend' as 'assistant'. Then she engulfed Edith. 'Will you be helping out here at
Delia's pet project?'

'I'll do what I can.' Edith made the sentence sound both posi-
tive and noncommittal.

'Now there's a sensible approach.'

'Mother, please.' The two words carried the weight of a lifetime
of arguments.

'I just don't understand your involvement with this group when
we are not in this war. Playing politics has never helped any career
and it won't help yours.'

'This isn't playing politics. This is lending a hand.'

Rhoda sighed with maternal forbearance. 'If you want to donate
to war relief, by all means, but—'

'I am. I'm donating my time.'

'Very well, but why you allow yourself to be the public face
of this group—'

Delia stamped her foot, looking every inch the juvenile lead.
'I'm not the public face. I've been in a few photographs. Alongside
Merle Oberon, and—'

'She's *English*, dear. That makes it a whole other kettle of fish.
Not to mention she already has an Academy Award nomination,
and a successful producer husband. That English fellow. Alexander
Korda.'

Korda, strictly speaking, was Hungarian. I wondered if Freddy Sewell had met Merle Oberon. If so, he probably already knew about the tea.

'The point,' Rhoda said, rounding out her case, 'is that she is established while you are not. At least, not yet. Why run the risk of offending some of your audience? Don't you agree, Edith?'

Edith deftly sidestepped the rhetorical trap. 'There's never any shame in putting one's skills to good use.'

'I suppose that's true.' After a quick pout, Rhoda changed tack. 'While we have you here, you should tell Delia how to dress.'

'She looks lovely.'

'I chose that outfit.' Rhoda permitted herself to preen. 'But I meant in pictures. The world's had enough of Delia the corn-fed gal. It's time for Delia the seductress.'

'Land sakes, Mother, I don't want to seduce a soul. I'd just like to put on a grown-up dress and kick up my heels in a picture. Nobody needs to be *tempted*.'

'You let me worry about that.' She placed her hand on Edith's arm. 'Paramount does loan you out on occasion, don't they?'

As Rhoda drew Edith aside to dissect her daughter's image, Delia turned to me. 'You'll have to forgive Mother. She means the best. Is your mother out here?'

'No, she passed when I was a child.' I stated the fact plainly, not seeking sympathy.

Delia provided it anyway. Her eyes moistening, she said, 'You poor thing', and hugged me like I was a character in one of her movies. Swaddled in the commingled scents of gingerbread and soap, I felt warm and secure. Which meant I also felt terrible, because I couldn't bring myself to ask Delia what black mark was on her character.

We said our farewells, Edith taking a good deal longer to extricate herself from her conversation with Rhoda. As we stepped outside, I almost collided with a man peering at the number on the door.

Arthur Davis immediately apologized, his strong New York accent hitting me like a gust from a passing subway train. An express. His rough-hewn face looked even more menacing in broad daylight. He raised his hat, revealing a thatch of thinning but recently dyed hair. His suit was cut in a style too fashionable for him, befitting a man married to a woman several years his junior and more famous to boot. I decided to be bold.

'Looking for Bundles for Britain? It's right in here.'

'I am, thanks.' He reached for the doorknob.

Be bolder. 'You're Arthur Davis, aren't you? We just spoke to your lovely wife.'

The flash of suspicion in his eyes gave way to pride. 'She's a charmer, isn't she? How'd a fella like me get so lucky?' He considered me. 'You from New York? Thought I heard something familiar in your voice.'

'Yes, Flushing. Something tells me you are, too.'

'Brooklyn and points north.' He pronounced it 'pernts', which took me back home in a hurry.

I gave him my name and Edith's. Already favorably disposed toward my fellow East Coast exile, I added, 'Your mother-in-law's in there, too.'

Davis stepped away from the door as if an alarm had sounded. 'Thanks for the warning. Maybe I oughta wait in the car till Delia comes out.'

'I doubt Mrs Carson would care for that,' Edith said.

'She makes an impression that quickly, hah?' Davis chuckled.

I was desperate to concoct a way we might ferret out a fact or two from Davis when Edith took my breath away. 'Unless I'm mistaken, I believe we have a mutual friend,' she said to him.

'That so? Who?'

'Glenn Hoyle.'

Davis blinked at her in confusion. 'You knew Glenn? That was sad news. He was still a young guy.'

I knew how to follow a lead. 'How did you know him?'

'I placed bets with him. Don't tell Rhoda or I'll never hear the end of it. I sometimes work as an extra in pictures – background stuff, ya know, atmosphere, it's how I met the wife – and Glenn, he had an in on some of the lots.' He studied Edith again. 'How'd you know him?'

'The same way,' Edith said brightly.

'You don't say. Ever win with him?'

'Not once. Every filly a bum steer.'

Davis roared. 'I was thinking it was just me. Poor guy. Anyway, probably shouldn't keep the wife waiting.'

'Or Mrs Carson,' Edith and I chorused.

Another laugh from Davis, another flash of rejuvenated hair as he tipped his hat, then he went inside, shivering slightly as he crossed the threshold.

I turned toward Edith expectantly.

'I had to try something,' she said. 'We're getting nowhere on this fool's errand for Lorna.'

'Agreed. Shall we throw in the towel?'

'I have one final notion in mind that won't be too taxing for either of us. Can I drop you somewhere?'

'No thanks. I'm off to throw a Hail Mary of my own.'

In a grimmer and less quaint section of Hollywood, I found Vi parked on a bench, paging through the latest issue of *Modern Movie*. She resembled a still from the magazine come to life, a fair-haired beauty in vivid pastel blue basking in the sun. As I paid the cabdriver, I watched a young sharpie size her up, then glide over to her. He said a few words, she smiled and shook her head. He said a few more, and she shook her head without smiling. He offered a parting riposte, but Vi had pointedly turned her attention back to the magazine, dismissing him. The wolf grumbled to himself as I passed him.

'Hi, toots,' I said to Vi. 'Have you scouted the place yet?'

'I did. I'm done. I saw your Mr Lymangood.'

'How'd you pull that off?'

'You said you were going to meet Delia Carson. I asked myself, "What would she do?" She'd be plucky, but without tears. I barged in there and said I had to speak to Mr Lymangood today, because I was performing this week. He heard me raising a ruckus, so he told me to come into his office.'

'Miss Webb, you're my hero.'

'It's not like he was particularly busy, your Mr Lymangood. There was no line of ingenues clamoring to see him. He gave me the usual lecherous look, asked the standard creepy questions, said he wished he'd met me a few years back. I paid that no mind and told him about the band and how he had to come see us this Thursday. I'll say this for him, he wrote down the date and the address. I wouldn't be surprised if he showed up. He also asked if we had any fiddle players.'

'Fiddle players?'

'He's doing a Western. Needs a band.' The magazine cover snapped up over her face, and I found myself staring into Myrna Loy's eyes. 'That's him there. Behind you.'

I glanced at the entrance. A man had emerged from the office building, his bulky frame wrapped in gray windowpane plaid. He moved with a bull-like tread toward the curb. He was, unusually, hatless, offering a glimpse of the graying stubble sprinkled across his scalp and his tiny, merciless eyes. My only thought upon seeing him was: *Central Casting, send me a villain.* Lymangood glanced in our direction. His unthinking hungry expression never changed as his gaze pawed me. He heaved himself into a waiting car and was gone.

At least I had a face to go with the name Earl Lymangood. I had seen all three people on Glenn Hoyle's list, even though I still had no inkling of what stigma they each might bear.

'Not a very pleasant fellow,' Vi said as the car sped off.

'He certainly doesn't look like one. I don't know how to repay you.'

Vi tucked Myrna Loy's face under her arm. 'With a slice of pie. Talking to that man gave me an appetite.'

TWELVE

The telephone call came during that warm, drowsy period after lunch, when dozing off at my typewriter was a constant threat. I missed the receiver the first time I reached for it.

'Did yesterday's Hail Mary yield results?' Edith asked.

'I can now pick Earl Lymangood out of a police lineup, if that helps. How about yours?'

'We'll find out later today. We've learned nothing about Mr Lymangood, so I suggest we consult Florabel Muir regarding him.'

Florabel was a reporter extraordinaire for New York's *Daily News*. I had been thrilled to make her acquaintance, having grown up reading her copy, which she now filed from Los Angeles.

'That's a smashing idea,' I said. 'Provided we can keep her off the scent of what we're working on.'

'We'll try, but I can't be overly concerned about keeping Lorna's business quiet. Can you come by this afternoon at five?'

'I'll be there, with my file on the Whitcomb case.'

'Don't call it that.'

Armed with a stack of letters for Addison's signature, I went into the library. There I discovered Frederick Sewell on a settee, cast aside like a scarf it was too hot to wear.

'Hello,' he said absently, the way one might greet a cat that had wandered into the room.

'You're back.' The statement was more to confirm Sewell had at some point physically left Addison's house. I feared that he lived here now, having colonized the east wing.

Addison bustled in. 'There you are! You must hear the news Freddy told me.'

'Not news, Addison, merely rumor. Although from copper-bottomed sources.' Sewell swung his feet to the floor, the bulletin demanding that he be upright to deliver it. 'The Academy of Motion Picture Arts and Sciences intends to open a museum. They're sniffing around the Trocadero with an eye toward taking the space over.'

'It would be good if someone did,' Addison said. 'Wasn't the place vandalized recently?'

'Yes. Ruffians smashing whatever crockery didn't go on the auction block. Anyway, the project's in the preliminary stages.'

'Freddy says the Academy will throw in with Jock Whitney and the program he started at MoMA in New York.' Addison rubbed his hands together gleefully. 'A proper museum, here in the heart of the film world. Can you imagine?'

'Doesn't that steal your thunder?' I asked.

'Not at all. If the Academy puts their muscle behind the plan, so much the better. I can offer support, financial and otherwise.'

'Mark my words, Addison, the whole thing will come crashing down,' Sewell said. 'Not the Trocadero, although it might. I mean the museum. Too many egos, too many long memories. You can't start something like this until everyone is long dead.'

'But that's not what I want at all. Let's talk to these people while they're alive, celebrate them while they can enjoy it. Like Vernon Reynolds, the director I told you about.'

Sewell nodded. 'Yes. It would be rather fun to have a chat with him. Do you fancy having dinner at that restaurant again sometime this week?'

'Absolutely! Lillian, set that up.'

I made note of the request, starting to suspect that Sewell was no mere sponger but a grifter, padding his pockets with Addison's dreams. I handed the correspondence to my employer and told him that I'd be leaving for the day early.

'Again?' Sewell cried. 'I can't tell if you work awfully hard or awfully little. Either way, my hat's off to you.'

As I exited, I decided not to tell Sewell about the authentic English tea offered by the ladies at Bundles for Britain after all.

Edith's office had the fraught atmosphere of a peace negotiation, with all parties weary of combat but unwilling to forfeit their claim to a godforsaken patch of scrubland. I understood why when I saw who Edith was bargaining with. There was much about him to notice – the luxuriously thick black hair, the aristocratic features, the precise cut of his pinstripe suit – but the eye was drawn at once to his mustache. Its halves were set an indecent distance apart, like two arms welcoming you in to appreciate the brazenly bare philtrum. He projected a sense of unflappability, along with the implication that his recent activities would definitely leave concerned citizens flapped.

'*Count* Oleg Cassini.' He interrupted Edith's introduction to append his title. His sophisticated but geographically vague accent seemed drawn from all the priciest precincts of Europe at once. He swept over in a cloud of cologne and bowed above my hand. 'An honor to make your acquaintance, Miss Frost.'

I squeaked out a greeting as my guard went up.

Cassini turned to Edith, who looked surprisingly small behind her desk. 'I shall take my leave. Thank you again for your counsel. It will be of great help on the picture.' To me, he explained, 'A bagatelle about American football called, I believe, *Touchdown*. Is that the expression? I am dressing Virginia Dale and Lillian Cornell.'

'A fine first assignment for a junior designer,' Edith said.

Both halves of Cassini's mustache twitched, but if he longed to correct her, he restrained himself.

Feeling the need to contribute to the conversation, I told Cassini, 'I can't wait to see your work.'

'A chance to put all I learned from my mother into practice. It was she who taught me the secret of good fashion: how to be daring in a manner that is not inappropriate. It is an interesting path we have chosen, Edith. We are able to envision women as they long to be seen. We can help them create fantasies about themselves. In a way, it is a great responsibility.'

'I never thought of it quite like that, Oleg,' Edith said. 'How poetic.'

Cassini bowed to Edith, then took my hand again before departing. He stepped through the door as if he were climbing into a carriage.

'The only fantasy that Miss Dale and Miss Cornell have about themselves is that they're starring in something other than a B picture.' Edith pushed out a heavy sigh. 'He's a count. An actual count, not some charlatan. How am I to compete with a count? I was born in a desert mining camp.'

'You have years of experience here,' I protested.

'Which the powers that be will ignore at a moment's notice if the right person happens along.' She emitted an unprecedented second sigh. 'Do you know how Mr Cassini came by his position? A tennis match. He was paired at random in a doubles tournament at the West Side Tennis Club with one of our executives. They won. The executive promptly arranged an interview for him, and he waltzed into work here. A far cry from how I began. What's worse is he actually knows his way around clothes. His mother taught him well.' She picked up a pencil and made an angry scrawl on the sketch pad before her, a trick that perhaps allowed her to keep her voice level. 'I once heard Ernst Lubitsch say, "I have been to Paris, France and Paris, Paramount. Paris, Paramount is better." I shall have to take solace in that. I helped dress Paris, Paramount, and they won't soon forget it.'

To change the subject, I pulled out the file folder in which I'd collected what we'd learned. 'At least we'll soon get to the bottom of this business for Lorna. It's getting so I can't tell the players without a scorecard. I've taken to using shorthand when I refer to the people on Glenn's list. The producer, the starlet, and the has-been.'

'*Has-been?* You're not calling Vernon Reynolds a has-been?' An unfamiliar note crept into her voice – not of anger but of pain, even grief. 'Mr Reynolds did extraordinary work during his career, work that is still spoken of and remembered.'

I tried to sputter an apology, but Edith was roused to keep talking. 'This is a savage business. At some point, the telephone stops ringing for us all. I would prefer to be known for what I've done than for the fact that, at the moment, no one is requesting my services.'

I felt embarrassed, and worse, foolish, given that I'd just heard Addison's vision for a museum dedicated to that very idea. 'You're right. It was thoughtless. I won't do it again.'

Edith swiftly recovered her pep. 'I can hardly blame you. This affair has been rather confusing. Here's hoping Florabel will shed some light and we can be done with it.'

I was filling Edith in on the nascent plans for an Academy museum when Florabel Muir arrived. My uncle Danny would have described the veteran newshound as a 'handsome woman', the intelligent eyes – already scanning the room for a story – easily her most becoming feature. Her red hair was fresh from the salon. She wore a sturdy brown suit, ideal for rooting through dusty records in some municipal office, accented by a brooch shaped like a dagger but with a tiny clock embedded in the hilt. She could look down and see the time, plus defend herself at a moment's notice.

We exchanged pleasantries, Edith offering tidbits regarding various productions on the lot, Florabel responding with morsels about Errol Flynn's latest exploits. All of it prelude; it was as if we were at an auction, marking time until the item we sought was placed up for bid.

Edith cracked first. Casually she said, 'I was wondering if you're familiar with a producer named Earl Lymangood.'

Florabel, no fool, responded, 'Why do you want to know?'

'I'm not comfortable saying that just yet.'

'Suppose I'm not comfortable answering.' The grin on Florabel's face belied the threat. 'So long as you give me the details when you do feel comfortable. Of course you know I'm going to start looking at Lymangood, so by the time I come to you I'll only have follow-up questions.'

I pulled a sheet of paper out of my file, ready to take notes. I saw 'has-been' on the page and hastily crossed it out.

'Earl Lymangood acts the well-heeled newcomer to the picture business, but he's been in this racket for a while,' Florabel said. 'Decades, in fact. Started on the East Coast, but he kept his name out of it. That's because his main interest was bankrolling smokers.'

'Smokers?' I repeated, scribbling furiously.

'Stag films. Pornography.' Florabel pronounced every word with lip-smacking relish. 'It's said Earl has quite an eye for talent. Some of his early films star people whose names now appear in lights. People who very much want to keep those bygone productions under wraps.' She gazed at Edith, her eyes as sharp as the brooch on her lapel. 'Is that what this is about? Paramount signed some dewy young thing who needed the money in her youth?'

'I assure you,' Edith said, 'that is not the case *at all*.'

Florabel, already drafting the salacious story, looked skeptical. 'I've also heard Earl put the touch on some of his discoveries who have gone on to bigger things.'

'He's blackmailing them?' I asked.

'No doubt if I asked Earl, he'd say he's offering them exclusive distribution rights to a specialty film. He'd likely say the same in court if it came to that. And if I put the question to the actresses who have come across with money for him, they'd walk away without a word. But it's my understanding this lucrative little pursuit is helping to underwrite Earl's campaign to become a legitimate producer. Where he can prey on young women in the comfort of his office.'

I thought of subjecting Vi to his predatory wiles and shuddered in shame. Still jotting notes frantically, I pulled more paper out of the folder. The photograph that Kay had given me of Delia Carson and her happy family fell to the floor. Florabel retrieved it, studying it briefly.

'There you go,' she said, handing it back. 'It stands to reason Earl would be in business with a fellow like Heshie. I'm just surprised Heshie ended up in the blue movie racket. It's not what he was known for.'

'Come again?' I said.

'The man in the photograph.' Florabel pointed to Delia's devoted husband Arthur Davis. 'Herschel Rieger. Heshie.'

'Oh,' I said. 'Yes. Right. Heshie.'

Edith swooped in to save the day. 'We hadn't heard that nickname before. Then you know Mr Rieger as well.'

'Only by sight and reputation. Another relic from my New York days. He used to run with that mob that's all over the papers lately. Abe Reles and his boys, hired killers of choice for the syndicate. Murder, Inc.'

'You're telling me he's a gangster?' I scrutinized the photograph, partly to shield it from Florabel. Sure, Arthur Davis looked tough enough to be plausible as a hoodlum without a line of dialogue in one of his turns as an extra. But Florabel was saying he was the genuine article. I pictured Davis tipping his hat to us, griping about his mother-in-law like any other married joe. And he seemed so sincerely smitten with Delia.

Edith ahemmed. 'I should point out that this . . . Mr Rieger is unconnected to Mr Lymangood.'

Is that true? I wondered. We had no idea what unsavory facts Glenn Hoyle had pieced together.

Florabel didn't buy it, either. 'I see. He just happens to be in a photograph you have. With his ugly mug circled.'

The comment hung in the air. I shifted my hand to cover Delia Carson's face in the picture, praying Florabel hadn't identified her.

'The interesting thing about Heshie,' she continued, 'who once was quite the Manhattan playboy – had an interest in a number of shows, dated a string of actresses – is he hightailed it out of New York several years ago. The story is he went with some fellows to take care of a guy skimming from the syndicate. Heshie started thinking the job was a set-up, and the real target was *him*. So he bailed out of the car, ran into the woods, and was never seen again. Just up and vanished. There are people in New York who'd be very interested to know that Heshie is in Los Angeles. Some of them are with the DA's office. Some are being targeted by the DA.'

'When did he leave New York?' I asked.

'Around 1936. I'd have to check my records. But still, can you beat that? Heshie Rieger surfacing in Los Angeles. And, as you say, *not* working for alleged pornographer Earl Lymangood.'

'No,' Edith said. 'He isn't.'

Florabel smiled contentedly to herself, visualizing her next byline. Edith and I exchanged a look. Florabel had just handed us two of the three scandals on Glenn Hoyle's list. Maybe they were linked, maybe they weren't. But Florabel had also written herself into the story, and now we'd have her to contend with, as well.

Los Angeles Register   August 21, 1940

LORNA WHITCOMB'S
EYES ON HOLLYWOOD

Will we still be calling Orson Welles a 'boy genius' when he completes his first feature? I, for one, fear he'll no longer be a beardless youth by the time production wraps. Welles will delay filming his own scenes for a while. After a minor accident, he's temporarily wheelchair bound . . . Rest assured that reports of my demise are greatly exaggerated, and ditto for Friend Simcoe. A few too many so-called colleagues are spinning their own suppositions into 'facts' for their readership. These fiction writers feel free to cast suspicion on Friend Simcoe, who has shared everything he knows about Glenn Hoyle's unfortunate death with the authorities. It's past time the police are left in peace to do their job – provided they're interested in doing it . . . As part of the publicity for Columbia's *The Howards of Virginia*, star Martha Scott will be crowned Queen of the National Tobacco festival. The affair takes place in South Boston –Virginia, of course. We wonder, will Martha bring home a few cartons along with her sash?

THIRTEEN

Visiting the Lodestar Pictures lot didn't pack the same punch as being at Paramount. The pace felt sleepier, the air less fragrant, under pepper trees that weren't quite as verdant. Paramount had become my home team.

I'd staked out a spot under one of those unimpressive trees. I had an eye on a nearby soundstage and a newspaper to hold in front of my face. There were people on the Lodestar lot – a surprising number of them, I realized – that I didn't necessarily want to see. But I had to have words with Delia Carson as soon as possible.

Edith and I had reached that conclusion the night before, once we'd bid good evening to Florabel Muir. That farewell had taken some doing; the newshound had unleashed her inner bulldog in response to the story we had inadvertently revealed to her. She deployed every approach in her arsenal to pry additional details from us – bullying, cajoling, pleading.

'I'm sorry, Florabel, but we can't discuss it yet,' Edith said. 'There are innocent people involved.'

'Heshie Rieger is nobody's idea of a choirboy. You've got to talk.'

'As I said, as soon as we're comfortable—'

'*Get* comfortable. You know I'll be working overtime on this.' To me, she said for the third time, 'Give me another look at that photograph.'

'I can't, Florabel. You shouldn't have seen it in the first place.'

'But I did, kiddo. Enough to get an eyeful of Heshie, clearly the object of interest, and someone identified as Momma.'

Rhoda Carson. Dammit.

Florabel's pen flew across a pad of paper. 'Is Heshie's mother out here? Does Heshie have a mother?'

'I think he has to,' I ventured.

'You know what I mean. Is she still with us? Is her little boy hiding out with her? It'd solve a lot of problems if I could see that photo again.'

I clutched the file to my chest. Florabel hadn't seen Delia Carson in the photograph, and she had no idea who Rhoda was. Add in the fact that Florabel didn't know the West Coast alias of Herschel Rieger – he remained Arthur Davis to me – and we had some breathing room. But it wouldn't last. Florabel would know more than we did if Edith and I didn't act fast.

Meaning first, we had to unload her.

'You know what I think?' Florabel fixed a gimlet eye on each of us in turn. 'I think Earl Lymangood is a blind. He's got nothing to do with Heshie.'

'That's what I told you,' Edith said.

'I think you opened with Lymangood as a feint. Then you oh-so-casually present that photograph, trying to confuse me. A cagey play, ladies. But I'm not falling for it.'

Honestly, I dropped the picture by accident didn't strike me as a worthwhile rejoinder, no matter how accurate it was, so I stayed silent.

With tremendous effort and a solemn vow to share all with her exclusively, Edith and I finally coaxed Florabel out of the office. Edith braced herself against the door once Florabel left and held a finger to her lips. After a silent count of ten, she pulled the door open again.

Florabel had indeed left the premises.

'I wouldn't put it past her to listen at keyholes,' Edith said as she shut the door again. 'Given her profession, I intend that as praise.'

We hunkered down to discuss the new game we found ourselves playing. 'I don't feel obligated to Lorna in the least,' Edith declared. 'But if Florabel's claim proves out, that will create complications for Miss Carson.'

'Also known as Mrs Davis, who may be Mrs Rieger. That poor girl. Do you think Delia knows about her husband?'

'That's what I'd like to find out before we tell anyone – Lorna, Florabel, even the authorities – what we've learned.'

'I'll give it a go if I can get close to Delia again. Perhaps at Bundles for Britain?'

'It could be days before she returns there. We must move quickly. She mentioned she's shooting her new picture all week.'

'I'll stop by Lodestar before work tomorrow if you can finagle me onto the lot.'

'There'll be a pass waiting for you in the morning.'

'Any chance you could also have a plan regarding Delia laid out for me by then?'

'I can't do everything.'

I slipped onto the Lodestar lot wearing sunglasses and a black cloche hat that concealed my hair. Part of me insisted it wasn't a disguise, but deep down I knew better. Simon Fischer worked at Lodestar as a driver. The job provided cover for the far riskier assignment he'd undertaken, spying on Nazi sympathizers for an organization of prominent Los Angeles citizens, several of them studio moguls. I'd had a dalliance with Simon after I'd split up with Gene, one that had ended badly. I wasn't prepared to see him, so I'd donned my camouflage and kept my trusty newspaper at the ready.

The Nazis, naturally, had seized the front page. Their attacks on Gibraltar and British airports, the British hitting back. I decided to focus on more promising news. Congressman Martin Dies had publicly proclaimed that Humphrey Bogart, James Cagney, and Fredric March were not Communists, but rather easy marks whose donations to various worthy causes had been nefariously diverted. Lorna had been correct in dismissing the story. The article was full of quotes from Cagney that made him sound like a Cagney character: demanding either to be thrown in jail or given a clean slate, declaring that when you heard an individual was sick or in need, 'you don't ask his religion, his nationality, or his politics.' At least Father Nugent's Sunday homily had been written for him.

There was an abundance of activity around the soundstage where Delia's picture, *The Country Cousin*, was shooting, but the star herself had yet to put in an appearance. As grips and script girls bustled by, I couldn't help entertaining the notion of some passing bigshot slowing down, giving me the once-over, then exclaiming I would be perfect for his latest production. But I had given up on that dream years ago and never once regretted it.

Time had ticked on to nearly nine o'clock when Delia finally reported for duty, trailed by half a dozen other girls identically attired in bib overalls and floppy sun hats. I got to my feet and strode industriously past them as if on my way elsewhere, then executed a double take that Mack Sennett would have deemed too broad. 'Delia!' I cried.

She turned toward me with that absent Hollywood smile, the genial placeholder employed by luminaries while they shuffled through the countless faces they'd met until they remembered yours – and, if they did, decided how they felt about you.

'Lillian!' Delia said happily, a cue for the other girls to troop into the shadows of the soundstage.

'I happened to be on the lot' – that magical phrase that precluded all questions – 'and hoped I would run into you.'

'But in this getup.' Delia removed her hat and pantomimed

punting it. Her overalls were pristine, the patches at the knees wholly superfluous. 'It's for a dance number with scarecrows. The song's lousy. Lyrics about bumper crops of love and the harvest in your heart.' She stuck out her tongue and fanned herself with the hat. 'No mention of the other things you find on a farm. Like randy cows and horseshit.'

I was grateful for the sunglasses, which hid my eyes goggling at her vocabulary. Delia, apparently, was not yet playing her character. 'Probably nothing that rhymes with them.'

'I'll bet that's it. We need better writers.' She stepped toward the stage. 'I shouldn't keep the company waiting.'

'We met your husband the other night.'

'Artie?' Delia's face lit up in a way the camera couldn't hope to capture.

'He was going in as we were going out.'

'He didn't mention it.'

For some reason, I found that oversight interesting. 'He's a fellow New Yorker, so we hit it off.'

'Actually, he's from just outside the city. Yonkers.'

Not with that accent. Arthur, it seemed, had lied about his birthplace to his bride. 'It must be great for him to go home and show you off.'

Delia tucked her hands inside the overalls. 'We haven't had a chance to do that yet, if you can believe it. Arthur's focused on my career at the moment. And his. Plus he says Los Angeles is the future. That's all well and good, I tell him, but we don't live in the future. We live right now, and right now I want you to take me to the Stork Club. But he hasn't done it, the bastard.' She pouted beguilingly. 'Maybe I'll have to be mean to him. Withhold my favors. Men hate that.'

I slipped off my sunglasses to better observe her performance. She played a fine vamp, even in overalls. Maybe Lodestar was missing a trick keeping her cuddly. 'I wouldn't resort to that. Not yet. Arthur's over the moon about you. He couldn't hide it the other day.'

'I'm daffy for him, too. So smart. A man who's been places.'

'You both seem happy.'

'We are, whenever we're alone. Mother's always lurking. She's on the lot somewhere.' Delia edged a sisterly distance closer. 'Do you know how I knew Artie was the one for me? He didn't baby-talk me the way every other man on this lot does. Acting as if I was some virginal innocent and they were going to be the first to put one over on me. Artie treated me like an adult. Like a *woman*. He saw me, bought me a drink – a real one – and said, "You already know what you like, don't you?"' Her voice dropped to a whisper. 'And I did. And it didn't bother him, the big dumb sweetheart. We're two people who know what we want, and we take it. No matter what Mother says.'

Delia Carson, I now understood, was nothing like her onscreen incarnation. But she wasn't so sophisticated as she thought. She didn't realize her husband had hoodwinked her about his past, and was steering clear of his old stomping grounds in New York for a reason. Worse, she obviously thought she had him wrapped around her pinky finger, and I feared for her. Not because Arthur Davis might hurt her, but because the whole world would once the truth about him came out.

'Now I really must go.' Delia pulled me in for a hug. She smelled of Shalimar and cigarettes, a fact that surely would have shocked her impressionable young fans. 'Time to cut a rug with some scarecrows. I told them the idea's played out after *The Wizard of Oz*, but no one listens to me.'

As I neared the closest studio gate, I abruptly changed course and walked in the direction Delia had come from, toward her dressing room. True love would never speak a word against a swain, but a mother-in-law holds nothing back.

I saw Rhoda Carson from a distance, but Howard Hughes could have spotted her from one of his jets given her huckleberry-blue dress. The color would have been too vibrant on Delia; on Rhoda, it was borderline indecent. I waved her down. No sign of recognition registered on her face. I offered my name to no avail. Finally, I bit the bullet. 'I'm Edith Head's assistant.'

'Oh, of course! But whatever are you doing here?'

I told the truth. 'I'm afraid I'm not at liberty to say.'

Wheels not only turned in Mother Carson's cranium, they practically clanked as they churned out mad theories about Edith defecting to Lodestar to dress her daughter.

'I ran into Delia,' I said. 'That looks such a fun number she's shooting today.'

'It's a rehash of one she did in *Citywide Sensation*. This fellow directing the picture, Minot, seems clueless. Did Delia turn the air blue? Some fool told her Carole Lombard has the mouth of a longshoreman so now she has one, too. Does it mainly to irritate me. What I really hate is how bad she is at it. She sounds like she learned how to swear at Berlitz.'

'She was on her best behavior. I was telling her Edith and I met her husband as we were leaving Bundles for Britain.'

Rhoda pressed a bejeweled hand to her chest, the word 'husband' in reference to Arthur Davis still bringing on a bout of the fantods. 'I doubt he was on his best behavior.'

I couldn't resist winding her up. 'He did talk about gambling.'

'I'm not surprised. It's all the man does! But then he comes from that world.'

'What world, exactly?'

'Gamblers. Sportsmen. You know, the checkered-coat crowd. Loud fellows who reek of beer and only read the box scores. Reprobates and louts, the people he runs with.'

'What do they do for work?'

'What do you think? They're *extras*!'

I started to make my excuses, but Rhoda refused to let go of an apparently sympathetic ear. She complained about Arthur's accent (a mark against her in my book), his attitude ('He tells my Delia that success in this business comes down to *luck*, if you can imagine'), and his hours. 'A married man out gallivanting with the boys. I'm no puritan – dear Mr Carson had a Thursday poker game he'd never miss, bless him, and I'd make the sandwiches. But not on a Friday! That's when a man should be tending to his wife, especially when she's the breadwinner. The 'lucky' breadwinner. He's twice my Delia's age. *He's* the lucky one. You'd think he'd act like it. But no, every Friday night, without fail, he's gone.'

Glenn Hoyle had been killed on a Friday night. 'That's a shame. Every Friday?'

'Since the start of their marriage.'

'And he's out till when?'

'Once he didn't turn up till the cock crowed! He usually staggers in drunk around three or four in the morning. Heavens, I shouldn't be telling you this. You don't know any gossip columnists, do you?'

I smiled. 'Not one.' Technically, it wasn't a lie. I knew two of them.

Again, I made to leave. Again, I veered away from the studio gate. I was already destined to be late for work. Delia's yearning to be treated as an adult had inspired me. I stopped a bicycle messenger and asked for directions to the studio's transportation office.

The harried man at the desk scarcely glanced up from his clipboard. 'Help you, miss?'

'Yes. I'm looking for Simon Fischer.'

'He's not here.'

That figured. 'Could you tell him—'

'No, he's not on the road. He's not here. Doesn't work for us anymore.'

'He . . . since when?'

'I don't know. A few months, anyway. Think he was at the Christmas party, maybe.' The tenor of the man's words implied that Simon had been fired, likely because of his drinking or some other problem. The news only reinforced how long it had been since I had spoken to him.

I was still puzzling over the possibilities when the clerk finally made eye contact. 'Can I get you another man, miss?'

'No thanks. I don't need one.'

FOURTEEN

With Addison cloistered in his workshop, I didn't have to grovel and scrape for being tardier than I'd promised. Even better, Freddy Sewell hadn't set up camp on the property. I wasn't in the mood for his needling. I made a note to remind him that he'd be dining with Addison – and Vernon Reynolds – at Arturo's the following day.

Next, I dialed Edith, the routine task suddenly transformed into a gauntlet; the wardrobe department receptionist had me spell my name twice, then kept me waiting an inordinately long time. Edith greeted me with an accusatory 'Yes?'

'It's me. What gives?'

'Thank heavens. Lorna has been calling all morning, leaving a string of messages, each more insistent than the last. I had no intention of responding until we'd spoken.'

After hearing my report on the ladies Carson, Edith sighed. 'It would appear we've learned what Mr Hoyle discovered. I'll inform Lorna of this the next time she telephones.'

'You mean you're not going to call her?'

Edith sniffed, wished me a pleasant afternoon, and hung up.

The day's tasks beckoned, but I felt compelled to make one more call. I didn't need to look up Simon Fischer's home telephone number as I had the exchange and the digits committed to my memory. I hadn't yet worked out what I would say to him when a perky operator announced that the number had been disconnected. I was so thrown that I forgot to thank her before breaking the connection.

Mrs Quigley, my landlady of indeterminate age and perpetually sunny disposition, had ventured outside in her housecoat to sweep the building's porch with a balding broom. I knew what the charade meant: she had news for one of her tenants. Probably me. She waved frantically in my direction as I approached. 'Lillian! You won't believe who's been calling!'

I hazarded a guess. 'Lorna Whitcomb.'

She nudged me with the broom's handle. 'How did you know? Three messages. *Three!* It wasn't her I talked to, it was her girl. But still! I never miss her column. I wonder if she'd remember me.'

'A lot of people read her column, Mrs Quigley.'

'Not from that! We overlapped a little when I was on the stage in New York. She was a silly little thing back then. Man crazy. You'd never have thought she had it in her to go so far.'

'Oh, she's got it in her, all right. I'll change, then try calling her back.' I had no intention of taking the latter step, assuming Edith had already been in touch.

Before I could shuck my sandals, the lobby telephone sounded. Mrs Quigley's summons followed an instant later. 'A young man for you, Lillian.'

I ran downstairs, not sure what I was expecting. Could it be Simon? Had he somehow sensed I'd tried to contact him?

But the hard-edged voice that rang in my ear belonged to Sam Simcoe. 'Saints be praised! I finally raised one of you. Lorna's been after you and Edith all day and we hadn't heard a peep. I was about to organize a search party, complete with St Bernards carrying brandy. I've already secured the brandy. Lorna expects – demands, really – an update on your progress. She's out for the evening at a premiere of the new Bing Crosby picture, costumes courtesy of Edith, and deputized me to get the latest.'

'Very well. Get your pencil ready.'

'Hold on. The difference when you work with me is you at least get a cocktail out of it.'

'I don't think so.'

'Come now. I owe you something. And I'll catch hell from Lorna if I don't come across. Do you want that on your conscience? I promise, this will be only business and only one drink. Unless you twist my arm. Do you know a bar called The Ploughman?'

Saying yes seemed easier than mounting an argument. As I hung up the receiver, Mrs Quigley's persnickety Siamese cat Miss Sarah Bernhardt wandered out of her mistress's apartment and eyed me up and down. I twirled before her in my dress, a black floral print on white in rayon crepe paired with a bolero jacket. 'What do you think? Is this outfit good enough for one drink with a leg man? Or should I change?'

Miss Sarah presented her backside to me, tail aloft, and left to seek better company. Good enough it was.

The Ploughman was an upscale hole-in-the-wall, a dive with the good sense to know it had gotten lucky. No one came to appreciate its weathered wooden fixtures and dusty assemblage of Olde English memorabilia, and drink orders were kept simple. But its location, close to several Hollywood theaters and hotel ballrooms, made it a convenient spot for people of note to enjoy a snort or three before heading off to some high-toned event. The well-dressed clientele did not linger over their libations.

Sam Simcoe, in his standard spruce suit, flashed a few fingers at me through the gloom. 'What'll you have, on the Whitcomb account?' he asked when I elbowed my way over. I requested a martini. 'Hope you like gin, because that's all it'll be. The last

bottle of vermouth this joint had was used to spot-clean the bar.
And thus ends the small-talk portion of the evening.'

The bartender drowned an ancient olive in my glass, which I
took as a mercy killing. Simcoe gestured toward a secluded booth.
'So we can speak in private. Tell me everything. Lorna will want
to hear it later, by which I mean tonight. The woman only sleeps
three hours a day.'

I laid out the results of our endeavors. Delia Carson's fugitive
husband, Earl Lymangood's sleazy cinematic past, Vernon Reynolds's
medicinal means of moneymaking. As I spoke, Simcoe jotted down
maybe a dozen words but gave his eyebrows a vigorous workout.

'How'd you find all this out?' he asked.

Florabel Muir's contribution, I knew, had to hit the cutting-room
floor. 'You keep your sources secret. So do we.'

'A fast learner,' he said. 'Well done. Not only to you and Edith,
but Glenn Hoyle. He really did turn up some gems.'

'Will it be enough for Lorna?'

'Nothing's ever enough for Lorna. But she won't be able to
fault your efforts. Granted, none of this points us toward whoever
killed Glenn, but it gets us closer.' He drummed the tabletop,
translating his scrawled hieroglyphics. 'I'd bet the ranch on Arthur
Davis, aka Heshie. He's got the most to lose, and he has experience in the lead-pipe racket.'

I pictured Arthur mooning over Delia. 'He doesn't seem the
type,' I said.

'If they all seemed the type, we wouldn't need the police or
Charlie Chan movies and we'd be a damn sight better off. At least
if it's Arthur, it gives Delia a break.'

'How do you figure?'

'Lorna seldom features her in the column. Never took a shine
to her for some reason. Every item I hand her on Delia, she drops.
Doesn't think she's real box office because the younger crowd
loves her. Once this news hits, though, even Lorna will give Delia
plenty of play. And Delia will finally get the juicy adult lead she's
hankering for.'

I felt vaguely ill. Whatever charge I'd gotten out of the seamy
spadework of gathering gossip had long since faded. I could only
think of Delia, and how her name would be on everyone's lips for
the wrong reasons.

'Who'd be your second pick?' I asked.

'Lymangood. One, he doesn't want his past coming back to bite him. Two, a guy who moved in those circles has trafficked with hoodlums. Again, that counts for something.'

'Not Reynolds? If he wanted to mount a comeback—'

'Nobody comes back from Arturo's. Although he'd also know some unsavory types. I'd still bet him to show. If Glenn were with us, I'd lay money on it. But then if Glenn were here, we wouldn't be having this conversation.'

'So long as Lorna accepts it, I'll be happy.'

'I'll make her accept it. Again, I can't thank you enough. But I'll try. How about another round on Lorna?'

I nodded. He signaled to the bartender for the same again with offhand elegance, a true denizen of the night.

'She's not so bad, you know,' he said. 'Lorna. She's just broken on the inside.'

'Oh, is that all?'

'The cost of having expectations that were exceeded without ever being met.'

'I think I understand. She's as famous as anyone she writes about – for writing about them.'

Simcoe smiled. 'You do understand.'

Round two arrived. 'To our benefactor,' Simcoe proposed as we clinked glasses. 'Born Lora Lee Mackey. Started as a dancer. Never the most talented or the most graceful, but the one who caught everyone's eye. I looked up her notices. Don't tell her. Then she wangled herself a studio contract, bid goodbye to all that, and hied herself westward to become a star.'

'And it never happened.'

'And she never recovered. To this day, she'll see some studio's lauded new discovery and say to me, "I had more on the ball than she does." She's haunted by it. She was at a loose end after Paramount gave her the gate – the Bronson Gate, as it were. Ended up selling cosmetics for a time. Falling into a marriage with Doctor Jerry Whitcomb would have been enough for plenty of women, but not Lorna. She has this insatiable need to be known for something. And now she is. Clawed and scratched her way there. Here's to Lora Lee.'

I took a sip of pure gin. 'How is she to work for?'

'As tough as the steaks they serve here. But she never forgets my birthday, reminds me to call my mother, and even puts me in the column. She's taught me a lot.'

'I hear you're a big reason why her column works.'

'Modesty forbids me from agreeing wholeheartedly with that statement and asking where you heard it. Lorna's not the best organizer of material. Fortunately, that's an area where I excel.' He took a sip of his drink. 'I wish to hell I could organize this show she's doing.'

'First I've heard of a show.'

'Which likely indicates a problem. She got dragooned into doing a live performance. She pretends to assemble her column in front of an audience as a bevy of guest stars loaned out by the studios clamors to get into it. They provide the actual entertainment.'

'Sounds dreadful. Why on earth would she agree to do that?'

'Because Louella Parsons is at last on the verge of toppling, but Hedda Hopper remains in the way. Lorna needs visibility, and not the kind I've been providing lately. It's why I've been pushing her to give a fair shake to the new crop like Delia, attract younger readers. But Lorna won't hear of it. So she got talked into this boondoggle by her syndicate. It's all bravado all the time with her.' He lapsed into a fair imitation of his boss. '"I've been on stage, kid. I was an actress." But I've distinctly heard knees knocking in rehearsal. We have a tryout in Santa Barbara this weekend and we're nowhere near ready, Lord help us. This is the kind of thing I'll refuse to do when I get my own acreage in the nation's newspapers.'

'Then that's your master plan. A column of your own.'

'Picture it. "Simcoe Sez".' He spelled the second word for my benefit.

'What is it with you guys?' I asked. 'You always have the names of your columns ready to go. Like Glenn.'

'Like Glenn.' Simcoe frowned into his glass. '"According to Hoyle" would have been a good name. Would have been a good column, too.'

We continued chatting until Simcoe began listing gently to starboard, as if he'd taken on water as well as whiskey. After a moment, he righted himself, and a smile bobbed to the surface of his features.

'Confirm something for me. Who's the fellow who just muscled his way to the bar?'

I turned and spotted a wall of glen plaid. Then the scattering of gray hairs. When the man swung his bulk around on the stool to take in the room with those remorseless dark eyes, I immediately spun back. 'That's Earl Lymangood,' I whispered.

'Thought so. I heard he frequents this place. Why I chose it, in fact. In the event you hadn't learned anything about him. You should talk to him. Maybe he'll let something slip.'

'Me? Why not you?'

'One, I'm a known commodity. I'm Friend Simcoe, persona non grata. Two, I told you before, it's Lorna's preferred method. Use proxies whenever possible. Three, I have to call Lorna and report your bonanza to her. And four, he's your choice for the man who did the deed. Don't you want to see if you're right?' He leaned across the table. 'C'mon. You'll get a kick out of it.' He then slid out of the booth and took a roundabout route to the pay telephones, avoiding Lymangood entirely.

I stared hostilely at my martini. I didn't want to move. I thought of how I'd sent Vi to beard Lymangood in his den. I could at least make a similar attempt in a public place. Maybe Simcoe was right, and I'd get a kick out of it.

One last sip of courage and I wobbled to my feet. Lymangood spoke to the bartender with the lordly manner of a regular who tipped well. The stools on either side of him were occupied, but I twisted sideways and found room. Lymangood pivoted in my direction. His gaze felt sweaty.

'Earl!' I tried to sound happy to see him, but Bette Davis herself couldn't have pulled that off. 'How are you?'

Up close, Lymangood's eyes seemed hard, marbles scuffed on countless sidewalks. The corners of his mouth were moist. 'Better now that you're here.' He took a break from assessing my form and set his brain to work on remembering how he knew me.

'Last time I saw you,' I prompted, 'you were with what's-his-name. Heshie.'

He blinked ponderously at me, at an apparent loss. 'Who-shie?'

That didn't fly. Time for another angle. 'Maybe I got his name wrong. Then there's our other mutual friend. Glenn. You remember, with two Ns.'

'Sweetheart, I hate to say this, but I think you're confusing me with someone else. Another Earl. Luckier than me.'

'Really? I'm sorry.'

I edged away from the bar. Lymangood's hand shot forward with startling speed. It dropped like a dead weight, clammy against my bare skin. 'Hang on. That's a good thing. Gives us a reason to get better acquainted. What's your name?'

'Louise. Let me get my handbag. I'll be right back.'

I slipped into the gloom before he could protest – or notice that I already had my handbag on my shoulder. I'd grown up in New York. I wasn't about to leave it at the table.

Sam Simcoe hadn't returned to the booth. After a moment, a waiter scuttled over to me. 'Mr Simcoe paid the bill and would like you to join him outside.' His eyes flicked toward Lymangood. 'Care to leave through the kitchen?'

He kindly led the way, and a moment later I found myself on the street. Simcoe slouched against a sleek navy coupe. 'Did you get anything?' he asked.

'Only the overwhelming urge to take a bath.'

'It was worth a shot. I couldn't track down Lorna, but our paths will doubtlessly cross as I make my rounds. She'll be pleased with your work, and again, I'm thrilled with it. Can I drop you somewhere?'

I declined twice, wanting a moment alone after my encounter with Earl Lymangood. Simcoe motored off. I tarried on the sidewalk, stretching my arms into the fading orange sunlight, inhaling the fragrant evening air and expelling The Ploughman's dank atmosphere from my lungs. Slowly my martini fog dissipated, and my thoughts turned to dinner.

I searched the street for a taxi. A Buick sedan parked a few feet along the curb rolled forward until it came abreast of me. The beefy man at the wheel had perspired through his hatband. 'Care for a ride, Miss Frost?'

I backed away, prepared to bolt, to hammer on The Ploughman's kitchen door, to scream bloody murder. The man in the car reached into his jacket. 'I think you should get in.' He showed me an LAPD badge with one hand while he mopped his brow with the other.

'My tax dollars at work,' I said, and did as he suggested.

FIFTEEN

The drive disoriented for a multiplicity of reasons. The detective didn't say a word once I'd gotten into the car; the tight-lipped Rogers might as well have been at the wheel. And I soon surmised that he was ferrying me back to my own neighborhood. I resisted the impulse to wave at my building as we tooled past. Mrs Quigley's shadow danced in her apartment window.

The car drew into the curb outside Cavanaugh's, the local greasy spoon. The nameless detective leaned across me and opened the passenger door. Never one to ignore such gentlemanly behavior, I bailed out and strode into the diner.

Cavanaugh's smelled of onions and soup, each having nothing to do with the other. A thin layer of grime coated everything, from the counter to the bewhiskered men perched on stools in front of it, nursing mugs of black coffee for as long as they dared. A figure at the table farthest from the door stood up. Detective Gene Morrow adjusted his dark blue tie without straightening it. His relatively new suit fit him uncommonly well. It looked like someone had accompanied him when he'd purchased it, offering advice on tailoring which Gene had then wisely taken. His brown hair now sported the first strands of gray. They, of course, lent distinction to his appearance.

Glancing down at my clothes, I wished fervently that I had changed before meeting Sam Simcoe. Served me right for listening to a cat.

Gene smiled at me, and I felt a flutter in my chest. Faint, but undeniable.

'I knew I had you to thank for my taxi,' I said.

'We pride ourselves on our comprehensive service.' He pulled out a chair for me. 'Now that you've laid down a solid foundation of martinis, I thought I'd buy you dinner at one of your favorite haunts.' He eyed the room askance. 'Place seems to have changed a bit, though.'

'Old Mr Cavanaugh passed at the end of last year. His son took over.'

'Jesus, not the one who used to box?'

'Kiss-the-Canvas Cavanaugh. He's . . . let the place go.'

'We could eat somewhere else.'

'No, it's fine. I'm plenty hungry. And I want to hear why you pinched me.'

'I didn't pinch you.'

'The night's still young.' I flushed immediately. 'I don't know why I said that. It's been a long day.'

'Then you do know why you said it.' Gene smiled again. The gray hairs really did give him a presence. A gravitas. 'We have Friend Simcoe under surveillance. Takes multiple teams with all the running around he does. He knows every door to every night-spot in town. We almost lost him at Earl Carroll's the other day.'

'Slipped out the back way, I'll bet. That's his specialty. Who saw me?'

'I did. I'd tailed Simcoe to The Ploughman. No idea who he was meeting there. You made your entrance; I made my exit. Asked Calhoun to deliver you when you left.'

Deliver me, I thought. *Like a case of Scotch or a dozen roses.* 'You weren't surprised to see me turn up, then.'

'You mean, did I know you and Edith were enlisted by Lorna Whitcomb to help Simcoe's cause? Yes. We've been watching Simcoe for a while. Ever since Glenn Hoyle was killed.' Gene lit a cigarette. 'Also, Hoyle's neighbor telephoned in a panic about a strange woman who turned up on his doorstep and compelled him to tell us something he'd forgotten.'

'And you automatically assumed it was me?'

'Whenever I hear "strange woman", Frost, I always think of you.' He grinned through the smoke. 'Plus I asked Hansen about it, and he folded under questioning. Admitted he'd shown you and Edith around Hoyle's place.'

'Funny how the only people keeping quiet are me and Edith. I didn't know you were part of the investigation.'

'A late addition. Byron put me on it.' Byron being Captain Byron Frady, the former mentor who had renewed his interest in Gene's career after Gene had been cleared of a crime he'd long been rumored to have committed. I'd played a role in vindicating him, an action Gene had taken as an affront. It had spelled the end of our romance.

'Byron has you earmarked for big things.' I hoped the words sounded congratulatory. I meant them that way.

A waitress in a hairnet and heavy black shoes presented herself at the table. She said nothing, assuming we knew the reason for her appearance. I ordered the first thing I saw on the stained menu, meatloaf with mashed potatoes. Gene had the same. The waitress wandered off in the general direction of the kitchen. I hoped she'd get there one day.

'Why are you following Sam Simcoe?' I asked.

'Because he killed Glenn Hoyle.'

'Are you sure of that?'

'Reasonably so.'

'Why would he do it?'

'Professional jealousy. Or fear, if you like. Hoyle was poised to box him out of a job.'

'How was he going to do that?'

'You're doing it again.'

'What am I doing again?'

'Two things, actually. You're building your side of the conversation entirely out of questions, and you're acting like you don't know something I know you're well aware of. Lucky for you I find those habits endearing.'

At that moment, I desperately wanted a pile of mashed potatoes in which I could hide my face. To stave off further embarrassment, I plowed ahead. 'You mean the list of names found in Hoyle's place. Delia Carson, Earl Lymangood, Vernon Reynolds. You think Glenn learned something about one or conceivably all of those people that would have landed him a job with Lorna and threatened Sam's position.'

'That's the general idea.'

'Then it stands to reason you believe there's something to be learned about one or conceivably all of those people.'

Gene shifted uncomfortably on his chair. 'Sure.'

'But you don't suspect any of them.'

'We don't think it's likely they're involved.'

'I've been trying not to ask questions, but I've run out of room. Why do you think that?'

'Because Simcoe was there, and he has an easy-to-understand motive.'

'Have you at least considered those three people?'

'Of course we have. We consider everything.'

'But you're sticking with Sam.'

Gene shrugged. 'We flatfoots are a simple people.'

The food arrived, much too quickly for my comfort. The meat-loaf had gone cold in spots, while the gravy smothering the potatoes was hot enough to have been poured out of a smelter. I fell on it anyway, ravenous.

'Suppose you tell me why I should consider any of those people,' Gene said. 'Since that's what Lorna had you doing.'

This version of events ran unedited. Even Florabel Muir's cameo made the cut. I felt an intense and unwholesome satisfaction when, a few minutes into my recitation, Gene retrieved his notebook and requested that I take it from the top. The information I had to relay apparently came as news to him. He took particular interest in the revelation about Arthur Davis's past as Heshie Rieger, late of Murder, Inc. I shivered again as I thought of how Delia Carson would be hounded regarding her marriage, the questions lasting the duration of her career.

'We'll have to get on to New York to confirm this story,' Gene said. 'They'll certainly want to know he's out here. Don't suppose you have any pull back in your old hometown.'

'I can probably get you into a Knights of Columbus dinner in Queens if you give me enough notice. In light of what I've told you, are you going to look at the names on Glenn's list with fresh eyes?'

Gene snapped his notebook shut. 'No. Just these same tired ones. But you've given us something to think about.'

'Have you considered Lorna Whitcomb herself?'

'You think she could have killed Hoyle?'

'She's killed enough people in print. She did see Glenn the day he was killed and concealed that fact.'

'We talked about that, she and I. She was forthcoming. At least I think she was. What she told us didn't fundamentally alter my view of things.'

He glanced down at my plate, and I realized I was drumming the tines of my fork against it. I set the cutlery down. 'What about

Glenn's sideline as a bookie?' I asked. 'Maybe that could yield a motive for killing him.'

'Believe it or not, that possibility had occurred to us. We're looking into it.' He peered at me. 'You're not, are you?'

'Hell, no. Edith and I are through with this business now.'

'I'm glad to hear it. I don't have to warn you off then. We truly are looking at every angle, Frost. Including the possibility that one of Hoyle's old magician cronies did him in for blabbing the secret of the Indian rope trick. I even went to a memorial service that crowd threw for him.'

'Did they remember him fondly?'

'They did. No conjuror himself, they said. Didn't have a feel for the stage, unlike his old man. But behind the scenes, he was a marvel. One of the best at building equipment for magic acts. Whatever they needed, large or small, Hoyle could make. Without breathing a word of what he did or how he did it.'

Pincus, Hoyle's neighbor, had mentioned that to me. Glenn laboring in his garage, assisting others who followed in his missing father's footsteps, prestidigitation being something for which he apparently had no aptitude. I wondered if Glenn Hoyle came to hate show business for that reason; if that contempt subconsciously drew him toward the gossip trade.

'I know you and Lorna don't want to hear it,' Gene said, 'but we keep coming back to Friend Simcoe.'

'You haven't arrested him.'

'Pinching the leg man of a nationally syndicated columnist isn't advisable until there's no doubt whatsoever.'

I understood that was why Captain Frady had put Gene on the case. Gene had proven proficient at politics, able to walk tightropes with aplomb. With Frady's endorsement, he might well be on his way up the LAPD ladder. I wished him well, but at the same time felt a stone in my heart. Not a large one. A pebble. And smaller than the last time I'd checked on it. But a stone all the same. Whatever successes Gene achieved, I wouldn't be at his side for them. I'd only be rooting him on.

He stopped shoving the meatloaf around his plate. 'Grub's not very good, is it?'

'I haven't eaten here in months.'

'My fault for wanting to revisit one of our usual spots.'

Our usual spots. Why did the phrase make me want to cry?

'Places change, people don't.' *Listen to you*, I thought. *Such sophistication.* 'There are new spots I like just fine.'

'You'll have to tell me about them. For the next time I kidnap you for dinner.'

I provided him with a list as he settled the bill. Gene insisted on walking me home. He asked after several of my friends, and I put a few questions to him about work. Even with his inherent modesty, it was obvious that his prospects were on the upswing, an added advantage of having Byron Frady in his corner again.

'Steak next time, or at least pork chops,' he said as we reached the door to my building. 'That's a solemn promise.'

'I'm already looking forward to it.'

There was a long, pregnant moment while he hesitated over whether to kiss me goodnight. *Nuts to this*, I thought, and pecked him on the cheek to spare us both additional agony.

Mrs Quigley popped her head out as I hurried inside. 'Was that Detective Morrow? Where's he been keeping himself?'

'He's a man on the go these days. Goodnight.'

I wondered why I'd made the decision to kiss him as I readied myself for bed. I also replayed whether Gene had turned his face toward mine as we'd separated, or if I'd only imagined it. I thought about both questions even more as I lay in the dark, waiting for sleep.

Los Angeles Register   August 22, 1940

LORNA WHITCOMB'S
EYES ON HOLLYWOOD

Cecil B. DeMille had such fun working with Joel McCrea in *Union Pacific*, he's trying his darndest to snag him for his new picture *Reap the Wild Wind*. The actor, who is receiving excellent early notices for *Foreign Correspondent*, is said to be fielding numerous offers . . . We've all heard the stories about them. The women who fall prey to men promising a path to stardom, only to be featured in films destined for the back room of a beer hall. We might ask what possessed them to take such risks with their reputations. But I say: no more, ladies. Let us approach our modern maidens with an understanding heart. Let us instead excoriate those 'producers' who are merely purveyors of filth, whose untamed greed has them forsaking all others in service of mammon. Let us keep those unscrupulous men outside our walls while making a place for their victims, so they can say 'Today we live without being chained to shame' . . . The town is divided on that new Stratoliner flight with only three stops between Los Angeles and New York. Half love cruising 20,000 feet above the earth, and half only want to get that high on a bottle of rye.

SIXTEEN

Lorna's column made it difficult to concentrate on my morning toast. I repeatedly reread the baffling item intended for an audience of one – Earl Lymangood. Simcoe had obviously relayed the substance of our conversation to his boss, and she'd decided to lay the groundwork for exposing the first scandal on Glenn Hoyle's list. But she hadn't referred to Lymangood by name; was she issuing him a warning? And why on earth had she larded her copy with over half a dozen titles of Joan Crawford pictures – *the women*, *possessed*, the dead giveaway of *our modern maidens*? Was Lorna suggesting that the actress had appeared in one of Lymangood's blue movies? If so, what was her strategy?

I reminded myself the matter no longer concerned me. Still, I read the column one more time before leaving for work.

The telephone was jangling before I reached my desk at Addison's. Edith started in at once. 'I have no idea what Lorna is doing. This morning's column is playing with dynamite.'

'Is she implying what I think she's implying about the person I think she's implying it about?'

'I'm going to say yes. Not everyone will pick up the clues she dropped, but the relevant parties will. To what end, I don't know.

As for why she'd involve another person in this imbroglio, even
indirectly . . . I'm at a loss. I take it you spoke to her about Mr
Lymangood.'

'No. I met with Sam Simcoe – and then with Gene. It was quite
an evening. Care to hear about it?'

'I'm chockablock with fittings today. Any chance you can drop
by the studio this afternoon?'

After we made plans, I struck off in search of Addison. I found
my portly patron on the patio, clad in a gray sweatshirt and sky-
blue shorts, engaged in what he called his 'tension exercises.' He'd
explained the anatomical theory – rigmarole about pitting various
muscle groups against one another – but it resembled plain old
stretching to me. The practice hadn't melted the pounds away, but
it got him into the sunshine and allowed him to purchase an entire
new wardrobe of workout togs.

'Good morning,' I said. 'Just making sure you haven't strained
anything.'

'Lillian,' he panted, grateful for the rest. 'Freddy confirmed
dinner at Arturo's tonight. Would you care to join us? Perhaps
Freddy can pry some pearls from the oyster that is Vernon
Reynolds.'

Middling Italian food in the company of a supercilious bounder
and a purveyor of narcotics did not meet my definition of a dream
date. On the other hand, I had nothing else on the docket. 'Thank
you. Don't mind if I do.' On a whim, I asked, 'Did you read Lorna
Whitcomb this morning?'

'Never miss her,' he puffed. 'Couldn't make head or tail out of
part of it, though. Lillian, would you mind—'

'Ice water, coming up.'

At least this time when I interrupted Edith in conference, she
wasn't in a standoff with Oleg Cassini or mid-consultation with
an actress.

The art director Bill Ihnen was more than Edith's colleague.
He was a steadfast friend, always willing to lend an ear and advise
Edith on work matters. Soft-spoken and genial, Bill projected a
serenity that permitted Edith to relax. His charms were operating
at full force given that she had shed her tan suit's jacket, showing
off a white blouse with subtle blue stripes and a rounded collar.

Bill, seersucker jacket draped beautifully on his frame, embraced me. 'I don't know why I'm happy to see you,' he said playfully.

'He's upset that we've visited Orson Welles and he hasn't,' Edith explained.

'And after I introduced you! The nerve. Why, it should be me basking in his glory.'

'If it makes you feel any better,' I said, 'we scarcely spoke to him.'

'It does, actually.'

Edith swatted him. 'We're about to walk over to RKO so Bill can see the circus for himself. You're just in time.'

As we made our way to the adjacent lot, I summarized my previous evening and asked Edith if she'd spoken to Lorna. 'No. She stopped telephoning, presumably because Mr Simcoe had gotten in touch with you. I'd be delighted if I never heard from her again.'

'You may not if she persists with this Crawford nonsense,' Bill said. 'Is she hoping to get herself fired?'

I couldn't resist asking the question. 'Is it possible Joan Crawford was in one of . . . *those* movies?'

'There are stories,' Bill said.

'And they're exactly that, stories,' Edith scoffed. 'In any case, it's none of my business.'

Bill leaned close to me. 'Which only means Joan's not a Paramount star.'

Orson Welles had mastered his wheelchair. He spun tight circles in it outside the soundstage and around a woman with the mien of his dotty old aunt.

Edith saw her, stopped short, and seized Bill's hand. 'That's not—'

'It is,' Bill whispered. 'Louella Parsons herself.'

I had heard the famed columnist's voice on her radio show 'Hollywood Hotel' for years, and seen her photograph in the newspapers. But it had been a shock at one of Addison's parties to encounter the grand dame of gossip in the flesh. She carried herself with the bearing of an aging monarch accustomed to being fêted but not entirely sure who was honoring her. Now she giggled uneasily at Welles's antics. She wore a navy suit with a white jabot that likely looked sophisticated on the store's model but seemed old-fashioned on her.

'You know what the press agents say.' Bill kept his voice pitched low. 'One item in Lolly's column is as good as two. The first time when it appears, and the second when it's corrected.'

'I've seen her correct her corrections,' I said. Parsons, many a wag claimed, prized access over accuracy.

'Bill!' Welles turned a pirouette in his chair. 'Get over here! And bring your harem with you!'

We approached somewhat warily. Greetings were exchanged, which as usual in my case meant reminding Parsons of where we had met before.

'Louella and I are wrapping up a splendid five-course lunch,' Welles bellowed cheerfully.

'I hope you appreciate how lucky you are, Orson.' The curious instrument of Parsons's voice, combining flat Midwestern tones with a theatrical delivery, turned her every utterance into a pronouncement. It was like hearing the Ten Commandments read by a Sunday school teacher. 'I usually make people come to me.'

'I'm honored you made an exception in my case.'

'When you're out of that chair you must call on us at our lovely farm in the Valley.'

'A farm, you say? That's the only way to live. I grew up in the heartland like you, Louella. Booth Tarkington stuff. I was a veritable Penrod. Had an all-American boyhood.'

Somehow I doubted that, much as I doubted that Parsons had hay that needed baling on the back forty. But she tittered nonetheless.

Welles rocketed toward Bill. 'I've been telling Louella all about the picture.'

'I hope you understand it better than I did,' Parsons said.

'As I said, dear, it's a sort of portrait in mosaic. The story of a great man, as told by the people who knew him best. Or thought they did.'

Parsons nodded, more out of fear than comprehension.

'It's like the Duke of Wellington's quote about the history of a battle being like the history of a ball,' Welles continued. 'There's no one who dances every dance or fights every skirmish. Everyone has pieces but not the whole.'

Parsons looked even more confused. 'Then it's a war picture.'

'Yes. The war of a man's life.'

Fed up with being at sea, the columnist made for terra firma. 'I will say that the little actress in your company – Dorothy Comingore, is it? She's the spitting image of my great friend Marion Davies.'

'You don't say.' Welles made big eyes at me as he suppressed a grin. He may have been enjoying his little joke, but I recalled Lorna's advice to him about playing straight with his audience, and understood her point. I wished that he had taken her counsel to heart instead of making sport of the entire enterprise.

Parsons now homed in on Edith. 'You're fortunate to be dressing Paulette Goddard. I hope you're ready. A woman married to Charlie Chaplin and accustomed to the MGM treatment will prove a challenge.'

'I believe I'm up to it.' The expression on Edith's face wasn't quite a smile, but I didn't know what else to call it. 'Miss Goddard and I already have a solid working relationship.'

Welles beckoned me closer. I bent down to him. 'Wonderful girl, Paulette, but she has the heart of a cash register.'

'What did you say, Orson?' Parsons snapped toward him, her antenna aloft.

'I said I wanted to ask about your radio show. I'll always think of radio as my home, you know, and you're a veteran of the form, like myself. What was that slogan you used to have? The foundation garments people?'

Parsons blushed, her face beet red over the white jabot. 'The sponsor made corsets, but couldn't abide the word. We were forbidden to say it! We were forever talking about "avoiding abdominal bulge".'

Welles laughed heartily. 'There's not a sign of it on you, my dear. You remain a dewy young maiden.' As Louella girlishly waved off his compliment, Welles again spoke to me sotto voce. 'She once called Mussolini her favorite hero, the old bat.'

He thumped his hands on the arms of the wheelchair. 'Bill, old man, are you ready for the grand tour? Let's away before the whistle blows. Edith, are you coming?'

But Parsons had pounced upon her. I heard the name 'Oleg Cassini' mentioned. Edith told the boys she'd catch them up.

Welles turned expectantly to me. I begged off. Dinner with Freddy
Sewell lay ahead, and I needed a change of costume and a bit of
a lie-down to prepare. Welles, I knew, would understand.

SEVENTEEN

F reddy Sewell's laugh – chilly and dry, in contrast to the wine
at our table – had quickly become part of the supper
soundtrack, along with the clash of cutlery and the distant
Italianate music. That Sewell's discreet chortles accompanied his
own stories only made them more unbearable.

We had encountered Vernon Reynolds upon entering Arturo's,
and he had commenced fussing over us at once. *Such* a joy to see
Mr Rice and me again, how flattering to think we might become
regulars at the establishment, and what a pleasure to make Mr
Sewell's acquaintance. Addison dropped Alexander Korda's name
en route to what I presumed was now our favorite booth, and
Reynolds deftly scooped up the moniker. 'Mr Korda strikes me as
one of the figures in the mold of the founders of the picture business. Men of vision and action.'

'You describe him admirably,' Sewell replied. 'He holds the
work of you and your contemporaries in the highest regard. You
blazed the trail for him to follow.'

Reynolds was struck dumb by the praise. Sewell took the menus
from the maître d's frozen hand and gestured me into the booth.
Reynolds tried to sputter an apology for this unconscionable lapse,
but Sewell continued as if the incident hadn't occurred. 'I've long
wanted to ask you about your career, Mr Reynolds. Some questions Mr Korda and I both had about your films. If you've time—'

'This evening, perhaps,' Addison suggested. 'Another round or
two at Club Bali. I've had your friend Bruz Fletcher's lyrics in
my head for days. Not quite appropriate for singing in the shower,
though.'

Reynolds beamed, plans were made, assorted appetizers arrived
at the table, and Sewell found them all wanting. On that score, I
had to agree with him.

Sewell wove the Korda thread into the fabric of the evening's conversation, offering one anecdote after another about his efforts while in the producer's employ. Many of them took place in Europe or South America and seemed to have precious little connection with the film business.

'What exactly were your responsibilities for Mr Korda?' I finally asked, exasperated.

'A combination of researcher and scout, I suppose you'd say. On the hunt for material with a touch of the exotic, to be turned into pictures. Rather a specialty at the house of Korda.'

'If I may say,' Vernon Reynolds interjected on one of his frequent stops at our booth, 'Mr Korda handles spectacle like no one else. It's one of the many reasons I'm pleased he's making films in America now.'

Reynolds, I feared, had begun envisioning a glorious return to the picture business with Alexander Korda as his benefactor. Sam Simcoe's voice chattered in my ear: *Nobody comes back from Arturo's.*

In addition to highlighting his illustrious past, Sewell alluded to his promising future. He brought up Addison's proposed museum in conjunction with Vernon Reynolds or various people he'd met on his travels; as far as I could tell, he knew everyone from Vladivostok to Visalia. He never specifically requested a job but always underscored how a man of his experience would make an invaluable asset to such a mammoth undertaking. It was, I hated to admit, a compelling performance, the pressure constant but never intense, like a river smoothing the surface of a stone. Addison nodded along avidly, utterly ensorcelled. The notion of being manacled to a cad like Sewell in my work life wore me down, too. I excused myself from the table. Reynolds descended instantly to whisk me to the powder room.

'A most impressive man, Mr Rice's friend.'

'Yeah, he's the bee's pajamas.' I pushed into the ladies', leaving a bewildered Reynolds behind me.

I took a moment to inspect my wardrobe, a silk floral dress in pinks and blues with a blue grosgrain belt. No stains yet. I emerged into the hall, still not prepared to return to the table. A dim alcove just past the ladies' room had been transformed into a lounge with the addition of a settee and a few paintings of Mediterranean scenery. I plopped myself down and pondered how long I could hide out here. Addison likely wouldn't notice my absence for some time, not with Freddy Sewell regaling him with tales of the empire.

From down the hall came the sound of hurried footsteps. A voice further along called out, 'Vernon, there's a problem.'

'Not now,' Reynolds said, his voice uncharacteristically tight. He didn't stop moving.

The first man, obviously a waiter, persisted. 'The couple at table six are unhappy. They're asking for you.'

'They can wait,' Reynolds snapped. I could see the sleeve of his tuxedo jacket as he turned toward the waiter. I pressed myself against the settee. 'They were unhappy when they came in, for Christ's sake. I need two minutes. *Two minutes.* Not everything in this dump is an emergency, and I can't handle every emergency myself.'

He stormed past without glancing in my direction. A moment later I heard a door open, and light briefly spilled into the alcove. A moment after that, the unseen waiter called Reynolds a name that, had I said it, would have occasioned a trip to Father Nugent for confession. He then left to face down the unhappy couple at table six alone.

And a moment after that, I followed Vernon Reynolds outside to the restaurant's parking lot.

I caught the door as I exited and eased it shut, so I initially didn't realize I'd planted my left foot in a puddle of murky water that had been tossed out by someone in the kitchen. I refrained from groaning and stepped out of it, only to land in a larger, more unpleasant puddle when I ducked behind a truck parked alongside the restaurant.

Across the parking lot, Reynolds trotted toward a brown Ford Town Car. He hadn't spotted me, or so I hoped. He slid into the car's passenger seat – it took him two tries to wrench the door open – next to the driver. The two men exchanged words, then Reynolds emerged. Only now he carried a smallish package, wrapped in brown paper.

The Ford backed up carefully and took a wide swing around Reynolds. The front of the car had been designed with showmanship in mind, baroquely swooping fenders coming together like a locomotive's cowcatcher to enclose an elongated, heart-shaped grille. But the car had seen better days; one of those fancy fenders was dented, and some of the vehicle's brown coloring was an accumulation of dust. This glimpse of luxury on its last legs saddened me for some reason, but it didn't disconcert the driver in the slightest. A thickset man with a pug nose, he had a face that in repose drifted naturally toward a smile. Judging from his pursed lips, he appeared to be whistling.

I scuttled back behind the truck to avoid Reynolds. But instead of making for the restaurant's door, he broke toward the front of the truck. I scrambled to cover, which meant plunging both feet into that disgusting puddle again. I willed the ripples I'd created in the water's surface to still themselves.

The puddle acted as a grimy mirror. I could see Reynolds carefully opening a corner of the package, inserting a finger, then raising that digit to his nose. The sniff that followed sounded unnaturally loud, and in the scummy water I could see Reynolds's shoulders shudder and then slump forward, almost in gratitude.

'Jesus,' he exhaled, and after a coughing fit fell against the truck's hood. Then, to my consternation, he started to talk.

'Addison. Frederick. Addison.' He repeated them like an incantation, giving my employer's name greater weight. He laughed several times – first politely, then uproariously – dropping a few linking phrases between each outburst. *That reminds me of a story. You're too kind.* He was rehearsing his repartee for Club Bali, I realized, boosting his confidence with a sample of whatever the delivery man had provided. He viewed tonight, at the very least, as an opportunity to be who he once was, a man of substance with tales to tell, and he wasn't about to let it slip past him. As I watched in silence, I couldn't deny that I felt hurt he hadn't bothered to throw at least one 'Lillian' into his practice session.

Finally, Reynolds pushed himself off the truck. He slid the package into his jacket pocket as delicately as if he were serving a poached egg, tugging on the hem to smooth the garment's lines. Satisfied, he walked toward Arturo's back door. I circled around the truck to stay out of sight. The door closed behind him, and I counted to fifty to give him a head start. The setting sun cast a tiny rainbow over the surface of the puddle.

In the ladies' room, I scrubbed my shoes as best I could. At least I no longer had to take Ready's word as gospel. I had seen Vernon

Reynolds accept a package of drugs, likely cocaine, from the jovial fellow in the Ford, an amount too great for his personal use, no matter how many headaches the couple at table six gave him. He was indeed a purveyor of narcotics. Again, I felt gossip's sickening thrill, at once toxic and enthralling.

I opened the ladies' room door and Freddy Sewell backed away from it. 'There you are, Miss Frost. I was about to knock.'

'Sorry. I suppose Addison is looking for me.'

'As was I. You've been gone some time. We were concerned. I offered to make sure you were feeling well.'

'I – oh – thank you.'

He studied me a moment. 'Are you? Feeling well, I mean.'

His unexpected kindness flummoxed me. 'Yes. My fault, I'm afraid. I-I ran into someone I know and the two of us got to gabbing. You know how we girls are.'

He smiled, implying he did. 'Yes, well. I trust you'll still be up for more conversation with Mr Reynolds. I'm determined to hear the truth about those early credits tonight.'

'If you and Addison don't mind, I think I'll beg off that leg of the journey. It's been a long day. I'll leave you gentlemen to yourselves.'

I expected him to gloat at the prospect of monopolizing Addison for the evening, with visions of moving into my office by morning dancing in his head. Instead, Sewell said, 'I'm disappointed to hear that. You'll be missed.' He presented his elbow. 'Allow me to escort you to the table so we can break the bad news together.'

Addison insisted that Rogers drive me home while he and Sewell strolled to Club Bali to await Reynolds. I had just changed into my most comfortable if slightly tatty bathrobe and fired up the radio when Mrs Quigley hollered my name.

'It's her!' she whispered hoarsely, the telephone's receiver buried in her bosom.

'Who's her?'

'Lorna Whitcomb!' She thrust the phone at me and ran back to her apartment with her hands aloft like a sinner at a revival meeting.

'Was that your mother?' Lorna cracked when I said hello. I heard music in the background.

'No,' I said flatly.

'Good. You know what they say about apples and how far they fall from trees. I need an update *tout suite* and I can't get a hold of Edith. I think she's avoiding me.'

'I gave you an update. Through Sam.'

'Sometimes I want to hear it straight from the horse's mouth.' The S's gave her a little trouble; she didn't sound drunk, but drunk had definitely appeared on the horizon. 'This is one of those times. Come see me. I'm at The Players.'

'It's late.'

'No, it's not. Actually, for Los Angeles, it is. Everyone turns in early here. Not like New York. In New York at this hour, when I was a dancer, they'd just be getting started. But The Players is still open. Tell 'em you're with me. Don't keep me waiting.'

I tried arguing, but she'd already hung up.

EIGHTEEN

As the taxicab inched along, I refrained from rubbernecking. I hunkered in my seat, fearful that Addison and Freddy Sewell might have opted to promenade from Club Bali and would spy me back on Sunset Boulevard not long after cutting my evening short. I had retrieved the moon-and-stars dinner dress from my closet, still presentable after its last outing. Perhaps not fancy enough for tonight's occasion, but I wasn't about to outshine any noteworthy names I might encounter.

Preston Sturges had chosen the location for The Players well, with the Chateau Marmont looming overhead and the Garden of Allah hotel, sylvan and mysterious, across the road. I finally sat up as the taxi pulled in. The Players didn't look like a nightspot so much as a home lit up for a gala party. It resembled a Spanish mission-style house, but only from the middle up, as if the structure had been hoisted out of the earth. The bottom level featured a drive-in restaurant, with carhops shuttling out with hamburger sandwiches to patrons in the parking lot. The scent of freshly grilled meat had my stomach growling. Another reason for me to hate Arturo's Ristorante: this marked the second time I'd had a mediocre meal there before going someplace I'd rather have eaten.

A two-story fine-dining restaurant stood above the drive-in. It crackled with the chaotic energy typical of a night out in Hollywood: everyone playing at having a wonderful time with almost nobody genuinely enjoying themselves. Most of those in attendance would probably have preferred to be at home with their feet up, listening to the Jimmie Lunceford Orchestra on the radio.

As I pushed through the crowd, the joint's owner called my name. Preston Sturges's hair stood in greater dishevelment than usual; even his mustache looked unruly. He'd knotted a necktie around his forehead, but not his own. That one still dangled around his throat. I wended my way over to congratulate him on his recent good fortune, but he started talking before I reached him.

'I hear you've visited Orson Welles,' he half-roared. 'Tell me, is he actually shooting?' When I nodded, he said, 'I've heard about this picture. The life of a captain of industry, remembered by the people close to him. I already did that, with *The Power and the Glory*, and the town didn't grind to a halt to offer hosannas. Nor did I expect it to! If Welles wants to do something truly difficult, let him open a restaurant!'

Or work as a headwaiter at one, I thought.

Sturges's rant continued unabated. 'I interviewed a hundred and fifty people for jobs here. Do you know the first person I hired?'

'The chef?' I ventured.

'No. The only one who pushed in his chair when the interview was over.'

I took that as my cue to praise The Players. 'Started as a house owned by William Morris,' Sturges said. 'Not the agent, the actor. Although his son Chester made a bigger impression. It had an inconvenient hillside, so I got rid of it.'

'You got rid of a *hillside*?'

'Had it carted off. William Morris's basement is now my first floor, the first floor's now the second floor, and so on. Possibly ad infinitum. Thinking of adding a spot for a helicopter to land, sort of suspended above the roof. Get the fish to the kitchen faster.'

I initially assumed I'd misheard him. Then I recalled Edith's observation about Sturges's genius being fueled by excess. Having little to contribute on the topic of helicopter landing pads, I steered the conversation to movies. I told him how much I was looking forward to seeing his directorial debut. 'Edith can't wait to get started on your next one. She said there'll be clothes galore.'

'They're essential to the story. About a con woman who masquerades as royalty, and a rich boob blinded by love.'

I stared at him, again thinking our signals had somehow gotten crossed. 'It's . . . what's it based on?'

'Nothing. It's wholly original. The studio bought a story, but I scarcely read it. It's all my own.' He tapped his temple, briefly startled by the necktie that was still there.

'Not anything else?' I couldn't think of a circumspect way to say it sounded inspired by the incident that had brought me into Edith's orbit years ago, a story involving an old roommate of mine that Sturges had heard firsthand.

'Nope. A yarn of my own invention. Only way I want to work now. I feel liberated. It's—' A waiter sidled over with a silver dish bearing a slip of paper. Sturges consulted the note. 'I'll pick it up. He's a good fellow, down on his luck. When his next script hits, he'll be in here every night and we'll make it back tenfold. Solomon has spoken!' The waiter nodded and vanished into the crowd.

Sturges waved to a newcomer then turned back to me. 'Stop by the bar, if you can find it. It's nice and dim. Bars are meant to be dim. I'm off to tend to my friends. That's the trouble with owning your own place. Suddenly, the whole world's your friend.'

A fashion show welcomed me to the restaurant's second floor. Among the gowns galore: one with a red skirt and a shocking pink bodice, and a striped stunner twirling by with navy, green, and cocoa brown on white. Lorna, as I'd anticipated, had staked out her position with a sniper's care, her table offering a view of every other diner and the small but busy dance floor. She surveyed her surroundings through a lorgnette embossed with rhinestones. Unless I was mistaken – and I wasn't – she wore the same dress that had hung in her office the other day, only in burgundy instead of black. Buying one in every color undoubtedly saved time. She sat by herself, but she wasn't alone; someone had abandoned a plate of rare roast beef at the second place setting, the blood-red juices congealing around a mound of potatoes. Perhaps it was just as well I'd already had my dinner.

'Here's Cinderella, late to the ball. I was starting to think you were going to disappoint me.' Lorna's S's were a touch looser now. She downed the last of her martini, hoping to set those sibilants free.

I was tired, and not in the mood to make nice. 'Why am I here, Lorna?'

'I told you. I want a report in person.'

'What happened to proxies?'

'Sometimes they're not good enough. So tell me—'

'You tell me something first. What the hell was that shot across Joan Crawford's bow in your column this morning?'

Lorna's smile curdled on her lips. She waved the empty coupe glass before them in embarrassment. 'Sometimes you have to stir the pot a little. People didn't seem to care for it. It's why I'm sitting here alone.'

And that's why you called me, I thought. *What's a queen without her court?*

'What was the point?' I asked. 'What exactly were you implying?'

'It's a rumor that's circulated in this town for dog's years. There have always been whispers that Billie – that's Joanie to her intimates, you know – made a stag film in the bloom of her youth, back when they first invented electric light, and she's been paying through the nose and other orifices ever since.'

'And you think she made this picture for Lymangood?'

'Darling, I have no idea. I just obliquely referred to an old saw well-known in certain circles with the new information you and Edith provided. Those who get it, get it.'

'To what end?' I snapped.

Finally accepting that her martini was no more, Lorna lowered her glass to the table. 'To strike fear in Earl Lymangood's heart. To let any women who paid him off know that retribution is on its way. To twit Joan for the beastly way she treated me at *The Shining Hour* premiere. And, as I've said, to stir up trouble. Can't have people thinking this business with Sam has made me go all timid. Now. Tell me everything you've learned. Start with Lymangood, the swine.'

I did, speaking quietly and quickly, again leaving Florabel Muir's role out of it. I lavished the most time on Arthur Davis's hidden past as triggerman Heshie Rieger. I didn't bother telling Lorna I'd laid eyes on Vernon Reynolds's drug source, the encounter still too fresh for me to process.

When I finished, Lorna sniffed. 'Hogwash.'

'Excuse me?'

'Codswallop. I can't go to press with any of this.'

'I don't care about your going to press. Edith and I are trying to clear Sam Simcoe.'

But Lorna spoke right over me. 'There's no name tied to Lymangood. That's why I threw Billie's out there, to see if it would stick. Though Billie tends to stick to most things. Everybody sells happy pills, so this Reynolds story nets me nothing. As for silly little Delia Carson, if she's being rooked by her husband then she's the victim here. None of this points us toward Glenn Hoyle's killer, and none of it is fodder for the column.'

A waiter presented her with a fresh martini. Lorna scarfed down the olives at once. 'I would have thought you'd rush Delia's story into print,' I said.

'Quite the contrary. The first thing I intend to do is let various higher-ups at Lodestar know they have a sizeable problem on their hands. I would counsel them to have Delia's marriage annulled. And if she insists on standing by her man, I'd have them grant me an exclusive interview with her. "I Still Want to Believe in Love".' Again, she laid out the headline in midair. 'One way or another, Lodestar will give me material I can use. It's about horse-trading, my dear. One damaging story for five interesting ones. Because Lodestar and I, every studio and I, we're on the same side. I don't want to destroy people. I want to praise them and this industry. The picture business as we know it is something only America could build. It's this country at its finest. And I celebrate that.' She addressed her comments to her martini, her only solace in a confounding world. 'No one understands this job. It's not about tearing down. It's about building up. I know so much more than I've revealed. I've buried more dirt than has ever appeared in the column. That's because I sing the song of Hollywood. I root for the entire team, and I keep the players on their best behavior. I don't drive stakes through hearts, I give slaps on wrists. It's taken me years to learn that balance. Sam knows it. Glenn Hoyle didn't. The poor boy had no idea.'

My only response was to flag down a passing waiter and point at Lorna's martini. I admired a woman behind him in white organza with a print of rambler roses.

When my companion cocktail arrived, Lorna spoke again. 'Someone on that list is the reason Glenn was killed. You need to tell me why.'

'I just did. Whoever it is didn't want him exposing their secret. Anyway, it's a police matter now. I told them what I told you, and they *still* think Sam did it.'

'Of course they do.' Lorna snatched a roll off a plate and tore it into pieces as she spoke, tossing each one back onto the china. 'They have a story they like. I have stories I like, too, but they must make sense. You have to dig into them, see if they hold water. So often they don't. The police should do the same.'

'They are.'

Lorna flung the next chunk of dough with enough force that it bounced off the crockery and caromed off the table. 'Hell, I'm more likely to have killed Hoyle, if only to protect Sam. That's how much I need the boy, and you *cannot* tell him I said that. Sam keeps this train running on time. And he's the only person with nerve enough to tell me when I've gone too far.'

'Did he tell you the Crawford item was going too far?'

'He did, as a matter of fact. Which only proves my point. Sam didn't kill Hoyle.'

But you might have, I thought. 'Don't you have a stage show this weekend?'

Lorna squinted at me. 'How'd you hear about it?'

'Sam told me.'

'Painted a pretty picture, I'll bet.'

'If it opens tomorrow, shouldn't you be getting ready?'

'I *am* ready. I still have the chops from when I trod the boards in New York. That kind of training you never forget. Rust flakes off, you know. I'm not worried.'

Which meant she was worried.

'Why do you think I'm using these rolls for target practice instead of eating them? I'm jowly enough as it is, thank you. Stage lights are so unforgiving. And they've got me sitting behind a desk for most of the show when my legs are the best things I still have going for me. Maybe I'll play the second half perched on the desk, give the audience a thrill and the director a coronary.' She cackled once, popped the last bit of roll into her mouth in victory, and brushed her hands clean.

'Why do the show?' I asked.

'Why not? It'll be fun to bring a touch of glamour to the wider world. But the truth is I'm doing it to feather my nest. It's hard to live like a star when you don't get paid like one. And poor Dr Jerry's getting on in years and not seeing as many patients as he used to. That's partly my fault. So many people stopped going to him because they're afraid he'll give me an exclusive on their test results – tell me before them.'

'*What?* He wouldn't do that, would he? Violate a confidence?'

'You've read my column, yes? The demand for material is relentless. I always need more, and I'll take whatever I can get. Some comical ski-trip injury, a blessed event for an actress or producer's wife. One time . . . speak of the devil. There you are. You left me alone long enough. Jerry, Lillian Frost.'

A burly man approached the table, his uneven gait owing more to age than alcohol, although a highball or two had surely contributed. He'd been packed into a white sharkskin dinner jacket with a shawl collar. His face was pink with exertion all the way to his bald crown; a fringe of gray hair stubbornly clung to the sides of his head. I took in his broad, jovial features. The pug nose. The lips primed to whistle. He smiled at me, his features in repose drifting naturally in that direction.

I had seen Doctor Jerry Whitcomb earlier, dropping off narcotics for Vernon Reynolds a few blocks away. Running a minor errand before dinner with the wife.

I seized the closest glass of water – Lorna's, judging from her glare – and forced some of the liquid down my dry throat. I sputtered, swallowed some more, and apologized.

'You should have that cough looked at,' Dr Jerry said, still smiling. 'Take it from me, I'm a doctor. Glad to know you.'

Lorna leveled a gaze at her husband. 'I'd have sent your meal back to the kitchen if I'd known you were going to be that long. What kept you?'

'I was dancing with Carole Lombard.' Dr Jerry waggled his

head, inordinately pleased with himself. 'Two numbers. A rumba and a sumba.'

'You mean a samba, and it wasn't that, either. You realize she only propped you up on that dance floor to get to me.'

Dr Jerry made a swift, exaggerated search of the table, even checking under the tablecloth. 'If that's so, darling, why isn't she here?'

'An excellent question. I think I'll go find out.'

As she started to rise, Whitcomb pulled out the table for her. 'Don't make a scene,' he cautioned.

'I don't make scenes. Even if I did, who'd write about it?'

Lorna left. Dr Jerry chuckled warmly as he watched her go. 'She's a handful. But she's my handful.' He sat down before his dinner, long gone cold, and scooped up a forkful of potatoes. 'How do you know my wife? If you're an actress I'll fess up and say I have a terrible memory for names and faces. Ailments, that's how I remember people. Gallstones. Angina.'

I mumbled something about working for Addison. Forcing myself to stop gazing at my martini as if it were a crystal ball, I looked into Dr Jerry's genial, open face. He hadn't seen me. He didn't know that I'd tumbled to his extracurricular activity, supplying drugs for Vernon Reynolds to sell.

The doctor's eyes brightened at Addison's name. 'He's a big wheel, isn't he? Lorna's told me about his parties.'

'You're always welcome to accompany her to one.'

'Doctors' hours. Up early. Usually to play golf.' He gave a practiced chuckle along with the canned line.

I needed to hold up my end of the conversation, so we chatted idly about the restaurant. When we hit a lull, I blurted, 'Lorna was telling me about the stage show she's doing this weekend.'

'Could you mention it to her again? Speaking of doctors' hours. The lady ought to be getting her beauty sleep. Has to be awake at the crack of dawn so she can get to Santa Barbara for rehearsal, then it's curtain up. Looking forward to the show myself. I've never seen her perform.'

Lorna reappeared, making her way back across the room toward us. She passed a man in white tie and tails who seemed to recoil from her. Lorna caught the movement and spun on her still-slender legs to face him. She commenced turning on the charm, leaving the poor fellow nowhere to run.

'You don't think she's performing now?' I asked Dr Jerry.

'Point taken. But it's not the same. It's not with an audience. She was the belle of the ball back in New York, at least to hear her tell it. I want to see that for myself.'

Mr Soup and Fish had surrendered, bowing low and kissing Lorna's outstretched hand. She strutted the rest of the way to the table. 'Good Lord, Lombard really does have a mouth on her. But I calmed her down and all's lovey-dovey. As for that pipsqueak producer Cal Hendry at Lodestar, he can—'

'I hate to break this up,' I interjected, all at once desperate to be away from Lorna and her husband, 'but I have an early day tomorrow. As do both of you, I believe.'

Lorna waved me off with disdain. 'Please. Jab me with a hatpin at sunup and I'll be ready to go on. Jerry's the one who has to operate in the morning. I suppose he told you to say that.'

Dr Jerry raised his hands. 'Leave me out of this. Although it wouldn't be a bad idea to call it a night. I can bring the car around.'

'You know I won't be seen in that heap.'

'Heap? It's a Brewster body!'

'Then treat it like one. Wash it on occasion.'

I superimposed my goodbyes over their bickering. Lorna called some word of advice after me, but I didn't hear it. I thundered downstairs and made straight for a pay telephone, cutting ahead of a woman waiting for the booth. I coveted her column dress with alternating panels of black satin and white lace while I dialed Edith at home.

When she answered, I didn't waste time. I told her about my two run-ins with Dr Jerry Whitcomb. 'Maybe Lorna knows what he's doing and maybe she doesn't,' I said. 'The question is, did Glenn Hoyle know? Could he have had something on Lorna?'

'I think it could be considerably worse than that,' Edith said.

Someone hammered on the booth's door. I ignored the racket and pressed the receiver so close to my ear it hurt. 'What did you say?'

'I said don't breathe a word of this to anyone. Not even the police, not yet. I'll do some digging and call you tomorrow. You get home safely.'

The hammering hadn't relented. I turned, and Preston Sturges manhandled the door open, a second necktie now knotted around his noggin. He thrust a cordial glass at me. Some of the emerald liquid within sloshed onto his thumb.

'Green chartreuse,' he intoned. 'The nectar of the gods. The secret formula known only to a clutch of French Carthusian monks, their wives, and their patent attorneys. On the house. You look like you need some.'

I accepted the glass and threw the liqueur back. Sturges's eyes goggled. 'It's better if you sip it.'

'Who has the time?' I took two steps forward and almost sat on the telephone booth floor as the chartreuse hit me. I reached for my host's arm. 'I wonder if you could call me a cab.'

Sturges gazed at me with pity in his eyes. 'You, my dear Miss Frost,' he said, 'are a cab.'

Los Angeles Register   August 23, 1940

LORNA WHITCOMB'S
EYES ON HOLLYWOOD

A reason for studio executives to tremble? A report out of New York says the Columbia Broadcasting System intends to begin color television broadcasts in January of next year . . . Your dedicated correspondent is a touch apprehensive today, dear readers, and for good reason. This weekend at the Varsity Theater in Santa Barbara, I'll be sharing the stage with some of filmdom's famous names. We've organized what one might call a 'live version' of this column. Yes, you heard me right, and if you buy a ticket you'll see me all right too. I'll be joined by movie stars, vocalists and an orchestra. But don't worry, I'll leave the singing and dancing to the professionals. If you've ever wondered how this column is composed, swing by and learn a thing or two . . . Is Bette Davis really grousing about 'her' roles being given to Ida Lupino? The star denies it all, saying she has nothing but respect for the young Warner Bros player.

NINETEEN

The sun drummed relentlessly on my eyelids. My chartreuse nightcap had left a taste on my tongue as thick and woolly as tweed, yet I craved more. Fortified with aspirin and coffee, I set off to work.

I'd been at my post for over half an hour before Addison tiptoed in, looking rather ragged. He hadn't quite succeeded in taming his hair, and his necktie was askew.

'I'll regret asking this,' I said as I adjusted his collar, 'but how was the rest of your evening?'

'Astonishing and exhausting in equal measure. I adjourned to Club Bali with Freddy and Reynolds. A most peculiar fellow, that one.'

'You mean Mr Reynolds? Couldn't Mr Sewell pin him down?' The thought of Sewell flustered amused me.

'He tried his best,' Addison said, 'but Reynolds ducked out to greet friends every few minutes. The man's incapable of sitting still. "Invite them to stay," I said. You know me, always happy to meet new people. But Reynolds insisted on popping out of the booth. Freddy matched the man drink for drink. I waved the flag early on, but didn't want to leave because Reynolds kept tantalizing us with tidbits from his past. Right when I thought he was ready to yield, Bruz Fletcher planted himself at our table. Turns out he and Freddy know a multitude of people in common, mainly in New York.'

'Mr Sewell seems to have connections around the globe. He's a one-man Travelers Aid.'

'Naturally, their conversation kept us out even later. It's a good thing Maude's in Arizona. She'd have blanched if she saw when I came in. And Reynolds never did reveal much about the early days of the picture business.'

'You tried your best.'

'We're not licked yet. Freddy swears he can make Reynolds crack. He's going to keep in touch.'

My feet shifted under my desk as I recalled standing in that puddle of water, watching Reynolds have a car-seat confab with Dr Jerry Whitcomb.

'You might want to keep your distance from him,' I said.

Addison frowned. 'From who – Reynolds? Or Freddy?'

Maybe both, I thought.

'Vernon Reynolds. It could be he's tight-lipped for a reason.'

'Perhaps you're right. At any rate, I don't fancy eating at that restaurant again. I might have some bicarbonate. With an aspirin chaser.'

'I might join you.'

In short order, the telephone no longer sounded like the crash of cymbals next to my eardrum. I still snatched it up as soon as it rang, in the hope it would be Edith with news. Alas, the calls proved the usual household business.

Until I heard Gene's voice. 'You're at your desk? I heard you were burning the midnight oil at Preston Sturges's swank nightspot The Players.'

'I'll have you know I was home well before midnight. Let me guess. You're watching Lorna.'

'We're aware of her movements. Hard not to be, considering she advertises her whereabouts in her column. So? How was it?'

'I still haven't eaten there yet. It's annoying.'

'One of these days. Did Lorna say anything interesting?'

I knew more – a *lot* more – than when Gene and I had last spoken, but Edith had asked me to keep quiet. At least I could answer his question with complete honesty. 'No, she didn't. Anything new on your end?'

'The New York DA's office laughed when we told them Heshie Rieger might be out here trying to crash pictures. They found the notion unlikely. Then they called back in a matter of hours with greater interest.'

'What changed their minds?'

'They heard Florabel Muir is barking up the same tree. Now they're afraid of getting caught with their pants down, so they want to eyeball this so-called Arthur Davis themselves. They're sending a man out this way. We're sitting on Davis in the mean-time. He seems none the wiser.'

'And if Arthur is Heshie?'

'We arrest him and ship him back to your hometown.'

'Delia will be heartbroken if that happens.'

'It's not her fault. And it's not your problem. I know how you get, Frost. Don't work yourself up into a lather over this.'

'That's good advice. I should try to take it.'

'It's Friday. Any plans for the weekend?'

'I'm playing it by ear at the moment.'

'That means packing as many pictures as you can into the next two days with a break for mass on Sunday.'

'What's wrong with that?'

'Not a thing. Give me a call if you feel at a loose end. Maybe you can use your pull to get me into The Players and I can buy you that dinner you missed out on.'

He tried to toss the invitation off, with the result that it came across too measured in its casualness. I appreciated it nonetheless and told him as much, even though I had a sixth sense I'd be unable to take him up on the offer.

The next call was from Edith. 'Can you take some time off this afternoon?' she asked without preamble.

'Yes.'

'Good. Meet me at the studio, quick as you can. And bring a bag. We're taking a trip.'

Addison thankfully had a light weekend planned – a party at a friend's tonight, dinner with the now-ubiquitous Freddy Sewell on Saturday – so he accepted my early departure. 'You've missed a good deal of work lately,' he observed with mild reproach.

The Good Lord and the man who pays you aren't in the market for excuses, my uncle Danny counseled. 'I have, and I'm terribly sorry about that.'

'You're up to something with Edith, aren't you?'

'Yes, but I can't really talk about it. Only because I'm not sure what's going on.'

'When you are, you must tell me. Give Edith my love.'

My appearing at home in the middle of the morning triggered palpitations in Mrs Quigley. I changed into appropriate travel wardrobe, a linen suit with a lilac jacket and a full pleated skirt with lilac and aubergine stripes. I tossed a few other items into an overnight case, told Miss Sarah to behave, and flagged a taxi.

It was hard enough swimming upstream against the Paramount lunch rush without luggage. I shouldered my way through a stampede of starving starlets and had almost reached safety when my case snagged on the handlebars of a parked messenger bike. I spun around, almost toppling.

Fortunately, a cloud of cologne – one tinged with bergamot and cardamom – caught me. The fragrant fog resolved into the form of Oleg – scratch that, *Count* Oleg Cassini. Dressed in a navy blazer, scarlet ascot, and gray trousers, he gave the impression of a man who'd left his yacht double-parked at the studio gate.

'Hardly an auspicious start to your Friday afternoon,' he said as he righted me. 'A tumble to the ground.'

I thanked him. Cassini's hand slid along my arm, checking me for injuries from the spill I didn't take.

'Edith tells me you hail from New York,' he continued. 'Yet you've made this city your home.'

'I like it here. Very much.'

'As do I. But then America has always fascinated me, since I was a child. My father believed in reincarnation, and he told me I had been an Indian in a past life.'

I glanced down. His hand remained on my arm. 'You don't say. Which tribe?'

'I always hoped it was the Crow. They're the dandies of the plains. I wonder, Miss Frost, if I might impose upon you. I'm new to Los Angeles, somewhat unfamiliar with its customs. Perhaps you might share your expertise with a fellow transplant like myself.'

The count, I believed, was asking me out. The second such offer I'd had in a matter of hours. All at once, I was drawing men like flies. Then I recalled what drew flies, and it wasn't always honey. Nothing like an unvarnished perspective.

I couldn't resist. 'You mean tonight?'

'Ah, yes, well, tonight I fear I have plans.'

'Tomorrow, then?'

'Again, I am spoken for. Although now that I think about it, I could perhaps adjust my schedule—'

My needling had gone far enough. 'Actually, tomorrow wouldn't work for me, either. And right now I'm late to meet Edith. I hope you're enjoying working with her.'

'It is an education. She's uncommonly gifted.'

'She is. I adore her costumes.'

Cassini chuckled, his fingertips dancing lightly on my arm. 'I did not mean her costumes. Although she is certainly a capable enough designer.'

I replied with one of Edith's patented thin smiles on her behalf.

'Her true skill is as a diplomat,' the count continued. 'She speaks to actresses, producers, directors, executives in a language I've never heard before. One they all understand, even agree with. Somehow she convinces them that the costume she has designed is exactly what each of them seeks. It is most extraordinary. A tongue I must myself master.' He shook his head in bewildered awe. 'She is wasted here, I think. We should send her to Europe. Allow her to negotiate with statesmen. All hostilities would cease, and every woman on the continent would be in a shirtwaist dress.'

'And you'd be here to hold the fort, naturally.'

'I stand ready to take on whatever task is required of me. That includes reluctantly letting you go.' Cassini kissed my hand. 'When the stars align and our schedules permit, you must show me the city you have come to love.' He stepped away. His cologne lingered. He'd served up hooey, but it was high-thread-count hooey. Edith needed to be on her toes.

Edith, a vision in a silver-gray rayon dress with a thin black belt and a Bakelite necklace of flat red discs, stood by her office window. 'I saw you talking to Mr Cassini. What did he say?'

'He asked me out.'

'Obviously. But what did he say about me?'

'He praised your talents. Thinks you could dress all of Europe.'

She eyed me, her spectacles only magnifying her skepticism. 'I'll decipher that comment later. Meanwhile, I've learned a great deal. We need to discuss it with Lorna. Face to face.'

'She's in Santa Barbara to premiere her stage show.'

'Hence the trip. If we leave now, we'll be there in plenty of time.'

I felt myself whiten. 'I don't know if I should—'

'We're taking the train. I'm aware of how you feel about my driving.'

'I thought I'd hidden it.'

'Not very well.'

I was proud of the dandy job I'd done compressing a weekend's worth of clothes into a small suitcase. Edith reached behind a divan and hefted a grip large enough to hold the outfits for Radio City's Rockettes, complete with costume changes.

'How long are you planning on staying?' I asked.

'I don't know what kind of theater it is. One wants to be prepared for any eventuality.'

'Let's switch bags, for crying out loud. We'll never make it to the station with you lugging that thing.'

We had almost breached the studio gate when a voice trilled Edith's name. Before I shut my eyes in despair, I noted that Edith had already closed hers. We both knew those dulcet tones.

Hedda Hopper stood some distance behind us. She wore a navy dress with lace accents. As usual, her hat commanded the attention. A simple pillbox, it had a not-so-simple bevy of ostrich feathers swirling around the brim. She probably had a falconer on call in case it flew away under its own power.

It was an apropos chapeau, given that Hopper placed a premium on the pecking order. She hadn't budged an inch, expecting us to come to her. I hoisted the bag and moved toward the columnist. She possessed a birdlike quality herself, sharp-eyed and watchful; of the gossiping crows on a telephone wire, she was the one at the end who heard the full story. Her makeup, I noted, was elaborate and flawless.

Air kisses were exchanged. Hopper asked after Addison, her gaze never leaving the suitcases at our feet. 'I was next door at RKO, visiting Orson Welles. I'm not buying that boy's line. Acts like he can take on the town with half his brain tied behind his back, and his every answer is as crooked as a dog's hind leg. Where are the two of you off to? Sneaking away early? Don't worry, I won't blab to Mr Zukor.' Hopper's speech highlighted her elocution lessons; there was a 'K' in the dead center of 'Zukor,' and by God, she wanted you to hear it.

'Some afternoon chores,' Edith said.

'With suitcases?' Hopper raised an eyebrow so high it almost got tangled in the feathers of her hat.

'We're bringing some things back to Western Costume across the street,' I chimed in. Edith signaled her thanks.

Hopper shrugged. 'I was wondering if you were off to help the competition. I hear you two are lending Lorna a hand.'

'You mustn't believe everything you hear, Hedda,' Edith said.

'I don't. I *do* believe everything certain people tell me. What's the story with Dr Jerry's little woman? What was she thinking with that jab at Joan Crawford yesterday? The whole town's buzzing about it. Joan herself is furious.' She at last deigned to move closer, slipping into a stage folksy accent that telegraphed she was just one of the gals. 'What's going on there, really? Is Lorna on the skids? Are they going to arrest her leg man? Or her?'

I glanced at my watch. We had a train to catch.

'Honestly, Hedda,' Edith said, 'I don't know a thing about it.'

'If you say so. I understand Preston wants to use Barbara Stanwyck in his next picture. Seems a bad idea to me. No one will believe Stella Dallas in ball gowns.'

'She'll be great,' I said without thinking. 'Edith knows exactly how to dress her.'

'Thank you, Lillian, but the decision is Preston's. I'll do as he asks. We don't want to keep you.' Edith picked up her bag – which was actually my bag – and inched toward the gate.

'Yes, I should be off,' Hopper said. 'Can't leave Mr Cassini waiting.'

Edith wheeled back around. She'd bitten on the hook, and Hopper had snapped the line taut. 'You're here to see Mr Cassini?'

'The count invited me. Wants to talk about how Hollywood needs to lead the way in what women are wearing. Shake off its fusty standards. Exciting stuff. He's a smooth talker, that one. Not hard to look at, either. Anyway, don't let me keep you. Western Costume will be closing its doors any moment.' She tossed off a salute and strolled back toward Edith's office.

Edith stepped after her. 'They won't hold the train for us,' I said.

'Hedda featured me in her column the other week. She wrote that Mary Martin restyled my hair for me and the studio offered me a screen test as a result. Ludicrous.' When Hopper vanished into the Wardrobe building, Edith lifted the bag again. 'Let's go.'

TWENTY

Santa Barbara boasted an ocean breeze scented with salt and possibility. I knew the same wind caressed the shore in Santa Monica and Venice, but somehow it didn't seem as fresh there. That breeze was only interested in signing with William Morris and went through your pocketbook when you weren't looking.

Edith and I rolled through the quaint downtown in a taxi from the train station. She had explicated all she had learned during our two-hour-plus ride along the coastline. Such a trip would usually lull me to sleep. But her revelations so jolted me I'd had no need of the dining car's coffee, bounding electrified onto the platform at our destination.

The Varsity looked to be Santa Barbara's third grandest theater at best. Its marquee proclaimed *Lorna Whitcomb with Hollywood's Future Stars Plus Feature Attraction*. A plain brown brick façade gave way to an interior styled to resemble a Spanish hacienda. Cobwebs spanned the high-vaulted ceiling above a threadbare red carpet, and a pervasive odor of mildew hung in the air. The Varsity's best days lay a decade behind it.

Edith told a helpful usher we were with Lorna. He fetched the unhelpful house manager, a sallow-faced martinet every bit as starched as his collar, who said Miss Whitcomb was not expecting anyone and we could purchase tickets when the box office opened. Edith raised the suitcase in her hand and said we had the costume changes that *Mrs* Whitcomb had requested. The manager walked away only to return a moment later lightly chastened. He asked us to follow him.

Sam Simcoe had established camp in a dim dressing room made glorious by a profusion of flowers, at least a dozen bouquets of every hue. He stood over a table, scribbling on a scrap of paper with the intensity of a founding father affixing his name to the

Declaration of Independence. After a moment, I realized he was only trying to keep the wobbly table level.

'Sure, sure, they're with the company,' he said in response to the manager's unbridled suspicion about us. 'Now could you put something under this table to get it on an even keel? I've asked twice already.' The manager shuffled out in a huff.

'What brings you ladies to the hinterlands?' Simcoe said. 'Couldn't wait for the reviews?'

'We must see Lorna,' Edith replied. 'At once.'

'She's in her dressing room sweating bullets. So much for her vaunted training. She took one look at the stage this morning and tightened up. Now she's raising hell over the schedule. 'Can't do two shows a night,' she says. She has to do *four* tomorrow, a fact she conveniently forgot. I've been holding her hand all afternoon when I'm supposed to be punching up the script for this fiasco. Do you really need to see her?'

Edith pointed her chin at him. 'Would we have traveled this distance otherwise?'

'Good point. Give me one second.'

I couldn't resist reading the cards on the bouquets closest to me. 'She's certainly received her quota of well-wishes. These are from Mary Pickford, Joan Fontaine . . .'

Simcoe finished at the table and attached the card to a stunning arrangement of roses. 'And these come courtesy of the king himself, Clark Gable.'

I stared at him. 'But you just signed the card.'

'Why shouldn't I? I bought the flowers. Well, technically, Lorna did, seeing I charged them to her account. I have discretion over the office purse strings in addition to my leg man duties. And I didn't buy all of them. Pickford did send those, and a few others are from admirers. I told you she's fragile right now. She needs to feel appreciated. Those flowers are a legitimate business expense.'

Edith looked amused. 'Won't she recognize your handwriting?'

'Please. I've had years of practice and all those photos on her office walls to draw from. Some of which I signed myself. Anything to buck her up and get her through tonight. I'll tell her you're here. Try not to crush her spirits, would you?'

*   *   *

I wandered around the dressing room, which had been decorated in cost-efficient fashion with vintage handbills. The faded colors conjured the ghosts of performers who had played the Varsity when it was a stop worth making. Reading one roster of names, I froze. A chill rolled down my spine and along my arms as I blinked furiously to confirm I wasn't hallucinating.

But the lettering didn't change. Buried at the bottom of one bill was the name *The Great Horatio*. Glenn Hoyle's magician father, performing one final trick, manifesting his presence some one hundred miles from Los Angeles.

When I'd regained my voice, I pointed out the poster to Edith. She leaned in close to it, seemingly as spooked as I was.

'A coincidence, I should think,' she finally said.

'Are you sure?'

'No. I'm seldom sure of anything. But I always act as if I am. It's gotten me this far.'

'What kind of show do you think this is?' I asked her.

'A lousy one,' called a voice from the doorway. 'If I were you, I'd get your money back while you can.'

I knew the voice, as did Edith. Brenda Baines beamed at us. The brunette, one of Paramount's most promising starlets, had become a friend thanks to our shared New York heritage. Edith had dressed her in a number of pictures. Brenda had cornered the market in playing ultra-efficient secretaries and shopgirls who cracked wise all the way to the last reel, when the second male lead finally took notice of her – usually after she'd whipped off her glasses, a move that had become her specialty – and swept her off her feet. Roles that, little wonder, spoke to me personally.

She hugged us both. 'What are you doing here?' I cried.

'It makes more sense for me to ask you that. I' – here she took a bow – 'am one of Hollywood's future stars.'

'Of course you are,' Edith said. 'Had we known—'

'I wasn't on the bill until yesterday.' Brenda stepped closer and spoke in a whisper. 'It's my understanding more than a few people dropped out of the show in the last week. I guess with Lorna's name appearing in places other than her column, some of the future stars begged off. I'm replacing Susan Hayward, I heard. And I was told Ronald Reagan would be the master of ceremonies only to get here and find out we're saddled with Burt Dunston,

Lodestar's great white hope. Known to all as the Octopus Twins, because he seems to have more than eight hands. Heaven help you if you get too close to him in the wings. The other girls in the show and I form a phalanx when we pass him.'

'You're the perfect person to explain how this show's supposed to work,' I said.

'Lorna's at her desk pretending to write her column, and we come in and pitch ourselves for coverage. There's some singing and dancing. I don't do either, so I get to tell some jokes, the best ones written by her leg man, Sam, the one who's in all the trouble. I don't know who wrote the rest of the show. There's a number that rhymes "Lorna" with "gonna", so it's sung "gorna".' Brenda held her nose and mimed waving away a foul stench. 'I don't think we're far enough out in the sticks for this corn to play, but what do I know?'

Edith eyed Brenda's floral print green cotton dress. 'What are you wearing?'

'The studio said I could borrow wardrobe for the show, so I grabbed that gorgeous gown you designed for me to wear in the Jack Benny picture. The jade jersey one?'

'With the jet brooch on the belt that gives the impression of holding the material in place. An excellent choice.'

'I didn't have time to ask you first, so I chose my favorite. In the closing number I stand in the back and sort of sway, and that gown moves so well.'

'Let me know if any last-minute alterations are required.'

'I have to ask,' I said. 'Why do the show?'

'It's a weekend out of town, all expenses paid. I could use a break. My horoscope said it would be an auspicious day, so I thought why not? Plus there's an astrologer here I wanted to see. He's set up a kind of campus here in the hills outside town. Dedicated not only to the stars, but how they affect the natural rhythms of the earth and the body. They're all connected, you know.'

She said the words with such deadly earnestness that I could only nod in a similar fashion. Brenda had cast aside her New York cynicism and embraced Californian free thinking. Every time we lunched, she was espousing some new philosophy or touting a recent self-improvement book.

'I had planned on going out to the campus myself,' she said with a pout, 'then I learned we're doing four shows a day! I invited Claude – he's the astrologer – to see the show, but I doubt he's *gorna* think much of the entertainment.'

Simcoe popped back into the room and brightened at the sight of Brenda. 'You were wonderful in the run-through this afternoon. I'm going to rewrite your intro, tailor it to mention the picture you have coming out with Ray Milland.'

'That would be fantastic. I'll see you two tonight.' Brenda moved in to kiss my cheek, only so she could speak into my ear: 'Keep your expectations low.'

Lorna's large, well-appointed dressing room was the closest the Varsity had come to reclaiming its heyday. The scent of mint, from some unseen source, had largely banished the mildew. Lorna sat before a mirror ringed with lights. A bulb in the lower left corner had burned out, and she had positioned herself so that she could avoid looking at it. She wore a dressmaker suit of light blue wool with a black velvet collar, several degrees nicer than the ones we'd seen her in before. With blue eyeglasses to match, natch. She made contact with us using the mirror as a medium. 'Sam tells me you come bearing news. I hope it's of a typhoid epidemic and we're not going on tonight.'

Edith folded her arms. 'We felt it was necessary to see you in person.'

'Before a show. Why not?' Lorna's laugh, edging toward a shriek, betrayed her nervousness. 'We're doing four-a-days, did Sam tell you? The glory days of vaudeville have returned, and apparently I'm Eddie Cantor. It's some dire lineup we have. We lost Ronald Reagan. He's affable enough, but no great shakes as an actor. I don't see much of a future for him. Burt Dunston at least has some authority. Later, there's a juggling act. That's why people read my column, it seems, for the latest news on the competitive world of juggling. I swear—'

'Lorna.' Edith's voice pierced Lorna's prattle. 'Lillian and I have come a very long way.'

'All right.' Still Lorna hadn't turned from the mirror.

Edith glanced pointedly at Simcoe.

'Sam stays,' Lorna declared. 'I have no secrets from him.'

Or anyone, I thought.

'We've discovered why Glenn Hoyle had Vernon Reynolds's name on his list,' Edith began.

'Yes, I know, Lillian told me. He's selling drugs.'

'We have since learned that his source for those drugs is your husband. Taken from his medical practice.'

Simcoe gasped. Lorna crumpled a little and gazed down at the arsenal of cold creams on the counter before her. Her face visibly blanched under her stage makeup.

'No,' she said. 'You don't know that.'

'We have a witness who saw it firsthand,' Edith said.

'I hear from witnesses all the time. Believe me, they're seldom reliable. This one better be unimpeachable.'

I resisted the urge to step forward, to clear my throat, to do anything smacking of melodrama. I simply said, 'It's me.'

Lorna's eyes flicked to mine in the looking glass. She had aged a decade since we'd entered the room. She plucked a tissue out of the box, then a second, then a third. She balled them up and cast them aside.

'Goddammit. I knew his practice had run onto the rocks, but I didn't think it was sinking this fast. Is it cocaine? It's cocaine, isn't it? It has to be. He keeps some on hand to prescribe to those neurasthenic patients he sees. I told him to stop, I told him—' She cut herself off and stared at me again. 'You're certain?'

I nodded, determined to keep the histrionics to a minimum.

Lorna closed her eyes and placed her palms flat on the countertop. Simcoe looked concerned, so I was, too.

After a moment, Lorna looked at us again. 'I can understand why you'd want me to know. Although I don't appreciate hearing it before I perform. I hope you had a pleasant trip. If there's nothing else—'

'There's more,' Edith said. 'A good deal more.'

'Christ. Then let's have it.'

'It has to do with Arthur Davis. Whom, we have ascertained, is a former New York gangster named Herschel Rieger, or Heshie.'

'I thought that hadn't been proven,' Lorna said, 'but go on.'

'When Mr Rieger lived in New York, he had a financial involvement in several stage shows and a personal involvement with several performers in those shows. Dancers, to be precise. We have independently verified' – via Florabel Muir, who had called various sources in New York the night before and this morning – 'that the longest-standing of these relationships was with a performer then billed as Lorelei McKay.'

Sam Simcoe sank into a chair, flabbergasted. He'd heard the name before. He understood what it meant.

Lorna retrieved the ball of tissues she'd made and began tearing pieces off, casting them amidst the multitude of makeup containers on the countertop. Snowfall on a tiny, abandoned town. 'I was born Lora Lee Mackey,' she said softly. 'I thought Lorelei McKay had more of a ring to it. Sounded classier. Your bosses at Paramount christened me Lorna. Then I met Jerry – poor Jerry – and he did the rest. World, meet Lorna Whitcomb.'

After a pause, Edith said, 'Given your indirect connections to both Vernon Reynolds and Delia Carson, I would posit that all three of the scandals Mr Hoyle unearthed are in some way tied to you. That the true target of his efforts was, and always has been, you. Am I correct in this assumption?'

Lorna exhaled slowly through her nose. At some point she had become like alabaster, cold and impervious. She turned to her leg man. 'Sam, would you tell that nitwit manager to push back the first curtain? I'll likely cry in the next few minutes. Not much, but enough that I'll have to redo my makeup.'

TWENTY-ONE

'I might as well start by answering the question on all your minds,' Lorna said. 'Yes, I appeared in one of Earl Lymangood's grubby little movies. It's called *One Moonlit Night*. At least that's what they told us back in 1924. It's probably known by a dozen grubby little titles. I'm only in it for a few minutes, wearing nothing but pants like you'd find in a Persian harem and a smile. Other girls wore less. I've never seen the finished product, but I must admit I'd like to. It was shot right before I broke through as a dancer. I looked awfully good back then. It would be nice to be reminded of that.'

She paused to sip champagne. Before telling her tale, she had asked Sam Simcoe to open the bottle – 'sent for opening night by Tyrone Power, so it should be of quality' – and the leg man had pressed a flute into my hand. I sipped from it. The circumstances didn't seem to warrant champagne, but whenever presented with some, I drank it.

'At any rate,' Lorna continued, 'I put that episode behind me – or so I thought – when I became a chorus girl. Although I became Lorelei McKay first. Around that time, I met Heshie.' The exhalation that followed wasn't a dreamy sigh so much as a remembrance of dreamy sighs long past. 'Once I made a name for myself, Lymangood started sniffing around, asking for money. Heshie put the fear of several gods into him and he scarpered off.' A bitter chuckle. 'I could use Heshie now.'

'But,' I said slowly, 'Heshie *is* around now.'

'That's true. I suppose I should explain. Heshie and I went around for, oh, quite a few years. We had fun. We were maybe even in love. Then I met a scout and got the offer to come west. Heshie balked. It's one thing when your girl's in a line of dancers and you can bring your pals around to ogle her. It's another when she's across the country pulling down real money. He told me to choose. I chose. I came here, alone, and got none of the breaks. I couldn't exactly go back, could I?'

In other words, I thought, the quintessential Los Angeles story, as common to the territory as sagebrush. I'd heard it many times and even told it myself on occasion. Only in my version, I'd gotten every break.

'When did Mr Lymangood resurface in your life?' Edith prompted.

'After my reinvention as Lorna Whitcomb. I landed a beauty column, which became a show-business column, which became a national column. One day, he turned up outside the office to chat about old times. He remembered them more fondly than I did. This time, I had no Heshie. And I wasn't about to inform Jerry of this sad, singular episode in my past. Earl made it plain he still had a copy of *One Moonlit Night*. In pristine condition. So I started paying him off. Sometimes with money, sometimes with information he could use to further his film career. He kept pushing me to plug him in the column, but I drew the line at that. I wanted nothing connecting us in print.' She snorted. 'That was six years ago, before you joined the team, Sam. Six years I've been under that louse's thumb. You'd think in all that time he'd at least have offered to screen the damn picture for me. Give me a gander at what I'm paying to hush up.'

After a moment's silence, Edith said, 'And then Mr Davis reentered the picture.'

Lorna peered at her, baffled. 'Mr Rieger,' Edith clarified. 'Heshie.'

'Jesus, I never think of him by that Davis name. I don't know what happened to him in New York, why he hightailed it out of there. He's never explained it, and I've never asked. I figure he had his reasons. I heard about it when it happened, and I wished him well. We'd had our squabbles and I hadn't left on the shiniest of terms, but I still felt for him.'

She drained her flute. Simcoe immediately topped it off. I wondered if she still intended to go on tonight.

'Months later,' she continued, 'I heard from him out of the blue. He'd made it to Los Angeles, planning to slip over the border. He needed help, and I was the only person out here he could trust. He said he never missed the column. Even when he was on the lam.' A girlish pride flooded her voice as she repeated this claim, Heshie's loyalty meaning more to her than word that Spencer Tracy was her most devoted reader. 'I told him he had to stop running sometime. I offered to help him start over here instead. Gave him some money, some advice, but told him we couldn't see each other. We tried to stick to that, anyway.' A swirl of the glass, a small smile. 'One day he told me he'd gotten work as an extra. You're nuts, I said. Who hides out by appearing in public? But he got another job, then another. It's his look, you see. Perfect for pictures. Faces with character you don't find so much. Tough but tender.' She shook away some fond memory. 'I told him the Carson girl was wrong for him, raised all kinds of hell about it. But if Joan Bennett doesn't listen to me, why would he?'

'She looks like you,' Simcoe said.

'Who does? Joan Bennett?'

'Delia Carson.'

Lorna recoiled. 'You're batty, Friend Simcoe.'

'No, she does. It's the eyes. She has your eyes. And the same shape face. Funny how I never noticed it before. Heshie certainly has a type.'

Lorna ran a fingertip around the rim of her champagne flute, considering Simcoe's point. She shifted on her seat, deciding to be flattered by the comparison.

'As for my husband and Vernon Reynolds,' she said, 'I was in the dark until you told me just now.'

'But surely you suspected Mr Reynolds had some connection to you when you heard about the list,' Edith said. 'As Miss Carson and Mr Lymangood did. You must have known that Mr Hoyle had been excavating your past.'

'I hoped it was some other story he was working on. But if it wasn't, I needed to know what the connection was. I also had to know how easy it would be for anyone else to follow in Hoyle's footsteps and find out about me.'

'And so you pressed us into service,' I said.

'I could hardly take on the job myself. I already knew how Delia and Lymangood were tied to me. And as I've explained, it wouldn't do to appear overly concerned about the bad publicity the column was getting. I've given that advice in print often enough I had to follow it myself. Then Sam mentioned you two.'

Proxies, I thought.

'Oh, and of course I wanted to clear Sam's name,' she added.

If Simcoe resented his putative innocence being consigned to an afterthought, he didn't show it.

Edith adjusted her glasses. 'What did actually happen the day you met with Mr Hoyle?'

'I was on the level about that,' Lorna insisted. 'He asked if I'd hire him if he delivered a scandal. He never said the dirt he had was on me. Never even implied it. The truth is it didn't occur to me. Not until I heard about the list. Even Sam hadn't met every skeleton in my closet. And all of that stuff – well, most of it – had happened to a different person. But Hoyle, the little bastard, was determined to prove himself to me, and he did. Now the both of you have, too.'

She set down her flute, as resolute as a regent. 'But I should have known. I should have suspected it. A person like me is the only one Hoyle could destroy. I'm out here on my own. There's no studio willing to horse-trade to protect their investment, or apply pressure. I'm a one-woman show with no recourse. My syndicate would cast me aside at the first hint of trouble and hand my column to some flack with an ax to grind. Some *man* with no sense of the give and take, who only wants to bulldoze. Everyone in this town is afraid of me when *I'm* the one who's vulnerable.'

The sentiment would have been mawkish if she hadn't uttered it with such icy finality. I set my champagne aside. I'd lost the taste for it.

Lorna looked at Edith and me in turn. 'I need you to believe me. I went to Glenn Hoyle's place only once that day, and he was alive when I left. When Sam found him, he was dead. Someone else visited him in between. Someone tied to that list. Tied to . . . to my past.'

'There's nothing more we can do to help,' Edith said.

'I know that. I just need you to believe me.'

If Edith nodded, I didn't see it. She then said, 'We'll have to tell the authorities what we've learned.'

'Still sticking to that, are you?'

'That was our arrangement.'

'Never let it be said Lorna Whitcomb doesn't honor a deal. That goes for Lora Lee Mackey as well. The poor, dumb kid.'

She sat up straight, back to her usual gimlet-eyed self. For at least part of that conversation, we had been talking to Lora Lee. Now Lorna had returned to tidy up. 'You're not going back to Los Angeles at this hour. Stay and see the show as my guests. And here.' She scribbled on two cards and handed them to us. 'My home telephone number. If you think of anything – anything – call me direct. I should get ready.' She checked herself in the mirror. 'How about that? I didn't cry once.'

'I heard you had your tear ducts soldered shut,' Edith said. 'A surgery down in Mexico.'

Lorna smiled. 'Well, I *am* at work. Can't let them see you sweat.'

Sam Simcoe led the way through the labyrinth of the theater. He moved with the solemnity of a child who'd witnessed his parents arguing, his slight stature only adding poignancy. Finally, he said, 'Getting her home number is a rarity. You're in select company.'

After another few hollow footfalls on the carpet, he continued,

'I always wondered why she never gave Delia Carson a tumble in the column. At least that mystery's solved. And I knew Dr Jerry was hapless, but *this* . . . I'm shocked. Stupefied.'

We reached the lobby, where a handful of early arrivals milled. 'I have a few last-minute changes to make to the script,' Simcoe said, 'so if you'll excuse me.'

'I have to ask,' I said. 'Did Tyrone Power really send that champagne?'

'Of course not. I did. But Lorna paid for it.' He stepped one way then reversed course, lost in a fog.

Edith marched over to a plush bench in a sparsely populated corner and sat down. I joined her. The cushions seemed to be the primary source of the mildew scent plaguing the Varsity, but we didn't budge.

'Am I wrong,' I began slowly, 'or is Lorna now the most likely suspect in Glenn Hoyle's death?'

'No, you're absolutely correct.'

'Isn't it also possible that Sam could have learned what Hoyle was up to and killed him out of a sense of loyalty to Lorna?'

'Yes, that's possible.'

'And yet couldn't Lorna be right, and someone with a connection to her past be responsible?'

'She could indeed be right.'

I nodded. Then thought. Then nodded again.

'And with that squared away,' Edith announced, 'what say we check into our hotel? I made reservations before we left. I plan to change clothes before we see this show.'

Santa Barbara's finest packed the house at the prospect of clapping eyes on Lorna Whitcomb in person. White gloves had been donned, the finest hats removed from their boxes. As a tourist I couldn't be certain, but it seemed like the event of the season.

Our seats were front row center. Edith had changed into a striking midnight-blue rayon dress with a pleated bodice, accessorized with silver bangle bracelets. I stuck with my trusty travel suit, accessorized with a liberal dose of perfume. We had just settled ourselves when a man lumbered along the aisle. I rose to let him pass, and looked into the face of Dr Jerry Whitcomb. He squinted at me.

'Oh,' he said. 'Hey. From last night. You didn't say you were coming.'

'I didn't know myself.' I introduced Dr Jerry to Edith.

'If you know my wife,' he said, 'I apologize for not recognizing you. I have a terrible memory for names and faces. Ailments, that's how I remember people.'

Gallstones, I mouthed along with him. *Angina*.

As the curtain started up, Dr Jerry led the cheers and applause. Lorna, I had to admit, did not look like a woman whose life had just crashed down around her, and who had then chased the news with several flutes of champagne. She stood on the stage absorbing the adulation, blew a kiss to her husband, then moved to her 'desk' and proceeded to sell the contrivance of the show with gusto. She found multiple reasons to get out from behind the furniture and showcase her fabulous gams. Burt Dunston hammed it up outrageously. Brenda put her gags over with aplomb, but they were beneath her talents. I felt pity for her – and a strange, growing respect for Lorna. I glanced at Edith, watching Lorna avidly, and sensed that she felt it, too.

As Brenda took a bow, Edith leaned over to me. 'That dress doesn't look at all bad, considering it was designed for the camera.' I nodded in agreement.

Santa Barbara Gazette   *August 24, 1940*

LORNA WHITCOMB ON STAGE

Screen Stars Highlight New Revue

In the run-up to Lorna Whitcomb's show, reporters heard the gossip columnist hadn't set foot on a stage for twenty years. That proved difficult to believe when watching her last evening. Whitcomb commanded the Varsity's stage as if she'd been doing it every night of her life. She was a delightful presence in a somewhat silly but completely engaging evening's entertainment.

The production begins with Miss Whitcomb sitting at a

desk 'composing' her column. Throughout the evening she's joined by up-and-coming stars familiar from your local motion picture screen.

Burt Dunston's jovial demeanor as master of ceremonies holds the show together. Acquitting themselves particularly well were Lloyd Michaels and Brenda Baines, who swapped wisecracks in a sketch about newlyweds on a Hollywood honeymoon. Also impressive, the comic capering of jugglers the Garza Brothers.

But there's no question whose show it was. Lorna Whitcomb's presence suffuses each moment and makes this revue sparkle.

TWENTY-TWO

On went my weekend-getaway wide-legged brown linen slacks and a light green rayon blouse. As I strolled from the Moorish-themed hotel in which Edith had arranged our accommodations – 'I've stayed here before, it's very good' – to a café she'd recommended for an early solo breakfast, the cooling ocean breeze and the passing friendly faces stirred the usual vacation reverie. Maybe I could relocate to Santa Barbara. Live at a more sedate pace only a brief train ride from Los Angeles.

Sure, cracked a sharp voice in the back of my brain, one that sounded like half the nuns who'd schooled me at St Mary's in Flushing. *It'll be a piece of cake to find a millionaire in this neck of the woods who needs an easily distracted social secretary. Unless there's some other kind of work you're cut out for.*

Halfway through my little thin hot cakes with a side of sausage, I'd abandoned this fantasy. Instead of perusing the local 'girl wanted' ads, I returned to the hotel, secured a hillock of loose change, and took over a pay telephone booth in the lobby.

Gene was still at home. 'On my way out the door. Why are you up this early on a Saturday? Fishing for that dinner at The Players?'

'Not tonight, I'm afraid. I'm in Santa Barbara.'

'Nice town. What brought you up there?'

I proceeded to explain. As I did, I could picture Gene drawing up a chair, pulling out his notebook, mussing his carefully combed hair in vexation. I counted two sighs and one muttered invocation of our Lord and Savior. Not bad for a Saturday morning. Perhaps I needed to make a habit of waking up earlier.

'I agree with your assessment,' Gene said after my recital. 'This bumps Lorna to the top of the list, and it doesn't actually help Simcoe's case.'

'I still think there are other possibilities.'

'Why?'

Because, to my own astonishment and in spite of herself, I believe Lorna, I thought. But I said, 'Because all the people implicated in what Glenn Hoyle discovered have something to hide. Including Lorna's husband.'

'Doc Whitcomb is one to take a look at,' Gene grudgingly admitted. 'As is Lymangood. But it's Arthur Davis – or Herschel Rieger – who appears more interesting by the day. He's on the run. And he's suspected of killing before.'

The very argument advanced by Sam Simcoe. 'Speaking of Heshie, any word from the New York contingent?'

'Their guy's not here yet. I get the sense they think Los Angeles is a hick burg like all New Yorkers.'

'Watch it, pal.'

'Present company as always excepted, Frost. Florabel Muir has thrown a scare into them, but I doubt they're taking this seriously. They're having a hard time buying that a fella on the lam from Murder, Inc. would hide out in pictures. So am I, if we're being honest. But criminals aren't exactly known for careful planning. And we still have eyes on Davis.' Gene paused, weighing his next words with care. 'What I'd like to know is what you and Edith plan on doing about this business now.'

'Nothing. We're through with it. We told Lorna that. My last duty is to relay all this information to you.'

'Glad to hear it. When are you coming back?'

'Today.'

'My offer stands if you're bored this weekend. Just give me a ring. In the meantime, bring me a souvenir.'

'Like salt-water taffy? Or a driftwood sculpture?'

'Whatever strikes your fancy.' Another pause, then Gene said,

'Nice work on this' before hanging up. Which only upped the odds that I'd call him.

I exited the phone booth as Edith emerged from an elevator like summer incarnate in a white dress dotted with blue. Snapping off a salute, I said, 'Reporting to Gene as promised.'

'I spoke with Mr Groff first thing this morning. I'd say he was pleased, but with him it's difficult to tell.'

'I asked at the front desk about trains back to the city. We have a few options.'

'Don't worry about that. I've already taken care of our transportation home.'

Before I could ask our departure time, another elevator disgorged the familiar sight of Bill Ihnen. He wore a sport coat in a plaid of green and white, plus the abashed expression of a boy caught raiding the cookie jar. 'Sorry I didn't get to see you last night,' he said as he bussed my cheek.

'I telephoned Bill yesterday to see if he'd care to accompany us,' Edith explained.

'I have friends in the area,' Bill added.

'And he paints here.'

'Regularly. Only I couldn't get away in time.'

Edith clapped her hands. 'So he drove up later.'

'Had to miss Lorna's show. Which, to be honest, doesn't sound like my kind of thing.'

'Still, Bill and I were able to take a late supper together.'

'And I can drive you back. No need for the train.'

'Isn't that a lovely surprise?' Edith asked.

I had developed a crick in my neck from tracking the tennis match between them as they overexplained Bill's presence. 'When are we leaving?' I asked.

'We haven't had breakfast yet,' Edith said, making it sound like an admission of guilt. 'But right after.'

'I'll run upstairs and pack. You two have fun. If you go to that little café you told me about, drop my name.'

Having Bill at the wheel on our drive back put my heart at ease, although a few vertiginous turns had it racing. We exhausted talk of Lorna quickly, and soon were discussing the news from Europe,

Bill's recent assignments as an art director, and places he'd stopped
to paint along the scenic coastal roads.

Then a cloud scudded over our discourse when the name Oleg
Cassini came up.

'Count Oleg Cassini,' I said.

'Don't you start with that,' Edith clucked. 'Imagine him inviting
Hedda Hopper to the lot so he can expound on how we're failing
American women. A canny bit of self-promotion, that. Not to
mention he has the studio brass eating out of his hand with that
Continental manner of his.'

'Don't mistake that for something it's not.' Bill kept his voice
breezy and his eyes on the road. 'He's a man about town, Cassini.
Those conversations are simply boys being boys. They don't
threaten you.'

'Any conversation I'm excluded from threatens me. It's one
fewer arrow in my quiver.'

'What really worries you, Edo? His talent or his ambition?'

Edith turned to him, lightly startled by the question. 'He's
certainly talented enough. But he wants my job.'

'No. He's even more ambitious than that.'

'Whatever do you mean?'

'Cassini wants the prestige that goes along with your job, but
not the job itself. While you only want to do the work. Frankly,
I'm amazed you went to Santa Barbara. I know you. You'd much
rather be in the workroom or sketching away.'

'I *did* bring my sketch pad. To develop a few more ideas for
Barbara Stanwyck in Preston's picture.'

'I noticed. Cassini will try to steal your thunder, because that's
what his type always does. You concentrate on the lightning. Eventually, he'll set his sights elsewhere. His type always does that, too.'

Bill had dropped his hand to the seat between them. Edith shyly
took that hand and squeezed it.

'You're also overlooking the obvious,' he said.

'What's that?'

'That job is a fantastic way to meet beautiful women. Once he
meets the right one, he'll be out of your hair.' The words brought
her instant comfort, and she slid closer to him. I gazed out the
window at the view.

*   *   *

'Door-to-door service,' Bill said as he pulled up outside my building. I begged off the late lunch he and Edith suggested; it had been a long trip, and I felt Bill had additional counsel to offer Edith that I didn't need to hear. I thanked them both profusely and went inside.

Mrs Quigley called out a hello and assured me all had been quiet on the western front. I toted my grip upstairs, threw myself on the bed, and contemplated my plans for the rest of the day.

An hour later I awoke to the sound of Mrs Quigley yelling that I had a telephone call. Miss Sarah, stretched out at the foot of the stairs, gazed at me in bemusement. I caught a glimpse of myself in the hallway mirror – hair matted, makeup smudged, a line from the pillow scrimshawed into my cheek – and could hardly blame her. I picked up the receiver, still fuzzy in the mouth and brain.

'This Lillian Frost?' said a familiar voice, gruff and unforgiving. I told him he'd struck paydirt. 'My name is—'

'Earl Lymangood,' I finished for him, the synapse firing just in time. I felt wide awake now.

The low, rumbling noise that followed I took for Lymangood's laugh. 'Then the rumor's true.'

'Which rumor? There are so many going around.'

'The one that says you're working for Lorna Whitcomb.'

'I'm not working for her. I'm helping her. And Sam Simcoe.'

'Let's not split hairs. What matters is I'm right. You're the person I should be talking to, since Lorna's made herself scarce. I'm calling to say enough, all right? I've had it. You can tell Lorna that from me.'

He paused to let me talk. Too bad I didn't know what to say. I finally came up with, 'Tell her what, exactly? I'd hate to deliver the wrong message.'

'Don't get cute, OK? She delivered her message, loud and clear. I got it. Tell her that. I'm trying to establish my bona fides as a producer here and don't want her fouling that up for me. She can call off the dogs, all right? She'll never hear from me again.'

There was no percentage in acting like I knew what on earth he was talking about. Besides, I couldn't carry it off. 'I'm not playing dumb, but if Lorna sicced dogs on you, they have nothing to do with me.'

Throughout the lengthy silence that followed, I could hear

Lymangood sizing up situations and playing angles. 'We should talk, you and me. I'm in the office today, even though it's a Saturday. That should show Lorna and anyone else how seriously I'm taking this new career. Come by and we'll hash this out.'

'I'm not about to set foot one in your office, especially on a Saturday.'

Another chuckle that sounded like someone sifting gravel. 'OK, OK. We'll keep it aboveboard. There's a place called the Viceroy next door to my office. Which is at—'

'I know where your office is.'

'Let's say six o'clock, then. The cocktail hour. I suppose you'll recognize me. But how will I know you?'

'You'll know me. We've already met.' I hung up on those words to let him mull over their meaning.

Then I dialed Gene, this time at work. 'I can't do The Players tonight,' he said airily, 'but hamburgers are a distinct possibility.'

'I have plans for drinks tonight, and now so do you.' I told him about my imminent assignation with Lymangood.

Gene adopted a matter-of-fact tone at once. 'Show up a few minutes late. It'll give us time to scout the Viceroy. I won't have you going in blind. I'll be there when you arrive. You may not spot me, but I'll be there. Anything the slightest bit off, send up a flare and I will get you out of there, safe and sound. Understood?'

I knew he was only doing his job, being thorough, but it still took me a moment to work my reply around the lump in my throat.

Saturday afternoon bled over into the evening. In the drab stretch of Hollywood where Earl Lymangood had opened up shop, a scattering of people drifted along the sidewalks like tumbleweeds, blown by the breeze. That same wind would carry them to another part of the city by nightfall.

My taxi turned the corner in front of Lymangood's office building. Police cars lined both sides of the street, their doors open and lights ablaze. Curious faces peered through the smeared front window of the Viceroy. From the exterior, it didn't look like an appealing place to bend an elbow.

The cabbie stopped so short I lurched forward. 'This the place?' he asked dubiously. 'You sure?'

I paid him and bailed out of the car.

An officer raised his hands as I ran to Lymangood's building. Gene, waiting by the lobby door, nodded at the patrolman, who let me through. I knew what Gene was going to say, and he knew that I knew. The essential information had been transmitted by an emotional telepathy, words now needed only to convey details.

'A cleaning woman found his office door open,' Gene said. 'He'd been shot.'

Somehow, I'd known he was going to say that, too.

TWENTY-THREE

There was never a good time to go to a police station. It seemed particularly sad at the start of a summer Saturday evening, before drinks had been imbibed, passions inflamed, trouble let loose. A fellow loitered in the lobby dressed in tuxedo trousers and a bloodied undershirt, leaving me to wonder if he'd gotten into a donnybrook over cufflinks. His punch-drunk expression indicated he still held out hope he could reverse the course of his day, determine where he'd gone wrong, and proceed with his night as planned.

Upstairs, closer to Gene's desk, sat a brunette, unselfconscious in a faded paisley housecoat with a hairbrush poking out of the pocket. She should have been weeping but she wasn't, staring at the smoldering end of her cigarette as if it were on the distant horizon. I prayed she and the gent downstairs weren't connected.

Gene had been on the telephone for several minutes, his end of the conversation consisting of occasional grunts and half-finished questions. 'What about . . .? Did you talk to . . .?' He'd forbidden me to enter Earl Lymangood's office, saying I didn't need to see what had transpired there. I didn't protest.

Hansen skulked over to deposit a scrap of paper on Gene's desk. Gene glanced at it, raised an eyebrow. Hansen elevated two in response. Gene shook his head. Hansen shrugged. An entire Russian novel, conveyed in their gestures.

Next, Hansen turned to me. 'Supposed to be taking the missus to the pictures tonight.'

'I'm sorry about that.'

'No, I'm thanking you. She's nuts for that actor from *Rebecca*, Larry Oliver, and was hellbent on dragging me to his latest. Can't understand what anybody sees in that guy.'

He wandered off. Gene continued making broken inquiries into the receiver. A man in a grease-stained coverall rushed over to the woman in the housecoat. Upon seeing her, he burst into tears. The brunette stood up, said a few words to a detective, and led the coveralled fellow away. She still hadn't cried. At least she wasn't leaving with the Beau Brummell bruiser in the lobby.

Gene hung up the telephone then lifted his hands gingerly, afraid of spooking it. 'That could go off at any time. There's a lot happening here, all of it unclear.'

'Can you tell me anything?'

'For starters, we confirmed what you found out about Earl Lymangood. The kind of pictures he used to make.'

'Stag films,' I said. 'Smokers.'

Gene chuckled. 'Listen to you. Little Miss Hardboiled. What would the sisters at St Mary's say?'

'They've given up on me by now.'

'Not all of us have. As for the scene, Lymangood had an office safe. It was open when we arrived. Not forced. There were papers in it, along with some gold jewelry in a bag. No money, but there could have been.'

'And no film,' I said, thinking of Lorna's starring turn in *One Moonlit Night*.

'No, but again there could have been. Lymangood could have had the safe open and someone surprised him, or someone could have ordered him to open it at gunpoint. He told you he wanted Lorna Whitcomb to call off the dogs, is that right?'

'Yes, but I'm not sure what that means.'

Gene considered me curiously. 'To me it means Lymangood was being watched, if not pressured, and he knew it.'

'Maybe. I don't know if that's true.'

Another odd look from Gene. 'Something made him say it. Allow me to muddy the waters further. There's no way Lorna Whitcomb could have done it. Because at the time we estimate Lymangood was shot, she was on stage in Santa Barbara.'

'Four-a-days,' I said. 'Like in vaudeville.'

'We also know Sam Simcoe couldn't have pulled the trigger because he was seated down front, making sure the changes he'd made to the script were going over. We've got a whole theater full of witnesses to alibi Lorna, and at least a couple of rows for Simcoe.'

'Then they're both in the clear.'

'I'm not prepared to say that. Not yet. Either of them could have had an accomplice.' He stretched. 'I *am* prepared to say that Lorna – and you – may have been right all along, and it could be someone connected to that list. And by extension, Lorna's past.'

He tapped the paper Hansen had left. 'One reason I'm willing to say that is no one in this esteemed department knows where the hell Arthur Davis, also known as Heshie Rieger, is.'

'What?' I erupted. 'I thought you were watching him.'

'So did I. When Lymangood was found dead, I had the boys sitting on him confirm his whereabouts. They thought he was at home with his wife. Turns out he wasn't. He'd slipped out. The last actual sighting of Rieger was yesterday afternoon. We have no idea when he flew the coop. The New York DA's man is going to get here and think we're a bunch of clowns. He may not be far wrong.' He scowled at the paper. 'I'd chew these guys out myself, but my plate's full at the moment. Think I'll let Byron do it.'

Byron. Back on a first-name basis with Captain Frady, his former nemesis. How times had changed.

'Have you spoken with Delia Carson?' I asked.

'I haven't. Another detective has. She's frantic because she hasn't seen her husband since yesterday morning and can't think where he's gotten to.'

Rhoda must be overjoyed, I thought.

'It'd be grand if we could figure out where he is before the New York man shows up to get a gander at him. I mean, he did come clear across the country.' Gene cracked his neck, a habit I'd always hated. 'Gonna be a corker of a night. No sleep for yours truly. Let me get you out of here.'

'You don't have to do that.'

'I want to. Anyway, it's the only break I'm liable to get.'

As Gene swung his car onto the street, he asked, 'What gives between you and Lorna?'

'What do you mean?'

'She shanghaied you and Edith into helping Simcoe. Which was actually helping her. Yet just now, you were practically defending her.'

'Was I?'

'Practically.'

'I guess I was. It's strange. She twisted our arms and never told us the truth. But now I'm invested in this. Because in spite of everything, I like Lorna. I even feel for her. She built something all on her own, and now it's under siege with no one to come to her aid. Sam's on the hook himself, and her husband is useless. I wouldn't want to be in that situation.'

'You should try not to be.'

'Good advice. Tell me what you've been up to.'

'The usual. Keeping the city safe. Doing battle with hoodlums and white slavers on a nightly basis.'

'I meant in your free time, Hercules.' I hesitated, unsure about venturing into this territory. 'Are you seeing anyone?'

Gene's lips twitched, as if he'd barely prevented an answer from escaping. After a moment's debate, he said, 'Yes. The sister of the fellow who lives around the corner from me.'

Oh. 'Not the druggist who's a backyard naturist?'

'God, no. The mechanic who lives just past him. She's a telephone operator.'

'And?'

'And she has a lovely voice.'

'I imagine it helps in that line of work.' *Listen to this carefree banter. Lillian Frost, everybody's pal and no one's anchor.* 'What else can you tell me about this angel?'

'She's quiet. Sings in her church choir. Never gets into a lick of trouble.' Gene issued a reluctant sigh. 'Turns out that gets a little dull.'

'I thought you were in the market for dull.'

'Put it this way. I've taken to walking the long way around to sneak through my own back door so I can avoid her brother. Like he's the neighborhood bully.'

'And you a grown man with a badge and gun and everything.' I settled back in the car seat, enjoying myself enormously. 'Maybe you should move.'

'Maybe I should. I've been thinking about it.'

'Really? You grew up in that house.'

'Reason enough to leave it.' He sighed again, this one honest, not meant for show. 'It feels like I need to do something. Ever have that feeling, Frost? Like your life's been the same for too long?'

I allowed that I had.

'You got comfortable and didn't realize it,' Gene continued. 'Only you didn't actually get comfortable. You just got used to things. Truth is, you're not comfortable at all. You only thought you were.'

'So what do you do?'

'You make a change.'

I nodded, thinking about my half-planned impromptu relocation to Santa Barbara. That had been this morning, yet it felt like a week in the past. 'The question is, what change do you make? What's the right one?'

'You never know. Sometimes any move is the right one.'

My thoughts were awhirl as I went inside, almost neglecting to say good evening to Mrs Quigley. Gene and I had been able to preserve our easy repartee after we'd stopped keeping steady company because we genuinely liked each other – but I also believed it was partly due to Gene's relief at slipping the cuffs of our relationship. Perhaps I had that wrong. Maybe he missed being together. Did I? Was I comfortable with my life, or had I simply gotten used to it?

I changed into a housedress and resolved to think about any other subject. The first to come to mind was the late Earl Lymangood. One of the threads from Lorna's past had been cut, with a second – Heshie Rieger – possibly responsible. That made me speculate about the third.

I fished Lorna's card from my purse and trotted downstairs to the telephone. Lorna's home telephone rang several times, and I hoped it would trill the night away.

Then, as I pulled the receiver away from my ear, I heard Dr Jerry Whitcomb say, 'Hello.'

'Oh,' I said, unable to keep the disappointment out of my voice. 'You're home.'

'Why shouldn't I be? And who is this?'

'Lillian Frost. From the show last night.'

'Ah. Of course. How are you?'

'I'm well, thank you. I was calling to leave a message for Lorna. I didn't think you'd be home.'

'I wasn't supposed to be. I started to feel under the weather last night. Too much sea air, probably. Either that or the champagne.' He chortled. 'I decided to come back from Santa Barbara first thing this morning, before I became worse for wear.'

'You sound in the pink now.'

'Wouldn't you know it? The drive fixed me right up. I'd prescribe that as a treatment to my patients if it wouldn't cost me money. I hated missing Lorna's shows today, but I'd already seen her perform. Wasn't she fantastic?'

'Swell.'

'Lillian Frost. I'll have to remember that name. Ailments, that's what I keep track of. Gallstones.'

'Angina,' I said.

'That's right!' The good doctor erupted in laughter. 'Now I definitely have to remember your name.'

I asked him to thank Lorna for the tickets to her show and hung up. Miss Sarah prowled past. She sensed my distress and, in a rare show of pity, allowed me to scoop her up and nuzzle her. I took a seat in the lobby, listening to the sounds of Mrs Quigley's radio. Gene needed time to get back to his desk before I could telephone to say we had a second suspect in Dr Jerry, who'd been back in Los Angeles all afternoon.

Los Angeles Register   August 26, 1940

MANHUNT FOR NEW YORK GANGSTER

Movie Extra Sought in Homicide

Los Angeles, Aug. 25 (AP) Los Angeles police are searching for movie extra Arthur Davis, wanted for questioning in connection with the murder of film producer Earl Lymangood. Lymangood was found dead in his Hollywood office on Saturday.

Davis is married to film star Delia Carson, who was not available to reporters. Davis is believed to be an alias for Herschel Rieger, a known associate of the criminal element in New York City, where Rieger was born.

Sources indicate that Davis is also wanted for questioning in relation to the August 9 murder of Glenn Hoyle, which remains under investigation.

WHITCOMB SHOW CLOSES

All performances of columnist Lorna Whitcomb's stage show at the Varsity Theater in Santa Barbara have been cancelled. A planned West Coast roadshow of the revue has also been indefinitely postponed. The show's producers declined to give a reason for either decision.

TWENTY-FOUR

I spent Sunday mass on the clock. I said a prayer on Lorna's behalf to Francis de Sales, patron saint of journalists, although that job description didn't seem wholly accurate in Lorna's case. Recalling her show, I also invoked Saint Genesius, who shepherded actors. Another tenuous connection, but Lorna would appreciate a roster of celestial all-stars interceding for her, and it happened to be Genesius's feast day, which struck an auspicious note. Besides, I had visited his chapel at St Malachy's Church off Broadway in New York after Joan Crawford had married Douglas Fairbanks Junior there, so I had an in.

Business attended to, I then joined the congregation in praying for the people of London, who had endured a full day of aerial attacks from German planes.

At home, I telephoned Edith and told her what I knew about

Earl Lymangood's murder, which wasn't much. She seemed every
bit as dumbfounded as I did. 'But then it isn't our concern anymore,'
she said. 'What are your plans for the afternoon?'

'I'm going to see the fruits of your labor in *Rhythm on the
River*.' I was as good as my word. Too bad I left Bing Crosby's
latest musical extravaganza humming the costumes.

An edge of agitation sounded in Edith's voice when she telephoned
me on Monday afternoon. 'I wonder if you could possibly come
by the studio.'

'I'm in the middle of a project for Addison right now. Is late
afternoon all right?'

'Ah.' An uneasy silence followed. 'It really does need to be
now. You see, Delia Carson is on her way over. She said she needs
to talk to both of us.'

'I'll be there as soon as I can.'

I finished the letter in the typewriter, then steeled myself to see
Addison. Naturally, he was in conference with Freddy Sewell; he
had invited the Englishman to lunch ostensibly to discuss Addison's
overture to the Academy of Motion Picture Arts and Sciences
regarding their proposed museum of film, but he confided that he
wanted to provide Sewell 'a safe harbor' in light of the deluge of
bad war news out of Britain. Freddy had appeared subdued when
I'd glimpsed him upon his arrival, but he'd regained his standard
insouciance. I walked in on him telling what I took to be a saucy
story about the British actress Wendy Barrie. Addison seemed
mildly irked by the intrusion.

I greeted Sewell and offered my sympathies.

'Thank you, Lillian. Afraid I won't know for a few days how
the family and friends have fared. Still, it was gratifying to read
in the newspaper this morning that we've gotten some of our own
back, bombing Berlin, taking aim at Hitler's chancellery.'

I opted not to mention a second story that had been on the front
page, in which British film producer Michael Balcon blasted his
fellow countrymen who remained in Hollywood after the outbreak
of hostilities as 'deserters' and 'war profiteers', including a thinly
veiled attack on a 'plump young' director who could only be
Rebecca's Alfred Hitchcock. Balcon might well have considered
Sewell in their company, but then I didn't know Sewell or his

story. In any event, it was hardly my place to judge anyone's behavior during wartime.

'I hate to do this,' I said, 'but Edith just telephoned me. There's a bit of an emergency I can't explain at the moment. If I could take some time to pop over to Paramount—'

'But we were going to draft my letters to the Academy and Jock Whitney,' Addison groused.

'Never fear, Addison.' Sewell stepped forward. 'I'm a dab hand behind a keyboard. I'd be happy to fill in for Lillian. Might be exactly what I need. Keeping the fingers busy occupies the brain. And I can edit the letters as we go.'

'That's fine by me. Carry on, Lillian.' He gently ushered me out, itching to hear the rest of Sewell's tawdry tale. I managed to slip in a thanks to Sewell as I left, despite my growing certainty that he would poach my position.

Interlopers were out in force; as I hustled toward the Wardrobe building, I spied Barney Groff chatting with Oleg Cassini, the studio strongman hanging on the count's every syllable.

Rhoda Carson waited in Edith's outer office, her hostility setting off sparks. 'There you are! What on earth is going on? Why does Delia want to see you?'

'I don't . . . I just got here,' I sputtered, blindly continuing toward the door to Edith's inner sanctum.

Edith, in a gray skirt with an ivory blouse, opened the door, seized my hand, and pulled me inside in a single motion. 'Thank you for your patience, Mrs Carson,' Edith said sweetly. 'We won't be long.' Rhoda, having none of it, barreled toward us. Edith closed the door in her face.

Delia sprawled on a sofa, bereft. She wore a simple blue dress and no makeup. In each hand she clutched a crumpled handkerchief, one per teary eye.

'Miss Carson asked to speak with us' – Edith used the measured voice of an adult trying to impart information without revealing it to the children – 'and I thought it best she do so in private, without fear.'

Translation: keep Momma out!

I said hello to Delia, who replied with a sob. 'I don't understand anything that's happening!'

'Why don't you tell me what's happening?' I suggested.

'You must know! It's in every stinking newspaper in the whole damn country! Photographers hounding me everywhere. Lying in wait outside our home. Lodestar shut down the picture today because of all this, this bother. I've *never* missed work before. I've sung and danced with a fever of a hundred and two and now suddenly I can't do my job because of this . . . this *goddamned nonsense*!' All delivered in a heaving, breathless rush. Delia inhaled deeply, then unleashed a fresh torrent of anguish.

'Arthur's gone! He's vanished completely! I haven't seen or heard from him in *days*. And the police are looking for him. Not because he's missing, but because they think he's some gangster from New York. It's not true. It can't be. He's Artie. *And* they think he killed some producer I've never even heard of.'

That's about the size of it, I thought.

Delia then let out a wail. An instant later, Rhoda pounded on the door, squawking about her daughter's welfare. Edith and I both yelled that she was fine, and Rhoda's protests subsided.

'I agree that's a lot to take in,' Edith said. 'Why, may I ask, did you want to see us?'

'Arthur told me to,' Delia sniffled. 'Last week he said if anything happened to him, I should go to the two of you.' She stopped crying and sat up abruptly, as if her director had called 'Cut.' 'I want to know why he said that.'

As did I. I had a theory – that Lorna and Heshie had still been in contact before his disappearance, and she'd told him that she'd enlisted us in her cause. He might even have known exactly who we were when we'd spoken to him outside Bundles for Britain. If so, he was too good an actor to be relegated to the background. He deserved more screen time.

Edith, who had obviously reached the same conclusion, cleared her throat. 'You are familiar with the columnist Lorna Whitcomb, of course.'

'Yes,' Delia said with a trace of petulance. 'Even though she never mentions me.'

It dawned on me that Sam Simcoe was right – Delia *did* resemble Lorna, which likely accounted for part of Arthur's attraction to her. An old flame in a new bottle.

'Lillian and I have been assisting Lorna on a personal matter.

It appears that Mr Davis – years ago, you understand – had a connection to her.'

'A connection?' Delia snapped. 'What kind?'

'At one time – in the past, in New York City – they were a couple.'

'*Artie?* And that shrew? Never. That's, that's impossible.' Doubt fluttered across her features, quickly replaced by fire. 'Wait a minute. Does this mean you befriended me under false pretenses?' Her nostrils flared as she settled on an answer to her own question. 'You don't care about me, or Bundles for Britain, or anything.'

'That's not true, my dear, not at all. Lillian and I admire your work as an actress and your commitment to war relief. Isn't that right, Lillian?'

Never had I nodded so vigorously. Still, Delia wasn't wrong, and I felt awful about that. Convinced of our insincere sincerity, Delia worried both handkerchiefs simultaneously.

'Can't you tell me where he's gone?' she implored us. 'What kind of trouble he's in?'

'You know as much as we do, I'm afraid,' I said. I didn't feel so bad that I avoided a thorny but necessary subject. 'Has Arthur ever disappeared before?'

'No!' She followed this with another wrenching cry. Rhoda stirred in the outer office, poised to assault the door anew.

'How about for shorter periods of time?' I asked. 'Does he stay out late, for instance?'

'Who told you that? My mother?' Delia looked daggers at the door with such intensity I half-expected Rhoda to shriek in pain.

'Yes,' I said. 'She said he goes out every Friday night, sometimes to all hours.'

'So what? Yes, he sees his friends, playing the horses and drinking beer. You don't think I wish he didn't do it on Friday nights? But he always comes home, and he only reeks of beer. Not perfume.' She pitched this last sentence at a volume even Rhoda could hear.

'Has he ever been gone this long before?'

'No. He's always back in the wee hours of Saturday at the latest. Always.' The frantic insistence in her voice indicated that there might have been an exception or two.

'And he does this every Friday?' I asked. 'Since when?'

'Since we've been going together. Except for the weekend we were married.' The way Delia brushed the hair away from her face – at once modest and seductive – felt like a violation of the Production Code.

'That means every Friday night this summer,' I pressed, 'he's been out?'

'Yes, because summer is when there are horse races and baseball games and cookouts, he says. I like those things. Or at least I tried to. Now Artie sees his pals on Fridays, and Mother and I go to dinner or the pictures. Lately, I've been spending my Fridays at Bundles for Britain. Mother doesn't come with me. But I like it, feeling like I'm doing something worthwhile. And on Saturdays, Artie takes me out. He makes a big production out of it. We go to the spots where I'll be seen, where the photographers are. He never wants to be in the pictures himself, even though I encourage him, and I—' She cut herself off, the nature of her husband's camera shyness abruptly apparent to her. Her Artie was on the lam. A split-second appearance in a movie might prompt a twig of recognition and the occasional 'didn't that fella look like . . .' moment among his old cronies. But his distinctive face, frozen alongside America's silver screen sweetheart in newspapers coast to coast . . . well, that was another matter entirely.

Delia slumped forward, as if a yoke bearing the weight of her problems had been deposited on her shoulders. Worse, she had no idea she'd added to her woes by confirming that her husband had been out the night of Glenn Hoyle's murder as well as Earl Lymangood's. Without intending to, she had tightened the noose around Arthur's – or Heshie's – neck.

'This is terrible,' Delia said in an eerie monotone. 'I never knew Artie at all. He had a whole life I didn't know about. A life he hid from me. Mother was right about him. Mother was right about everything. She keeps telling me that people only want to get close to me because of who I am, that I can't trust anyone other than her, that they're all liars.'

It was a monologue she'd evidently rehearsed in her mind countless times, finally uttered aloud in those lifeless words. Delia had ulcerated to play an adult woman, and now that the role had been thrust upon her, she wasn't prepared for its demands. I felt dreadful, because Edith and I, despite our best intentions, had in fact been as unscrupulous as she'd described – and worse, we'd proved Rhoda Carson right. Edith shared the sentiment, because she went to Delia on bended knee.

'None of that is true,' she said. 'We are honored to know you, and wish we could have met under better circumstances. What you are doing with Bundles for Britain is a noble thing, to be praised. Your husband kept his past a secret because he wanted to protect you. He wanted to be worthy of you. Don't listen to your mother. Listen to your heart.'

'I know I should. I can't bear the thought of her pouring such hatred in my ear right now. I wish I could be alone for a little while. I wish I could sit by myself and knit for the sailors for a few hours.'

'That can be arranged.' Edith rose and turned to me. 'Lillian, can you please show Delia the other way out of the office, through the salon?'

'I'll go you one better,' I told Delia, 'and have you taken to Bundles for Britain in a chauffeured Cadillac. Even the driver won't talk to you. Take it from me.'

TWENTY-FIVE

Once Rogers had ferried Delia to her destination, I had him whisk me back to work *tout suite*. Addison and Freddy Sewell had adjourned to Sewell's club – presumably for several rounds of pink gins and ribald stories – after drafting the initial correspondence regarding Addison's dream museum project. Which, I had to admit, struck exactly the right tone. The letters had even been typed neatly, dammit.

I stayed late to get an early start on the next day's chores, so I was still at my desk when Gene telephoned. 'Let me guess,' he said. 'You're applying a little extra elbow grease to make up for today's jaunt to see Delia Carson.' I admitted he was right, and he chuckled. 'That tears it. When I settle down, I'm marrying a Catholic girl.'

I had neither the inclination nor the energy to decode that statement. 'Why are you calling?'

'To find out what Delia said.'

I reeled off chapter and verse. 'She seems completely in the dark about her husband's history,' I finished.

'That was a nice thing you did, separating her from her harpy of a mother for a spell so she could go to Bundles for Britain.'

'I take it that means you followed her there.'

'Once I heard she'd gone to Paramount, I told the boys tailing her to be on the lookout for Addison's car. I know you, Frost. That Catholic thing again.'

I didn't enjoy being an open book, particularly when the reader was entirely too pleased with his ability to predict plot twists. 'Your turn. What's going on?'

'The New York DA's man is here and he's furious. And we're certain that Arthur Davis is on the run.'

'Because he'd been identified as Heshie Rieger? Or because he killed Earl Lymangood?'

'Why not both? And let's throw in killing Glenn Hoyle while we're at it.'

'I don't see why he'd do that.'

'To keep his past a secret. And to protect Lorna, because he's still carrying a torch for her.'

'Maybe. But don't forget Dr Jerry.'

'We haven't. We try to be thorough, no matter what the New York DA's office thinks of us at the moment. We don't want to tip Whitcomb off that we know about his side venture as a medicine salesman, but right now he's on his best behavior. Sticking close to his wife, being extra solicitous. She doesn't seem happy about him hanging around, I have to say. But our focus is tracking down Arthur, aka Heshie, probably known as something else by now. We find him, we solve several problems at once.'

'I hope you're right.'

'I do, too. Say a prayer for me, would you, Frost? To one of those saints of yours.'

I couldn't help smiling. 'How about St Jude? He's the patron of lost causes.'

Gene sounded like he was smiling, too. 'Got it in one.'

*   *   *

The dress, lightweight cotton with a Brazilian floral print, had quickly become a favorite. But in taking it off, I was locked in a life-or-death battle with the zipper on its back; such skirmishes were a constant in the lives of us bachelor girls. I had manipulated the zipper halfway down when Mrs Quigley sent up an excited cry. Unable to move the blasted fastener at all now, I shrugged on a sweater I didn't need and bounded downstairs.

My landlady flitted about the lobby in agitation, alternating between smoothing her housecoat and touching her hair to reassure herself it remained atop her head. 'Hurry!' she whispered. 'You can't keep your guest waiting!'

'What guest?'

She pressed a hand to her chest. 'Royalty.'

It wasn't the former Wallis Simpson sitting in her kitchen but Lorna Whitcomb, in a black suit with an embroidered collar. Her onyx eyeglasses came to points at the outside of each lens that gleamed like the tips of arrowheads. Instead of looking out of place in such humble environs, she appeared right at home, because she held Miss Sarah Bernhardt in her arms. Never had I seen the feline take to a newcomer so quickly. I gazed into Miss Sarah's eyes – their shape mirroring that of Lorna's spectacles – and understood that she'd done it solely to spite me.

Lorna and Miss Sarah purred contentedly at one another. 'Such a beautiful creature,' Lorna said. 'Regal. Must be why we get along so well.'

'We've been getting along, too!' Mrs Quigley chirped.

'Always a treat to talk to a fellow trouper from back east. We knew a lot of the same steps, and used them to avoid a lot of the same wolves.' Lorna spoke with the offhand absorption of someone who'd had a few drinks – rum, by the scent – and intended to have a few more. 'I'd love to stay and reminisce. I seldom meet people who remember the same headwaiters as me. But I must borrow Lillian for a while.'

'By all means,' Mrs Quigley said, as if I were a piece of jewelry that was hers to loan out.

Lorna blew a kiss at Miss Sarah before setting the cat down. She then stood up in a way that required her to swing her legs out from under the table with a flamboyant kick. The scent of her floral perfume mingled with the rum as she nudged me into the building's lobby. 'We're going to that restaurant,' she told me. 'The one where you saw my husband. I want to meet this partner of his.'

'Are you sure that's a good idea?'

'No. Not remotely. But I'm doing it, and I need you to show me the way.'

'You know where it is. It's around the corner from Club Bali, where Bruz Fletcher sings. I learned about that place from your column.'

'You have to point the man out to me.'

I toyed with the notion of saying no. But then I had visions of Lorna storming the place solo and embarrassing herself. I also smelled her breath again.

'I'll do it on two conditions. First, we take a taxi.'

'What? Fine, we'll pretend we're in New York. What's condition two?'

'You have to zip me up.' I dropped the sweater and presented my back to her.

'Thank God. I thought you were determined to wear that hideous thing.'

If our cab driver recognized his famous fare, he kept the knowledge to himself, chewing on his pungent cigar. I rolled down the window as we rolled toward Sunset Boulevard, airing out the taxi as Lorna aired her grievances.

'You saw that the show closed, of course. It got good notices, which I suppose is something. Although I've long said reviews don't make a damn bit of difference.' She waved a hand before her face. Our driver shifted his stogie to the far side of his mouth. 'It's falling apart. I can feel it. The police and the syndicate are after Heshie. My own syndicate "has concerns", a phrase you never want to hear. No one's returning my phone calls. Tips are drying up. Tomorrow's column is all filler, no meat. "Lorna's impressions of sunny Santa Barbara", God help us, plus material that normally wouldn't rate a second glance. The rest of the week looks worse. Sam's scrambling, trying to hold it together, insisting it's fine, but it's not. What I do is all smoke and mirrors. But the smoke's cleared, and the mirrors are cracked.'

I didn't know what to say in response. So I kept quiet.

'I'm not even sure why I'm fighting to hang on,' she continued. 'But of course you have to.'

'Why? Why do you have to?'

She gazed out the window at the lights coming to life. 'Because that's the way it is. You fight even if you don't like what you have. Even if you don't want it anymore. You can't let them take things from you. And if you walk away from it willingly, you may discover you were wrong. By then, it's too late. You'll never get it back.'

It sounded like a brutal, bitter slog of a life. But I didn't see the point in telling Lorna that. She already knew.

'Did you tell Heshie that Edith and I were helping you?'

Lorna nodded. 'Once I saw Delia's name on that list, I knew Hoyle had found out about Heshie and me. I had to warn him. I also wanted him to know I was trying to get to the bottom of this, so you two might be talking to Delia. He wasn't to let on that he knew.'

'Could he have learned about Hoyle before you told him? Hoyle had buddied up to him, took his bets.'

'Anything's possible, I've come to discover.'

'You also said Heshie had come to your aid the first time Earl Lymangood demanded money from you. Meaning Heshie knew you'd . . . you'd made a movie with him.'

'*For* him. I made it *for* him.' She set her jaw in a manner that would do Joe Louis proud. 'Is that what your boyfriend and his pals think? That Heshie . . . took care of Earl for me?'

It didn't seem the time to split hairs and say Gene wasn't my boyfriend. 'They're leaning that way.'

Lorna settled back against the seat. 'He did know. And he loved me anyway. Enough to stick up for me. Men like that don't come along very often. Naturally, I walked away from him.'

And then it was too late, I finished for her.

After a suitable interval, I said, 'I talked to Dr Jerry on Saturday night. He was home from Santa Barbara then.'

'What of it? You think that old man could have done this? You think he'd defend my honor? That's almost sweet.'

The taxi swung onto Sunset Boulevard, which had ignited its gayest lights for the evening. Lorna's eyeglasses reflected them dully back. 'They used to fear me up this street and down.'

Her words reminded me of the cavalier manner in which I'd written *has-been* in my notes, and I buckled inside.

'What's worse is this town needs me. I was about to do Orson Welles the biggest favor of his still-young career and force his hand. Get him to admit his picture is about Hearst once and for all. Put it out there, now, and dare the old man to attack him. Louella's too blind to see it, Hedda's too calculating. And the public loves an underdog. Would have been a fun scrap, and Orson could have come out on top. But no one will listen to ol' Lorna now.' She leaned toward me but spoke at the same volume. 'So who gets a jingle from our hack when he lets us out? Hedda or Louella? My money's on Hopper.'

In the front seat, the driver stubbed out his cigar.

The whispers began as soon as Lorna entered Arturo's. Craned necks, discreet finger-pointing, and a low but insistent hubbub marked her arrival. To her credit and my astonishment, she didn't care. I followed her like a lady-in-waiting, knowing I'd have no lines in this scene.

Vernon Reynolds was not at the front of the house, and for one wild moment I hoped we'd come on his night off. Then the kitchen door swung open and Reynolds in his tatty tuxedo appeared, only to spot Lorna and retreat at once.

Lorna turned to me and her eyes narrowed. 'You saw him, didn't you?' She went to the stand holding a superfluous reservation book and hammered on it mercilessly.

'Where's Vernon Reynolds?' She summoned a mighty stage cry that rang through the restaurant, raising the hair on the back of my neck and causing cutlery to clatter across the room. 'I'm not leaving this dump until I talk to Vernon Reynolds!'

The maître d' was propelled through the kitchen door, pushed by a heavyset, mustachioed man with a panicked expression. Arturo in the flesh, I presumed.

Reynolds wielded his remaining dignity like a shield before him. 'Ladies, if there's a concern, I'm happy to speak to you outside.'

'Jesus. A *concern*. Everybody has concerns these days. All right, let's go.'

The door closed behind us, and she tore into him. 'Tell me who started this idiotic racket, you or Jerry. And don't you dare act like you have no idea what I'm talking about or I'll dredge up every last rumor about how you killed those stuntmen on *Storm Cloud* and bury you with them.'

Reynolds tugged on his collar, but it didn't seem to help him swallow any better. 'We're both to blame.'

'Not good enough.'

'I mean it. I went to see your husband on a . . . a private medical matter, and we got to talking. I hinted about acquiring some' – he waved his hand in an indefinite gesture I assumed meant 'cocaine' – 'for my own personal use. He obliged.'

'He's obliging. That's his weakness. Then what?'

'I acquired more from him on other visits. Eventually, he asked me if I knew anyone who could sell said substance. I offered my services.'

'And thus was a partnership born. A regular Gallagher and Shean. Jesus. When's the last time you saw the good doctor?'

'Saturday.'

'What time? Be exact.'

'Early, before we opened for dinner. Around three.'

'When I thought he was home sick, poor baby. But then I suppose you had to stock up the pharmacy ahead of the dinner rush.' She paced around Reynolds in ever-tightening circles. 'Here's the latest, Vernon. My husband is out of that business effective immediately. Find yourself a new sawbones. If he calls you, hang up. If you see him on the street, run away. Into traffic, if necessary. If he comes in the restaurant, you have my permission to poison his food. That's all. You may go.'

Reynolds studied her, unwilling or unable to believe he'd gotten off so lightly. 'My apologies for any difficulties, Mrs Whitcomb.' He lowered his head and returned to the restaurant.

Lorna had already started striding toward Sunset Boulevard. I scurried after her. 'Son of a bitch,' she said over her shoulder to me. 'Jerry actually could have killed Earl Lymangood. Will wonders never cease?' She heaved a tiny sigh. 'I'll have to have it out with him, I guess. Tell him I know everything. For once, I do. Normally—'

Lorna's name was uttered like a peal of thunder cast down from the heavens. We both turned to the alarming sight of Joan Crawford striding out of a restaurant on the corner of Sunset Boulevard. We had wandered blithely past its windows like ducks in a shooting gallery, and the actress had taken aim. She had transformed her exit from the eatery into an entrance. People in passing cars couldn't have failed to notice her, dressed as she was in a peach halter gown with a pleated skirt, a colorful Mexican shawl thrown over her broad shoulders.

Lorna paled, but then slapped on a gladiatorial grin. 'Hey there, Billie. How's the chow in that place tonight? I never have any luck in there.'

'I want you to know, Lorna,' Crawford said, each word like an individual ice cube pried out of a tray, 'that I got that little joke in your column the other day. I didn't appreciate it one bit.'

'A harmless bit of fun, Billie. No names mentioned, no blood drawn.'

'Oh, bullshit. You don't have the last word on what's harmless. Spreading falsehoods in print is not harmless. It's my understanding no one in town appreciated it. I've asked around. But then you likely haven't noticed with all your other woes.'

'Oh, I've noticed. Believe me.'

Crawford weaved closer in dodges and feints, her movements as spellbinding as a cobra's. I couldn't shake the sensation that she was enjoying herself. 'Let's speak plainly, *Lora*. One busted chorine to another. That story you foisted off on your readers about me sounds an awful lot like one I've heard about you. Only I wouldn't think of repeating it.'

'Come off it, Billie. I *know* you've repeated it. Just like I know you'd like to haul off and slap me right here.'

Crawford smiled. 'Never, Lorna. Not even in private. This isn't a picture. In life, I prefer to take other steps. I find them more effective. And far more lasting.' The remark still refrigerating the air, she turned to me. Her smile widened but skittishly steered clear of her eyes. 'Lillian, how are you? Do give Addison my regards. That's such a fetching print on you.'

She pivoted on her ankle-strap shoes and went back to her meal. Through the windows we could see Crawford accepting a round of applause from her fellow diners. Lorna stood stock-still and took in the scene, including the withering glances from other patrons who now felt brave enough to show their scorn. She smiled crookedly through it all.

'It's over now for sure,' she said quietly. 'I've broken the only inviolable rule. I'm more scandalous than the people I write about. And for the record, that is a nice print.' She faced the processions of headlights streaming down Sunset. 'How does a busted chorine get a taxi in this town? I need to get back to my car.'

San Bernardino Lamplighter   August 28, 1940

KATHERINE DAMBACH'S
SLIVERS OF THE SILVER SCREEN

Darryl F. Zanuck had his eyes wide open when he plucked beauty Gene Tierney from the Broadway stage. Now the star of *The Male Animal* is making a splash in 20th Century-Fox's new *The Return of Frank James*. The movie's a fun one too, although I'm not fonda Henry Fonda in a mustache . . . Oh, Hollywood life, where you're up one day and down the next. No one can predict these vagaries of fate, nor escape them. What we can do is not kick someone when she's down, even when everyone else does. One of my sister scribes is going through a rough patch these days. She should know there are still people, including me, in her corner . . . Word is RKO starlet Linda Hayes will be making with the ring bearers and orange blossoms once her divorce becomes final. She's the latest to board the most popular ride in the screen colony: the marital merry-go-round.

TWENTY-SIX

A normal day spent applying my nose to the grindstone came as both blessed relief and alien experience. As I confirmed arrangements for Addison's upcoming address to a Long Beach inventors' club, I stayed poised for updates from Gene, or Edith, or *somebody*. But the day's barrage of calls pertained to my other major project: organizing Addison's Labor Day cookout, a relatively intimate affair in that he'd invited only five dozen guests.

The sole intrusion on my routine came late in the day, when Kay telephoned. 'I'm giving you a ring, kiddo, because I hear the mystery woman seen with La Whitcomb when Joan Crawford served up an earful the other night was a tall drink of water. I figure it has to be you. Any chance you can share Crawford's cutting comments? Feel free to tidy them up if necessary.'

'I wasn't there, I'm afraid.' Funny how Kay was the one person I could lie to and not feel bad about it. Scratch that; I felt a *little* bad. 'I have to confess, I was surprised to see you cutting Lorna a break in your last column.'

'Why stick the knife in when I'd have to hunt for a place to put it? She's washed up.'

Count on Kay to be the opposite of magnanimous. 'I still appreciate it. Everyone else is being horrid to her.'

'Another reason to play the different drummer card. Anything to stand out in this racket. Especially now that Lorna's syndicate is searching for her replacement.'

'Is that what you've heard?'

'Me and every other scribe in town. Lorna's through. If I play nice, maybe they'll give me a shot. I've seen enough minor league pitching. Time to bring me up to the majors. I'll sing Lorna's praises if it'll land me her job.'

I had to admire her mercenary instincts. Plenty of people would step over Lorna's body to claim her place, but only Kay Dambach would eulogize her while doing so. Lorna herself would likely salute the stratagem.

'C'mon, kiddo,' Kay wheedled. 'I know you were there. How did Crawford tell Lorna off? Give.'

'I wish I could tell you,' I said, and hung up sweetly.

On Wednesday, Addison set sail for Long Beach, leaving me to finalize the festivities for his upcoming barbecue. He wanted a south-of-the-border theme, and I had secured the services of Western Costume for wardrobe and booked a mariachi band. I walked the grounds with the workers who would transform Addison's estate into a temporary Tijuana and sampled the planned menu of spare ribs and baked beans. I was still in the midst of savoring it when a maid chugged across the lawn to fetch me. An emergency telephone call, she panted.

Gene came straight to the point in his crispest voice. 'We've got him. Arthur Davis. Or Heshie Rieger, whichever you prefer. I don't think he cares.'

'How did it happen?'

'No gunplay required. He turned himself in. Can you beat that? And here's the thing. He insists on talking to, and I quote, "the tall girl and the costume lady." Took all my well-honed detective skills to dope out who he meant.'

I gulped. 'Let me—'

'Edith's already on her way. I called her first. Get over here as soon as you can.'

The interview room was surprisingly spacious, in part because its furniture – a newish wooden table and chairs – seemed one size too small. The smell of freshly applied cleanser hung in the air. I flattered myself into thinking that the room had been spruced up for Edith and me, but even the stinging aroma couldn't cloak the welter of desperate scents beneath it – perspiration, defeat, fear. In a room full of stories with no good endings, despair had become part of the atmosphere. It reminded me of a confessional, not least because I knew I'd feel lighter when I left.

I picked up a trace of my own perfume, which almost came as an affront in these surroundings. In my short-sleeved navy dress with a white belt, I felt like an emissary from a distant land. Edith's gray suit, accentuated by a pink blouse, struck a more appropriately somber note. Gene insisted on accompanying us into the room, no matter what Arthur Davis had requested.

The man in question sat placidly at the small table, his hands in cuffs resting loosely between his knees, as if they were tired. Davis looked at home in the room but out of place in his clothes. He didn't have the face for a blue chambray work shirt and rough trousers. As a background player, Davis could portray a tuxedoed tough or a back-alley brawler, but you'd never buy him as a man simply trying to earn a living.

Edith and I sat opposite Davis while Gene planted himself next to the table, primed to leap into action if Davis even leaned forward. Davis never glanced at him. Upon seeing us, he sat back as far as the unforgiving chair would allow and relaxed. Only then did I notice the puffiness and bruising on Davis's face; at some point recently, he'd taken a blow or two. I glanced at Gene. He kept his eyes on Davis.

'Thanks for coming,' Davis said.

'What shall we call you?' Edith asked.

Davis pushed out a laugh; the question clearly hadn't occurred to him. 'How 'bout Arthur? My Los Angeles name. They'll be calling me Heshie soon enough. Herschel, actually, seeing it's the law. Only the law and my mother ever called me Herschel, and she's long gone now.'

Edith nodded. 'Why did you ask to see us, Arthur?'

'Couple reasons. First, to thank you for helping Lorna. And second, to ask you to look after Delia, if you can. She didn't do nothing wrong. I'm the one got her into this mess, and I regret it like hell. She's gonna need someone to hear her side of things. Christ knows her battleax of a mother won't.' His accent was as broad as the Grand Concourse now, with no reason to hide it anymore.

'We're happy to provide your wife with whatever support she needs,' Edith assured him. 'What can you tell us?'

'Only that Lorna was the one person who didn't turn on me when I left New York. And look at how I pay her back.' He lifted his hands. The cuffs clanked, shocking me with a reminder that he'd been arrested; he seemed so at ease. 'If I'd listened to her, everyone would be better off. Her, Delia, me. Don't try to be in pictures, she said. Don't hitch yourself to that little girl. Keep to yourself, lie in the sun, bank your money, and live your life, she said. Sounds so easy. But I told her no. I could figure a way to have it all. Didn't work. All of it up in smoke, like the bets I placed with Glenn Hoyle.' He waggled his fingers, to pantomime that smoke dissipating in the air. The handcuffs rattled again as he moved. I thought of Marley's ghost and shivered.

Gene ran a hand through his hair. Our agreed-upon signal.

'Did you know a man named Earl Lymangood?' I asked.

'Yeah. In New York.'

'That was through Lorna, wasn't it? And you knew how Lorna had met him.'

Davis's eyes shifted briefly to Gene, then back to me. 'Yeah. She was young then, you have to remember.'

'Did Earl Lymangood know you in Los Angeles?'

'Not as Arthur Davis, he didn't.' He smiled.

'Then he did know you,' I pressed. 'You saw him here.'

For the first time, Davis appeared anxious. 'You got a cigarette? I ran out, and the joker who brought me here only had Chesterfields.'

Gene dropped a brand-new pack of Lucky Strikes onto the table. 'When did you last see Mr Lymangood?' Edith asked.

Davis busied himself with the cigarettes. He'd clearly opened a pack in handcuffs before. 'Better make these last.'

'Who says I'm giving you the whole pack?' Gene spat.

'You gonna let 'em haul me back to New York without any? That's a hell of a send-off.' He lit a cigarette, then defiantly tucked the pack into his shirt pocket. 'Because that's what's next, ain't it? So be it. I'm ready to answer for those crimes. Or at least take questions on them. Because my life out here? Arthur's life?' He made the spectral gesture with his fingers again, amidst the plumes from his cigarette. 'Up in smoke.'

Gene touched the knot on his tie. Another cue to me.

'At least you can tell us about your last meeting with Mr Lymangood. What you took from his office.'

'A guy like that's got nothing I want. No class. No sense.'

'Just money,' Gene said. 'And lots of it.'

Davis removed a fleck of tobacco from his tongue with oddly delicate gestures. 'Not everything worth having can be locked in a safe.'

'Then you know Lymangood had a safe.' Gene's voice and eyes had both gone flat. 'How hard was it to open?'

'I wouldn't know about that. 'Cause if it happened, Arthur did it. And like I said, Arthur ain't around anymore.' He flashed Gene his best checkmate grin. 'Nobody left but poor old Heshie. In fact, that's about all I've got to say. I just wanted you ladies to be good to Delia. She's gonna need a friend.'

'I'm afraid Delia's a little sore at us,' I said.

'That'll pass. She can carry a tune but never a grudge. Heart of gold, that one. Better off without me.'

Edith nodded. 'Is there anything you'd like us to tell Lorna?'

'Yeah. Tell her I did it for her. For us. For old times' sake.' He looked at Gene again. 'That's it. I'm ready to go.'

Gene dexterously plucked the cigarettes from Davis's shirt pocket. 'Sit tight, Heshie. You're not going home just yet.'

We stepped into the bustle of a corridor. I felt a scrim of the room's residue on me that steel wool wouldn't remove.

Gene exhaled. 'Thank you both for doing that.'

'What happened to him?' I asked. 'He looked like he'd been beaten up.'

'It didn't happen here. That's the state we received him in.' Gene's inflection warned me not to pursue the subject. 'We learned enough. He as good as confessed.'

Edith adjusted her eyeglasses. 'To what, Detective?'

'To both murders. Hoyle and Lymangood. He wanted to protect himself and Lorna.'

'I'd hardly say we heard anything conclusive.'

'We didn't need anything conclusive. Fingerprints place him in Lymangood's office. He slipped up when he mentioned the safe. And he said he did it for Lorna. That's enough to get him for Lymangood, and Hoyle follows from that.'

'But what about Dr Jerry?' I asked.

Gene didn't respond. He glanced along the hall toward an office, where a barrel-chested, bullet-headed man in blue serge radiated impatience. I recognized the cross-against-the-lights demeanor of the born-and-bred New Yorker and pegged him as the district attorney's man.

'There's gonna be a squabble over who gets Heshie first if we can charge him with a pair of murders out here,' Gene said. 'I'd better let Byron know. Excuse me a moment.'

He walked toward the DA's man. Edith studied Heshie Rieger through the window. If he hadn't been puffing on a cigarette, I'd have thought he was sleeping.

'I'm sure that man's guilty of something,' Edith said quietly. 'But I'm not sure what.'

'Me neither.' Down the hall, the DA's man threw up his hands in disgust and Gene shut the office door. 'I'm going home to take a shower.'

'What an excellent idea,' Edith said. But she didn't move from her vantage point at the window.

TWENTY-SEVEN

My uncle Danny, a devout Catholic who also placed great stock in omens and portents, believed the Irish possessed a gift for prophecy. This alleged aptitude never helped him at the racetrack or when buying a sweepstakes ticket, but he'd harp on his every vaguely worded premonition ('Something feels off today, pet') that came within hailing distance of accuracy (an ice wagon pile-up three blocks away later that afternoon). 'Never ignore a pricking in your thumbs or a stirring in your blood,' he'd advised me more than once. 'Could be your ancestors communicating with you.'

I'd been antsy from the moment I'd cracked my eyes open – and I hadn't felt like eating breakfast, never a good sign. Even donning a new dress, maize-colored with buttons set in pairs down the front, didn't bolster my spirits. But it wasn't until Freddy Sewell sauntered into my office, hands tucked insouciantly into his trouser pockets, paisley necktie and pocket square providing a peacock note, that I felt the line of all the Frosts throughout the ages whispering, 'You're in for it now.'

Addison fairly skipped in after him, beaming. 'Wonderful news, Lillian! Our little family will be growing!' I eyed my employer's girth and refrained from asking if he was expecting. Jokes did not seem the order of the day.

'After some arm-twisting,' Addison continued, 'Freddy has agreed to come work for me.'

'Splendid,' I said through a transparently artificial smile. 'In what role?'

'An advisor, I suppose you'd say,' Sewell himself supposed. 'And general sounding board.'

Addison nodded, and I knew he'd rubber-stamped whatever Sewell had suggested. 'Freddy's sources say the Academy's museum may be some time coming, so I may start my own project after all. I thought it made sense to have Freddy on hand, perhaps set him up in the small study down the hall.'

Giving him a larger office than mine, I noted, while robbing me of the quiet room where I could take the odd break.

I stretched my synthetic smile to its very limits and congratulated Sewell.

'I can't say how long I'll remain in the post, the situation at home being what it is. Still, one does value a place to hang one's hat in times of strife. And this will allow me to continue to put an informal word in Mr Korda's ear on occasion.'

Addison excused himself. Sewell perched half of his posterior on my desk and gazed around the room, already planning what he'd do with the space once he'd planted his flag and annexed it. 'Addison speaks so highly of your abilities. I look forward to working together.' The words had the feel of a statement composed by committee and delivered under duress. 'Although I expect little overlap between your functions and mine.'

Defiance surged within me. I opted to sugarcoat it. 'Are you sure? Addison runs a democratic household. He tends to let everyone weigh in on every subject. He's more interested in the idea than the source.'

'Is he? A most American approach.' Sewell didn't frown, but he definitely considered it. 'I should think we'll be able to stay out of each other's way and get along harmoniously. And if you'd add me to the guest list for this holiday party on Monday. Sounds like a most curious affair.'

'Be sure to come early,' I told him, 'to have your pick of the best Western duds.'

'Yes,' he said guardedly, then raised his rump from my desk, pointed with approval at a painting on what I foolishly thought of as my wall, and left. I expected the artwork to be relocated to his new office within two weeks. Or a fortnight, whichever came first. The day had gone down the drain so quickly.

I was still grinding my teeth over this turn of events when Edith telephoned. 'You won't be surprised to hear that Delia Carson has been in touch again. She knows we spoke to her husband. Can you come by?'

'After work,' I said around the pencil clenched in my teeth.

'No chance of coming any earlier?'

'None. Those days may be over. I'll explain when I see you.'

*   *   *

Given the relative lateness of the hour, I expected to find Edith toiling over her sketch pad in solitude. Instead, she paced carefully around Barbara Stanwyck, eyeing the actress like an unearthed landmine that could be set off by the slightest jolt.

'Thank God, an audience,' Barbara crowed. 'You're just in time, Flushing. Edith's about to give me a list of my flaws. Pull up a pew.'

I couldn't spy a fault in her figure, currently swathed in an unfussy navy sheath dress, and said as much.

'That's not at all what I'm going to do,' Edith protested. 'You asked me – dared me, essentially, to reveal how I would dress you in Preston's picture. I'll do more than tell you. I'll explain the science behind my decisions.'

'The science,' Barbara cracked. 'Like I'm some top-secret bomber she's developing.'

'On the contrary,' Edith said with a close-lipped smile. 'I'm developing a bombshell, and it's you. If only you would listen. To begin with, you have the best legs in the business, bar none.'

'Better than your pal Lorna's?'

Edith settled her glasses on the bridge of her nose. 'Better than Dietrich's. But I will deny saying that.'

The compliment brought Barbara up short. 'Well,' she finally mustered, 'I *was* a dancer.'

'I would naturally highlight that attribute. At the same time, however, you do have a rather short waist.'

'I was undernourished as a child,' Barbara whispered loudly to me, pulling a forlorn face.

'This, unfortunately, compounds another issue, namely your . . . you possess a rather . . . I wouldn't call it a flaw, exactly . . .'

'Out with it, Jughead.'

'Very well. You have a low-slung derriere.'

Barbara's eyes widened. She strode to the three-panel mirror in the corner of Edith's office and analyzed her asset from every available angle. 'I haven't had any complaints,' she said with reluctance, 'but I see your point. Still, it's what God gave me. Good luck changing it.'

'I'm not going to change it. I'm going to camouflage it.' Edith tapped the sketch pad on her desk. 'I showed you how in the drawing.'

'And I don't get it.'

'Then I'll show you in person. Stay there.' Edith unfurled a roll of muslin. She draped the fabric around Barbara. I helped, mainly by holding a pincushion as Edith deftly fixed the gossamer material in place. In her skilled hands it took on a strange permanence, forming a ghostly garment over Barbara's own, one with a visible silhouette if not much personality.

'This is only an indication of the dress's design, but it will allow me to illustrate my point. What I propose is to give you an asymmetrical waistline. Higher and wider in the front.' Edith knotted a tape measure about Barbara's midsection, but on a diagonal. She gently pressed a fingertip to Barbara's stomach, about two inches above the makeshift belt. 'Imagine that the gown's waistline starts here then tapers downward in the back, like so. The result is something of a *trompe l'oeil* effect, creating the illusion of length in your waist. At the same time—'

'My caboose looks closer to the train,' Barbara marveled.

I stepped away from the mirror to better appreciate Edith's wizardry. The placement of the belt fooled the eye completely, making Barbara's shape more stunning. 'That's amazing,' I gasped.

'How did you do that?' Barbara asked.

'I'm good at what I do. As are you. Once I put you in dresses styled in this manner, you'll be able to pull off the role in Preston's picture.'

'I just might at that.' Barbara ran a hand over her rump, then caught Edith grinning. 'Now let's talk about you, Jughead. How come you never show any teeth on the rare occasions when you smile?'

Edith turned red so quickly I expected her eyeglasses to fog up. 'I'd rather not talk about it.'

'Come on, now,' Barbara coaxed. 'If we can talk about my flat backside, we can discuss Head's head.'

'I always wondered about that myself,' I put in.

'Oh, very well. Some of my front teeth didn't grow in properly.'

'I never noticed,' I said.

'That's because I seldom smile. I did when I was younger, and the other children called me names.' She flashed her ivories at us, a genuine blue-moon occurrence. In that instant, I noticed that two of Edith's upper incisors were indeed rather stubby, which made

her front teeth seem larger by comparison, in turn lending a certain
. . . beaver-like cast to her features.

As quickly as they had appeared, her pearlies vanished, Edith
snapping back to her usual inscrutable form. 'I've been self-
conscious about my teeth ever since.'

A litany of childhood slights came flooding back to me. 'Kids
are the worst.'

'Why not have them fixed?' Barbara asked. 'You can't just
throw a crooked belt around them, but they do have people called
dentists, you know.'

'It's not important.' Edith untied the tape measure around
Barbara's waist. 'I'm not an actress.'

'Don't be ridiculous. Everybody has to smile. What are you
going to do if Barney Groff falls down a flight of stairs? Tell
you what. If Preston puts me in this cockamamie picture, I'll
introduce you to my dentist. Hell, I'll pay to fix your choppers
myself.'

'I suppose I'd better get used to the idea. Preston wants to cast
you. Once he sees you in these clothes, he won't be able to use
anyone else.'

Edith and I removed the muslin, unwrapping Barbara like a
glamorous mummy. 'Going to Del Mar tomorrow?' the actress
asked. 'Bing's invited the whole studio to bid adios to the racing
season. Sounds like fun.'

'I missed the last big event. I may well attend.'

Barbara hugged us both goodbye. On her way out, she stopped
to study Edith's sketch again, then cast a final look at the mirrors,
her shape now without the benefits of Edith's ministrations. 'You
may just be on to something here, Jughead.'

'You're not going to have your teeth fixed,' I said when we
were alone. 'Any more than you're going to the racetrack tomorrow.'

'Don't be so sure.' Edith rolled up the muslin with care. 'I'm
capable of surprises. Now what did you mean on the telephone?'

My tale of woe about the imminent arrival of Freddy Sewell at
Addison's met only with scoffing from Edith. 'Nonsense. If I can
handle Mr Cassini, you can contend with the likes of this Mr
Sewell. Besides, it's imperative that you keep that job.'

'Believe me, I know. A girl's got to eat.'

'Yes, but now there's another reason. If Mr Rice means to build this museum, I need you on the inside to encourage him to preserve costumes.'

We had packed the muslin away when Delia Carson came in, preceded by Rhoda in full wet-hen mode. Momma glared at the two of us. 'After your little stunt last time, helping Delia slip down the back stairs like the mayor caught in a brothel, I'm not letting her out of my sight.'

'Mother, would you *stop*?' Delia stripped off her gloves and pressed them to her forehead. Dramatic gesture aside, she had regained some of her moxie. She wore a stylish white dress with emerald-green polka dots, the colors duplicated by Rhoda's green-and-white striped number. I wondered if the Carsons coordinated outfits and if so, who chose first, Momma or the meal ticket.

Delia stepped forward, planted her feet firmly, and gave her next line some zing. 'I know you two spoke to Arthur, and I want to know what about.'

'He was very sweet,' I said. 'He asked us to be there for you, in case you needed a friend.'

If her spouse's call for compassion moved Delia, her face betrayed no sign. 'You know how I feel about that.'

Edith spoke up. 'We do, and as we've said, we're sorry that we misled you.'

A mocking laugh from Rhoda.

'We understand your husband surrendered to the authorities,' Edith said.

'Yes, because I told him to. He telephoned me to apologize, and I begged him to turn himself in.'

'I'm shocked he listened to reason for once,' Rhoda spat. 'Born to be hanged, that one.'

Frustration – or was that anger? – sparked in Delia's eyes. She turned away from her mother and looked out Edith's window, her gaze on the stragglers departing the studio after a long day, their lunch pails glinting in the sun. 'I didn't want anything to happen to him, that's all.'

This time, Rhoda's laugh was a declaration of triumph. She rummaged in her purse. 'He's been playing a sick game all this time, your so-called husband. I had a friend in New York do some digging. She found a photograph of that Lorna Whitcomb, when she was a two-bit hoofer calling herself Lorelei McKay and going around with that hoodlum. She looked just like my Delia back then. It's perverse. I told Hedda Hopper as much this very morning.'

'Enough with that goddamned photo!' Delia stumbled slightly on the profanity, but there was no mistaking the fire in her voice. As Rhoda reluctantly closed her bag, Delia asked, 'Why do the police think Artie killed this man Lymangood?'

I couldn't bring myself to tell her the motive. Besides, another name interested me more. 'They can prove Arthur was in Lymangood's office. But they're also interested in his connection to a man named Glenn Hoyle.'

Delia frowned. 'Yes, him. I never liked him.'

'You *met* Glenn Hoyle?'

'Once or twice, and only for a few minutes.' Delia wrinkled her nose like a little girl smelling something foul. 'He was talking to Artie. Artie explained later that he sometimes placed bets with Hoyle.'

Rhoda clucked and dove back into her handbag, as if hunting for betting slips to submit as Exhibit A.

'Why didn't you care for Mr Hoyle?' Edith asked.

'Oh, he rubbed me the wrong way, that's all. He was too eager, too ingratiating.'

'I've told you time and again to be on guard against such riff-raff,' Rhoda piped up.

Again, Delia subtly pivoted away from her mother. 'He kept trying to impress me whenever we talked. With magic tricks, if you can imagine. He was also some kind of magician, I gathered from Artie. Not much of one, though. He'd pluck a coin from behind my ear and expect me to clap my hands with delight. I'm not Shirley Temple. I'm a *woman*. A married woman. He went to light my cigarette and did another trick, using that paper that bursts into flame. All it did was startle me.'

'Flash paper,' Edith said thoughtfully.

'I've asked you not to smoke in public, dear,' Rhoda added.

'I asked him, do you carry that stuff – that flash paper – around all the time, and he said in his line of work, it came in handy. What does that say about a person?'

Rhoda had her answer ready. 'It says he's a bum and a crook. No wonder Arthur palled around with him. He probably did bump him off.'

'Mother!' Delia's face flushed, her anger now close to the surface.

Too bad Rhoda ignored the signs. 'The only thing he did right was surrender to the police. That, and tell you to stick close to these ladies. Say what you will, they were trying to protect you. They had your interests at heart, while that louse never did. When I think of the sacrifices I've made to—'

'*No!*'

Delia uttered the single syllable with such ferocity I expected the glass in the window to tremble. All noise outside Edith's office seemed to go silent. The world was now the four of us within these walls, along with Delia's pent-up rage.

'I have had it with you running down the man I love. I don't care who he associates with, or what he did in New York, or even if he loves Lorna Whitcomb more than me. I don't care if he's killed anybody. He treats me like I'm my own person. He always has. When you don't, when the bosses at Lodestar don't, when my goddamned public doesn't. I'm determined to help Artie and you can go straight to hell if you don't like it.'

Rhoda reacted first with shock, then a cold fury. For her finale she opted for crocodile tears, and as her eyes moistened I thought, *Delia really is the actress in this family.* 'Is that how you speak to your mother?' she croaked.

'It is now. I speak for myself from now on, too. I don't want you gassing on to Hedda or Louella on my behalf.' Delia turned to Edith. 'For some reason Artie thinks you're a good influence. So tell me. Who should I talk to?'

I spoke up. 'Katherine Dambach.'

'She's nobody!' Rhoda cried.

'She's on her way up, now that Lorna's in trouble,' I said. 'She's younger than Hedda or Louella, so she'll take your side. She'll hear you out, tell your story. It'll help you and her both. That's how the game is played.'

'Lillian's right,' Edith said.

'Then that's what I'll do. Thank you.' Delia slipped on her gloves. 'Are you coming, Rhoda? Or would you prefer to hail a cab?' She breezed out of the office. Rhoda stared after her, apoplectic. Then she ran out, fearing her offspring really would leave her behind.

* * *

Edith suggested a cocktail at one of the bars abutting Paramount: 'I feel we've earned it.' I wished we'd had a bracer beforehand, because Oleg Cassini lingered outside the Wardrobe building, his usual picture of louche elegance.

'Good evening, ladies! I believe I just saw that lovely actress, Delia Carson. I tried to pay my compliments, but she appeared to be in a lather.' He raised his nose as if he could still detect Delia's scent on the air. 'I understand her husband is in some difficulty.'

To put it mildly, I thought.

'I must say, she's quite striking in person. Hardly the insipid child she plays onscreen. She stormed past me like the kind of woman who could inspire a duel to the death. That is, were the practice not banished because it became too expensive.'

'Expensive?' I fairly choked. 'That's why they stopped having duels?'

'Yes. An *affaire d'honneur* runs into astronomical sums. Your seconds risk arrest, so you must purchase gifts for them, extravagant ones. It's hardly the time to be ungenerous. The attending physician also requires compensation. And if one is fighting with swords, you take the contest seriously and hire an instructor for the night before. This is why only gentlemen engaged in the tradition. They alone could afford it.' He shook his head, lamenting the passing of a better age.

I gaped at him. Had Cassini actually fought a duel?

Before I could ask, he posed a question of his own to Edith. 'Shall I be seeing you at Del Mar tomorrow?'

'But of course, Oleg. I'm looking forward to it. Have a pleasant evening.'

We exited the lot and angled toward Oblath's Café. 'Are you serious?' I asked Edith. 'You're going to skip work?'

'There are times when a casual attitude conveys more than diligence does. Half the studio will be at the racetrack, including Oleg. My attendance will indicate I don't fear him. Besides, nothing will be accomplished here on the Friday before a holiday. You should come, too, as my guest. Unless you're afraid of this Mr Sewell.'

'Nuts to him. I have to work on Labor Day because of the cookout. Plus I learned a system from my uncle Danny for betting on the ponies. Not that it ever did him any good. I'd be delighted to come.'

We stopped at the corner to wait for the light. 'Did we learn anything from Delia?' I asked.

'Only that I don't believe this matter is over.'

'Neither do I.'

Los Angeles Register   *August 30, 1940*

LORNA WHITCOMB'S
EYES ON HOLLYWOOD

June MacCloy won't reveal the particulars but we hear she's recovering from a sprained ankle sustained during a love scene with Groucho Marx on the set of *Go West*. Didn't June replace Marion Martin in the role after Marion came down with pneumonia? Any more of this and starlets will be taking out Groucho insurance . . . A swell time was had by all, especially me, at my first stage performance in Santa Barbara. Many thanks to those readers who came to see the show. You diehards should stay tuned, because we have a big announcement coming in the next few days. Holding my tongue for now, but you won't want to miss it. I plan on keeping a tight rein on the news even at the Del Mar races with Bing Crosby this Friday afternoon . . . Scenario writers around town were livid upon hearing Clara Kimball Young will be ad-libbing her lines in Paramount's *The Round Up*. Although one wag told us: 'I'm not worried about an actress taking my job. One look at my paycheck and she'd run the other way.'

TWENTY-EIGHT

Dressing for a day trip to Del Mar posed a conundrum, given the occasion: the glorious start of a holiday weekend that also marked the end of the racing season, as well as the unofficial close of summer. Underneath lay a melancholy sense that the entire affair with Lorna and the list was, one way or another, nearing its own conclusion. A tall order for clothes to fill. But I was a tall woman, with a wardrobe worthy of the challenge. I chose a white tropic silk short-sleeved dress with green braiding on the collar and cuffs, along with a white hat sporting a brown ribbon and white gloves to complete the ensemble. I made a note to not stand anywhere near the track when horses were thundering past, kicking up clods of dirt, and crept downstairs as quietly as I could.

The sun, as usual the first name on the call sheet, was my only company at this early hour. Light streamed across the lobby floor, making even the most worn patches of carpet inviting, and I resisted the urge to do my Miss Sarah Bernhardt impression and stretch out in it for a doze. Edith had arranged seats on one of the special excursion trains running to Del Mar. With Edith at the wheel, a relatively brief drive to Union Station was infinitely preferable to an expedition clear to San Diego.

Behind me, the telephone rang. I hurried to it so it wouldn't rouse the whole building. Gene was halfway through asking for me when he realized I was already on the horn. 'It's because you're surprised I'm up this early,' I chirped.

He doused my mood at once. 'We have a problem. Hasn't been broadcast yet, but it will be any minute. Davis escaped last night. Heshie. Whichever.'

If the telephone hadn't wakened Mrs Quigley and my neighbors, my yelp of astonishment did the trick. 'How did it happen?'

'Still piecing it together. We've got one brained cop who's not able to talk yet, and another telling the dumbest story I've ever heard. It's looking like Heshie saw an opportunity and seized it. By all accounts, he'd been well-behaved.' He yawned into the telephone, and I joined the chorus. 'We've got people watching his place in case he tries to go home to see his wife.'

Plant Rhoda outside the house, I thought, *and he won't bother visiting Delia.*

'Considering that he asked to see you and Edith,' Gene continued, 'there's a chance he may come looking for you.'

'He'd better hurry. I'm going out of town for the day.'

'Where are you off to?' When I told him, he said, 'Didn't I read Lorna would be there, too? Stick to that plan. It'll save on manpower. Put two bucks on the best-looking nag for me and I'll cover it on payday. Let me know when you get back to town. Stay safe.'

By the time I hung up and returned to the window, Edith was idling outside in her roadster. She wore a linen sport suit in desert sand with brown buttons and trim. I climbed into the car, complimented her hat, and said, 'Have I got an update for you.'

Once again, Edith and I found ourselves riding the rails. A festive atmosphere prevailed even before the train left the station, the raucous crowd including people whose celebrations had commenced the night before. Many a hair-of-the-dog chased an aspirin. The later trains could likely chug their way down the coast powered by their passengers' breath.

The topic of horseflesh dominated conversation, but Edith and I concentrated on racing silks, namely the gaudy attire on display. All at once a familiar voice bellowed my name. Kay Dambach juddered up the aisle, impossible to miss in a cherry-red and navy plaid skirt topped by a red cotton sweater and matching beret; an outfit designed to make a horse buck before it got into the starting gate. Ready Blaylock, Kay's appointed escort to any outing, wore a rich brown western-cut suit. Appropriately enough, the veteran stunt rider looked like the only person onboard with any equine education.

'Fancy meeting you two here.' Kay fell into a seat opposite us, a smug expression on her face. Ready swayed in the aisle. He carried his hat, his fingers twitching against the brim like Bruz Fletcher's on a piano keyboard.

'Bet I know why you're looking so pleased,' I said.

Kay switched effortlessly from self-satisfaction to paranoia. 'What have you heard?'

'Only that you're talking to Delia Carson.'

'Oh. That.' A dismissive wave. 'She did mention you when we talked. We'll be sitting down for Sunday brunch.'

Ready winced as people squeezed past him. He looked jumpy, as if he'd been sunburned all over.

'I thought you meant the other news,' Kay trilled, baiting the trap.

Edith and I swapped a look. Could she be referring to Heshie Rieger being at large again? I wasn't about to bring her up to speed, so I asked the question Kay clearly longed to hear. 'What other news?'

'I'm not supposed to tell.' Apparently saying those words freed Kay from any legal constraints, because she leaned forward in best bean-spilling form. 'I'm taking over Lorna Whitcomb's column. Effective next week. She's out. I'm in. Got the final blessing from the syndicate this morning. Believe me, there's no better wake-me-up to be had.'

I fumbled my thoughts. Edith, as usual, did not, extending her congratulations immediately. 'An inspired choice. You'll be splendid, Miss Dambach. Next week! This came together quickly.'

'You're telling me. I spoke with the people from the syndicate yesterday, and their offer came this morning.'

'That shows great confidence in their selection. Do you know what happened with Lorna? Did she quit, or . . .' Edith trailed off meaningfully.

'I don't know what the story is, and it doesn't matter. The deal's done.'

'Indeed. I expect you triumphed over fierce competition.'

'Rumor is I bested a few names.' Kay preened. 'Sam Simcoe would have been a shoo-in if it weren't, you know, for that murder charge that had been hanging over him.'

'I'm not surprised he finished out of the running,' I said. 'I hope he gets another chance.'

'He will now that they've locked up Delia's husband for killing Glenn Hoyle. And without Lorna around to queer his chances.'

'Has she done that?' Edith asked.

'Sam's been up for other columns before. He was even in the running for mine a few years ago. But Lorna put the kibosh on that. I've heard she scotched other offers that came his way. Couldn't let him go. She needed him but didn't want to admit it. That's why I don't rely on a leg man. They have their place, but they also make you lazy. Speaking of which, I should see who else is aboard this train.'

Ready helped Kay to her feet. She moved into the aisle, then turned back to us. 'One more exclusive. Remember how I told you years ago I wouldn't tie the knot until I'd be covered in the other columns?'

'Yes,' I said, not comprehending. Edith again moved faster than me, leaping up to embrace Ready. He looked stricken as he accepted her best wishes.

As they spoke, Kay pulled me aside. 'It'll be a small ceremony, but of course you're invited. It's next weekend.'

'Next weekend? You're not wasting time.'

'You can't in this racket. Will you be there? I'm counting on you.'

'I wouldn't miss it.'

Edith and I switched partners. As she showered her regards on Kay, I whispered in the bashful bridegroom's ear. 'Are you seriously going to go through with this?'

Ready shrugged meekly. 'Reckon I have to, Lillian.'

'You don't have to do anything.'

'People at the studios where I ride are already looking at me funny, wondering why I ain't hitched. And I've had a few close calls lately. Dodged some questions, but only with Kay's help.' He peered over my shoulder at his soon-to-be spouse, now grilling Edith about wedding dresses. 'She's smarter than me. She knows exactly what she's getting into. Heck, we're gonna live our lives same as we are now. We'll just be under one roof with a piece of paper saying it's all square and legal.'

'But will you be happy?'

'Point's not to be happy. Point's to be yourself. With Kay, I have a chance at that.' He stooped down to speak into my ear. 'Plenty of the fellers I spend time with are married themselves. Least this way, I'll get pointers on what to buy my wife for our anniversary. Unlike most men, I ain't likely to forget.' Glancing again at Kay, he sighed. 'I just wish she'd listen to me when it comes to clothes. I begged her not to wear that get-up. Too much red. Good thing we're seeing horses and not bulls, or we'd be in a heap of trouble.'

Bing Crosby had immortalized the charms of Del Mar in a silly song called 'Where the Turf Meets the Surf'. It became apparent as we arrived that this dopey ditty did the place justice. The cool blue of the Pacific calmed the nerves as Edith and I were swept toward the racetrack's entrance by the steady stream of revelers, who brought an undercurrent of intensity to the otherwise idyllic setting. Summer would be all but over come Tuesday morning and, by God, they would enjoy themselves before then or die trying.

Pushing through the turnstile, we were received by none other than the old groaner Crosby himself, glad-handing all comers in his role as president of the Del Mar Turf Club. Natty in a white double-breasted jacket, he waved us over with his straw boater.

'Delighted to see you both for our blaze-of-glory send-off to this year's meeting,' he said.

'We wouldn't have missed it,' Edith said. 'The entire Paramount family will be down for the day.'

'Only appropriate, considering recent history. I invited Brother Hope and his lovely wife here two years ago. We had a bit of a *musicale* at the end of the night – I expect another may break out this evening – and Bob and I decided to rib each other for the faithful. Various studio pooh-bahs caught our joshing and got it in their beans to put us in a picture. Blew the dust off a script written on papyrus so ancient it was originally intended for my old pals Jack Oakie and Fred MacMurray. I still have no idea which of 'em I'm meant to be.'

'Then we owe *Road to Singapore* to this racetrack?' I asked.

'And the many films that should follow,' Edith said.

'I call that poetic justice, having this establishment better known for my pictures than photo finishes.'

Edith chuckled. 'I believe you promised some advice on wagering.'

'Don't get too attached to your money, and if you see Hope don't listen to him. Stick around for the fun and games after the races. Who knows? Maybe I'll get another picture out of the deal.' He waved at someone in the clamor behind us. 'Forgive me, ladies. Must greet the other paying customers.'

We ambled into the Spanish Mission-style grandstand. All of Los Angeles had apparently decamped the two hours southward. Barbara Stanwyck and Robert Taylor had claimed choice seats. Mickey Rooney, not looking at all boyish, rumbled toward the betting windows like a man possessed. I caught a glimpse of Pat O'Brien, the Turf Club's vice president, in the flesh, and blessed myself as if I'd just seen the Pope. Wait until I told Father Nugent.

'Are you going to bet?' I asked Edith.

'We did come all this way. And Bill gave me a few tips.'

'Don't be stingy with them. I need all the help I can get.'

We moved further up, out of the crush of spectators. Two men and a woman clustered by themselves at an elevation where the crowd and the air thinned, the last of the group in an eye-catching dress with a white chevron print on wine.

Edith squinted. 'I believe that's Lorna.'

'With those eyeglasses, you can tell better than me. Do you think she's heard about Heshie?'

'If she hasn't, I suppose we should tell her.'

As we struck off toward them, the third and shortest member of their party broke in our direction. Sam Simcoe, looking snappy in a summer suit topped with a straw hat.

'Thank God you're here,' he fairly gasped. 'Somebody has to say hello to Lorna. She's being shunned left and right.'

'Because she's leaving her column?' I asked.

'You *know*?' Simcoe plucked his pocket square and smeared his brow. 'That's perfect. The last thing Lorna needs today is to be scooped. Half the town giving her the silent treatment and now word's out she's sunk.'

'Not widely,' Edith amended. 'Why is she leaving?'

'I'll let her tell you. For the love of God, act like you haven't heard anything. She's already a terror this morning.'

'We will, as always, be the soul of discretion.' Edith waved at Lorna, who raised a weary hand in response. 'Not to jump into her grave, but do you know who'll be taking over her column? I trust your straw hat is in the ring.'

'Thank you for saying that.' Simcoe beamed, genuinely pleased. 'I'm holding out exactly zero hope. It's too soon. But mark my words, "Simcoe Sez" is coming. A whole new stink on the entertainment column. In which Edith Head will be quoted liberally.'

Even Simcoe's sensitive feelers hadn't picked up that Kay had pipped him at the post. Interesting.

He glanced back at Lorna and Dr Jerry. The couple seemed small, the distance alone not to blame. 'This isn't how her last hurrah is supposed to go, dammit. It's a hell of a thing. A hell of a day.' He stuffed his hands in his pocket and strode off toward greener pastures.

Edith indulged in some minimal primping. 'Shall we pay our respects to the soon-to-be deposed queen?'

'Son of a bitch, you already know, don't you?' Lorna roared the instant we were within earshot. 'I can tell by those hangdog mugs of yours, the grim set of your shoulders. Neither one of you can act a lick. At least you don't pretend to.'

Dr Jerry, his garish houndstooth jacket barking for attention, patted her arm. She swatted his affections away. 'Thought I'd have one final day on top, and now that's taken from me.'

'At least you look lovely,' Edith said.

'Fat lot of good that does if nobody comes over to tell me. As you can see from this crowd of well-wishers, I'm already persona non grata.' She turned to her husband. 'You might as well place our bets for the day. Two-dollar window only. You have my list?'

'Yes, dear.' Dr Jerry tipped his topper and toddled off down the stairs. Lorna watched him go, shaking her head ruefully.

'I guarantee he'll bet on the wrong horses. But with his luck, we'll probably finish in the money.'

'I imagine this is the big announcement you teased in your column,' I said.

'Yes. One last breaking bulletin from Lorna Whitcomb, announcing my premature retirement. Provided Hedda doesn't leap on it first, the witch.'

'Why are you stepping down?' I asked.

'Because the rumor mill is madly churning, and for once everything it's spitting out happens to be true.' She smirked. 'Word's out about me and Heshie, and how we both tie into Earl Lymangood. That's a tough hurdle to clear. I want to stay and fight, show this town what for. I didn't hurt anyone. All I did was help a friend, return a kindness from the days when I was struggling. Point me toward someone in Hollywood who can't relate to that! But I have to think about Jerry. I don't want his blunder coming to light. And there's his health.

This is too much for his heart. That, and we're damn near broke. Hence all today's two-dollar action. The time has come for us to push off to Palm Springs, where Jerry can open a new practice. I still hate the idea. I wanted to leave on my own terms.'

I couldn't resist. 'What would those be?'

'Dropping dead at my desk after filling a column. One with three genuine stories and two good jokes. Never say goodbye if you can help it. Just stop, let 'em remember you that way. Instead, now I get to wither away in the desert.'

'I grew up in the desert,' Edith said. 'All manner of beauty can grow there, if you know where to look for it.'

'Save the pep talk for the ingenues, Edith. My number's up.'

Edith shrugged. 'It was worth a try.'

'I hear your friend, the Dambach girl, was crowned my replacement,' Lorna said to me.

'So did I. Sam didn't know, though.'

'I haven't had the heart to break it to him. He'll get his chance. God knows he's earned it. Still, I'm glad they gave my slot to someone young. New blood's always a good idea. And another woman, too. Men tend to treat the whole world like a sporting event. Winners and losers. If you ask me, they're too mean-spirited for this work.'

'Even Mr Simcoe?' Edith asked.

Lorna's brow furrowed. 'Never gave it much thought. But I'd say he's the exception. Has a nose for nuance. Why?'

'Mere curiosity. Now we'll reverse roles. Lillian and I can provide you with news. Regarding Mr Rieger.'

But before Edith could proceed, Dr Jerry appeared, waddling up the stairs. Lorna peered at him. 'More bad body language. Now what?'

'Awful crowded by those betting windows,' he puffed when he reached us. 'Thought it made sense to wait. You haven't even looked at the horses yet.'

'I don't need to look at them. But I suppose a trip to the paddock wouldn't hurt.'

As she and Edith started down, Dr Jerry beckoned me closer. 'Did she feed you that line about my heart? Take it from me. My ticker's fine. It's Lorna's that broken.'

'Then why are you going to Palm Springs?'

'For her sake. She knows she can't have a column. And it's partly my fault. Taking her away is the only thing I can do.' He gazed lovingly at his wife, deep in conversation with Edith. 'If she has to be around all those picture people and not be part of that world, it'll kill her.'

The path to the paddock seemed to be paved with upturned noses and cold shoulders. Everyone gave Lorna the brush. She grinned imperiously and took her sweet time moving through the throng, letting each awkward moment expand. 'I may have to take you two prisoner for the rest of the day if no one's going to talk to me. I've heard all of Jerry's stories. Even Bing found cause to slip away when I arrived. The stories about that man I've kept secret.' She waggled her fingers at a well-kept woman who started in fright and ran away.

No horses perambulated in the circular paddock, but they smelled close at hand. Lorna leaned against the railing. 'What in God's name does Heshie think he's doing? Turning himself in was the right decision.'

'I have a theory,' Edith said.

I wanted to turn her way, but a figure emerging from a shed next to the paddock distracted me. He wore a coat too heavy and dark for the weather. A coat for a New York winter.

Heshie Rieger's expression also came out of that time and place. He walked toward us, with one hand thrust in his pocket.

TWENTY-NINE

He may have looked like a man on the run – hair in disarray, eyes sunk deep into his face with exhaustion, clothes rumpled as if he'd slept in them – but Heshie didn't move like one. He walked with confidence through the sunlight, refusing to hide in the shadows. Striding directly toward Lorna, he kept his hand clenched on the object concealed in his pocket.

Dr Jerry stepped in front of his wife, an act of gallantry I honestly didn't think he had in him. Lorna gazed into Heshie's eyes and gently nudged her husband aside.

'Lora Lee,' Heshie said, his voice a croak.

'Herschel.'

He nodded at the rest of us, then swung his focus back to Lorna. 'Told you I never missed a column.'

'You look spent. Why'd you run?'

'Stupid, I know. But I hadn't thought this through.' He ran his other hand through his hair in a misbegotten attempt to neaten it. 'I needed to see you first. I shoulda seen you first. That shoulda been my plan all along. But I never been too good at plans.' The hand in his coat pocket twitched. I decided to scream if Lorna did, but she simply stared at Heshie, waiting for him to act.

The air smelled of horses and the sea.

Heshie pulled his hand out of the coat. It bore a canister of film, so small it couldn't contain even a single reel. But it rattled as he held it out to Lorna; something was definitely inside.

She accepted the offering. 'Is this what I think it is?'

'The *Moonlight Night* picture, whatever it's called. Not all of it. Just the bit you're in. Lymangood had it in his safe. Shoulda come to you with it before I gave myself up. But I talked to Delia and she got into my head and I-I didn't think it through.' He slid his hand easily back into his pocket. He could have been waiting for a subway home. 'I couldn't let them pack me off to New York without giving it to you.'

'Heshie, you didn't have to do this. You didn't have to do any of it.'

'But I did.' He nodded at the film canister. 'Now your troubles are over, right?'

A wild laugh welled up in me at that sentiment, but I held it at bay. Lorna didn't crack, either. 'Sure they are,' she said.

'I didn't want to kill him. Lymangood.' Fatigue seeped in Heshie's voice now that he'd delivered his prize. 'I told him I only wanted the film. But some guys can't help themselves. He tried to get tough. And when that happens . . .' He shrugged, a man brought low by his own nature.

Lorna almost smiled. 'Delia didn't civilize you completely, then.'

'She tried her damnedest, though. She's tough. And she's got the goods. A real actress. You oughta feature her in the column more.'

I almost missed it: Lorna brushing away a tear. 'You know, I think I will.'

I spotted movement from every direction at once, policeman and detectives fanning out to surround the five of us. We had even drawn a crowd of onlookers, mostly racetrack employees and a few horses. Heshie had to be aware of the commotion, but he didn't care. He eyed the film canister in Lorna's hand. She took the hint and spirited the canister away into her purse.

Heshie then looked at Dr Jerry, the force of his gaze driving the doc back a step. 'You take care of her,' Heshie told him. Dr Jerry replied, 'I will', so softly I feared I alone heard him.

But Heshie nodded. Then raised both hands. 'All right, you got me,' he yelled. 'You bums make a hell of a lot of noise sneaking up on a guy. You wouldn't last ten minutes in Brooklyn.'

Heshie was docile as the flood of policemen converged on him, accepting the handcuffs slapped onto his wrists without complaint. To my surprise, Gene and Hansen bulled their way to the front of the pack.

'What are you doing here?' I asked Gene.

'We got multiple reports spotting Rieger south of Los Angeles. And as the gang's all here . . .' He turned to Heshie. 'One of our boys has a whale of a headache, thanks to you.'

Heshie didn't bat an eye. 'Had to be done.'

As Gene seized his elbow, Edith stepped forward. 'One moment, please, Detective. If I might ask a question or two?'

After deliberating, Gene said, 'Two.'

'Mr Rieger. Do you admit to killing Earl Lymangood?'

'Yeah. But like I said, I didn't plan to do it.'

'Did you kill Glenn Hoyle?'

Heshie looked as though his honor had been insulted. 'Why would I? I liked the kid.'

'That's two,' Gene said, tugging Heshie's arm.

'But I haven't asked the most important question!' Edith protested.

'Then you should've led with it.' But Gene had stopped pulling his prisoner away.

Seizing the moment, Edith spoke faster. 'When you told us the bets you placed with Mr Hoyle went up in smoke, you meant that literally, didn't you?'

Heshie blinked at her, perplexed.

'Did Mr Hoyle write down the bets he took on flash paper? Special paper that he made himself? For magic acts?'

The clouds parted. Heshie nodded. 'Yeah. Yeah. It was a gimmick he dreamed up. He explained it to me. If he got pinched, he could lose the evidence in a hurry. Right in front of the cops, if he had to. He'd ask if he could have a cigarette and then . . .' He waggled his fingers in midair again, as he had done in the interrogation room. Edith made the gesture along with him.

'Thank you, Mr Rieger.' She turned to Gene, satisfied.

'*That's* the most important question?' he asked, and with a weary shake of his head began to haul Heshie away.

'You might want to wait a moment, Detective.'

'Why?'

'You can apprehend Mr Hoyle's murderer as well.'

Gene spun toward her, poised to pepper her with queries or at the very least subject her to intense scrutiny. Then, just as quickly, he surrendered. He pointed his chin at Hansen, who tugged Heshie toward a now-open gate behind them. Heshie walked backward, his eyes on Lorna's as he was led away.

'Very well, Edith,' Gene said. 'Let's have it.'

But Edith said nothing at first. She looked sadly at Lorna and Dr Jerry Whitcomb instead.

Gene and his local law-enforcement colleagues commandeered a gatehouse near the paddock. The sun had been beating down on its roof all morning; the place was gaspingly hot before we crowded into it. It felt like the group of us was being subjected to the third degree. Lorna forced Dr Jerry to take the only seat. He shucked his jacket and fanned himself with his program. His protestations about the state of his heart had, perhaps, been exaggerated.

'Isn't there anyplace else we can go?' I whispered to Gene.

'We're trying to maintain a low profile here, Frost. We can't exactly arrange this through a travel agent.'

A San Diego County sheriff's deputy returned with water for the now-pale Dr Jerry, while two more bookended a bewildered Sam Simcoe. The leg man stepped into the gatehouse, forcing Gene into the doorway.

'Why did I warrant the police escort?' Simcoe asked. 'Put a fright into Bing Crosby, I can tell you that. I'd managed to button-hole him to chat about his racing stable.'

'Are you seeking material for your next column?' Edith asked, a touch too brightly.

Simcoe stared with concern at Lorna, hunkered alongside her husband, while he answered. 'I'm thinking about a feature combining the sporting life and show business. Have to figure out how to get the dames to read it, though. Do we need a doc for the doc? And who's this?' He pointed at Gene.

Gene presented his detective's shield and brought Simcoe up to speed. Then, with an element of reluctance, he nodded at Edith, yielding the cramped floor to her.

'Forgive me, Mr Simcoe,' she began. 'I wanted you here to provide confirmation of a fact or two. But first, a question. Do you read Conan Doyle?'

'Who's he write for?'

She tolerated his joke. 'One of his Sherlock Holmes stories famously features a dog that doesn't bark.'

'"Silver Blaze",' Dr Jerry said. 'I remember that one. About a racehorse, I think.'

'Yes, a striking coincidence,' Edith said. 'I'm reminded of it because our story features paper that didn't burn.'

'You've lost me,' Simcoe said.

'No, Mr Simcoe, I don't believe I have. You set this entire adventure in motion by finding that list in Mr Hoyle's residence. I've thought about that list, how fortuitous it was that you discovered it. You mentioned that Mr Hoyle made a practice of recording the bets he took on paper different than the kind he used for tracking his tips for you.'

'Sure. What of it?'

'Lillian and I belatedly learned the logic behind that choice, something I believe you don't know. Mr Hoyle had cause to be concerned about incriminating papers being found upon his person. Consequently, he engaged in elaborate precautions so that they could be destroyed at a moment's notice. Mr Hoyle, you see, regularly made flash paper for magicians. Sheets of tissue treated with acid so that they burst into flame, leaving no smoke, no ash – and no trace. An effective piece of stagecraft, and crowd-pleasing as well. Mr Hoyle ingeniously employed it in another of his side-lines, recording bets on them that could be instantly incinerated in the event of his arrest.'

'Much as I hate to say it,' Gene threw in from the doorway, 'it's a savvy idea. It better not catch on.'

'OK, so Glenn was smart,' Simcoe said. 'I told you he was. If you're saying something more, I don't get it.'

'I'm suggesting that anyone who regularly took such steps would have found a better way to dispose of that list than dropping it into the wastebasket in front of his killer. Mr Hoyle, we now know, was a thorough young man.'

'He'd have eaten that list before throwing it out,' I said.

'One hopes he wouldn't have gone to those lengths.' Edith's eyes flicked to Gene in the doorway then the sheriff's deputies outside the gatehouse. 'We've been operating under the idea that Mr Hoyle did not want his killer to see what was written on that paper. Whereas we should have considered the notion that his killer *needed* everyone to see those names. Isn't that correct, Mr Simcoe?'

Dr Jerry lurched forward, color returning to his face. 'Wait. Are you saying – you mean Sam really *did* do this?'

'We spoke of coincidences a moment ago, Doctor. The truth is, I've been suspicious about that list from the outset. I said it was fortuitous that you found it, Mr Simcoe. One might even say that, in and of itself, was a remarkable coincidence. I became more suspicious when we saw you signing cards for Lorna, purportedly from her various famous admirers, and you said that you'd signed many of the photographs in her office. At that moment, I realized that you could have forged Mr Hoyle's handwriting and composed that list yourself. You'd have time to practice, after all, while you waited in his residence alongside his body in order to create the illusion you'd found him hours later.'

Lorna pushed herself upright and flung an accusatory finger at Simcoe. 'Wait a minute. Which photos in my office did you sign yourself?'

But Simcoe only had eyes for Edith. 'This is preposterous. If you had these suspicions, why didn't you say anything? Why did you help Lorna? And why the hell would I kill Glenn?'

'If you'll permit me, I'll answer your first question last. Lillian and I helped Lorna because Lorna gave us no choice in the matter. Although now I'm pleased to have participated in some small way. As for why you killed Mr Hoyle, I have only a guess, but it's a sound one. In the course of doing your job, you stumbled onto the connections between Lorna and the three names on that list. You set out to investigate those links further. You embroiled Mr Hoyle in your effort – without his complete knowledge – because you used Lorna's own preferred approach against her.'

'A proxy,' I breathed.

Relentless, Edith pressed on. 'Mr Hoyle looked into those three names while you pulled the strings, kept your distance. Only Mr Hoyle got wise to you. He figured out that each of those individuals tied into Lorna – and that you planned on using this information against her. He set out to beat you at your own game, even approaching Lorna about the possibility of a job. But Mr Hoyle erred. Perhaps his brashness tripped him up. In any event, he showed his hand, and you killed him. How to protest your innocence while ensuring all your work hadn't been for naught? You proved yourself as cautious – and as devious – as your protégé. You forged the note. It guaranteed that if you were suspected of Mr Hoyle's murder, even apprehended for it, Lorna's past would nevertheless come to light. Further, you had the "brainwave," as you put it, of recruiting two more proxies to your campaign in Lillian and myself. Confident that every action Lorna undertook on your behalf would ultimately hasten her public ruin.'

Lorna waved her hands in the air, trying to dispel the accusations. 'No. No! Is this true, Sam? You wouldn't do this.'

Simcoe continued to stare at Edith, the corners of his mouth twitching as if fighting off a grin. 'You haven't answered my first question. Why didn't you say anything if you suspected me?'

'At first, I didn't. I merely viewed your discovery of the list of three damning names as . . . convenient. I thought you were Lorna's devoted leg man, which is what you wanted the world to think. Only when you let slip about your unique penmanship skills did it occur to me that you could have drafted that list yourself. At the time, I had no idea that Mr Hoyle would never have disposed of a critical document in such a fashion. But what truly stymied me was that, for the life of me, I couldn't fathom what possible motive you could have. Why destroy the person who meant so much to you?'

'And now you know.' Dropping any pretense, Simcoe smiled openly. 'All those people out there kowtowing to that hack Katherine Dambach told you. She has the job I should have had. A job I'd have landed years ago if Lorna hadn't sabotaged my every chance to break away on my own.'

'Sam, no!' Lorna pressed her palm to her chest and, even amidst the frenzy of the moment, it struck me as a calculated, melodramatic movement.

'Don't deny it,' he said. 'I'm a good enough reporter to know how many times you did it, too. Because I was *meant* for this work. I knew I had my teeth in a story when you asked me to balance your accounts – not part of my job, by the way – and I noticed those big withdrawals. Didn't take much to put together you were paying off Earl Lymangood. That's how it started. I knew I had a better story when I spied your nitwit husband consorting with lowlifes on the Sunset Strip. But I didn't have the trifecta until I found you with Delia Carson's husband. Now *that* one took a while to unravel. But once I did, I knew I had enough to bring you down. Maybe I wouldn't inherit your column, but some outfit would take a flier on me. I needed Hoyle to help me keep tabs on everyone. I thought I had him in the dark. Hell, I even planned on making him *my* leg man, the way he'd proven himself on this caper.' He chuckled bitterly. 'There's a lesson for both of us. Never trust the people you're bringing up behind you.'

'Sam, for the love of God, stop talking!' Lorna pleaded. 'You don't know what you're saying. I'll get you a lawyer, I'll say that you're—'

Simcoe spoke coldly over her. 'One, you can't afford a lawyer. Certainly not one good enough to defend me. Remember, I've seen your accounts. Two, I'll happily confess. I *want* to confess.' He turned to Gene, a manic glimmer in his eyes. 'I confess.' Spinning back to Lorna, he said, 'I'll admit what I did and tell everyone why I did it, because it means dragging your name through the mud. It's what I set out to do. I assumed it would be in my own column.'

Simcoe Sez, I thought.

'But if I can't write the story, then I'll be the story for once. Who knows? Maybe I'll like that better. And at least then I can get some rest. The hours in this job have done me in.' To Gene, he said, 'Go ahead and cuff me.'

'I don't think you need the publicity just yet. We'll walk out of here, quickly and quietly.' He signaled the deputies. They closed ranks around Simcoe as he stepped out of the hut and led him away. The leg man went without a look back.

Gene asked me to call when I got home, nodded his silent thanks at Edith, and joined the parade leaving the track.

Lorna buried her face in her husband's shoulder and sobbed. Dr Jerry held her, saying nothing. Finally Lorna, her voice muffled, said, 'We need to go now.'

'Of course, sweetheart. We don't have to stay for the races.'

'No, I mean to Palm Springs.' She looked up at Dr Jerry, her eyes and cheeks shining. 'Let's go now. Get someone else to pack up the house and leave straight from here.'

'If that's what you want.'

'It is. Forget Los Angeles and start anew.' She pulled the film canister that Heshie had given her out of her bag. 'We have a projector at the place out there, don't we? I'd like to take a look at this before I burn it. Remind myself what I looked like when I was young and gorgeous and had my golden future ahead of me.'

Dr Jerry caressed Lorna's face, clumsily but sincerely. 'You're still a knockout. And you've got plenty of time yet.' He tapped the film can. 'Can I watch it, too?'

'Why, Doctor.' She smiled at him. 'Yes. If you're a good boy.'

They left, arm in arm, making their way toward the vast parking lot. Edith and I meandered slowly toward the grandstand. Activity at the paddock had picked up as the first race drew near, horses trotting past, their jockeys adorned with vivid flashes of color. Edith tutted at some of the combinations.

In the grandstand's luxury seats, Bing Crosby chatted with Barbara

Stanwyck. One row back, Bob Hope jawed amiably with a flash of
red that I recognized as Kay, Ready standing diffidently by her side.
Other familiar faces, Mickey Rooney among them, lingered nearby
as she held court, waiting for their chance to speak with her. Word
had gotten out that the order had shifted, that Katherine Dambach
was a force to be reckoned with, and Hollywood assembled to pay
obeisance.

'What do we do now?' I asked Edith.

'I don't know about you,' she said firmly, 'but I came here to
win some money.'

Los Angeles Register   September 6, 1940

KATHERINE DAMBACH'S
SLIVERS OF THE SILVER SCREEN

Forgive the mess as I set up housekeeping here in my lovely
new home. I'm especially pleased that this humble column
will now appear in the pages of my favorite hometown
paper, the *Los Angeles Register* . . . Speaking of new begin-
nings, I'll be attending a wedding over the weekend. The
groom is Western stunt rider extraordinaire Hank 'Ready'
Blaylock, as handsome a man as ever waited for his sweetheart to walk down the aisle. The bride will wear a gown
designed by Irene and her heart will overflow with happi-
ness. How do I know? Because yours truly is the lucky girl
. . . By now we've all heard about Arthur Davis, a.k.a.
Heshie Rieger, the movie extra whose prior credits came
courtesy of Murder, Inc. Davis was arrested last week for
killing producer Earl Lymangood. His motive: the dead man
'said some things I didn't care for about the woman I love.'
Coming up in this column, a three-part interview with that
wronged woman, singing ingenue Delia Carson, now on her
way to becoming a huge star – and a grownup one at that
. . . Producer Walter Wanger's new picture *Foreign
Correspondent* is being touted as the first anti-Hitler movie.
To some of us it plays more like a recruiting film, aiming

to push America into a European war. The director Alfred Hitchcock has talent, but more films like this and his career in Hollywood will be short-lived.

THIRTY

Vernon Reynolds had definitely lost some of his verve. As he patrolled the dining room at Arturo's Ristorante, he looked quite haggard without his supply of pick-me-ups from Dr Jerry Whitcomb, now ensconced in Palm Springs. Reynolds had straightened up noticeably as our party had entered; in part, I assumed, to burnish his reputation with Addison, but also because I'd witnessed his dressing-down from Lorna. He retained that perfect posture as he presented the traditional offering of the house specialty sardines to accompany our quartet of salads.

'Is everything to your liking, Mr Rice?' he murmured.

'Yes, yes, fine,' Addison said. Reynolds surveyed the other diners, searching for signs of distress, then bustled off.

'I can't believe he doesn't recognize me.' Bill Ihnen sounded genuinely hurt. 'We did a picture together.'

'To be fair,' Edith said, 'you aren't very memorable. Neither was the picture, as I recall.' Her eyeglasses reflected the flicker of the candles in the center of the table, so I couldn't read her expression. But I heard the mirth in her voice. For a split second, I even glimpsed her two prominent front teeth, Bill being one of the few people in whose company Edith would, on certain rare occasions, smile.

She patted him on the arm. 'I'll introduce you when I talk to him. That's why we're here, after all.'

'It's certainly not for the food.' Bill eyed his salad skeptically. 'To think there's a wonderful little Mexican place down the street. No one knows about it. We'd have it to ourselves.'

I nudged the sardines closer to him. 'You'll want to dig into these, then. I can recommend them unreservedly.'

The evening out had been at Edith's suggestion. She had never

visited Arturo's, and she and Bill both wanted to clap eyes on –
and ideally talk to – Vernon Reynolds, a living link to Hollywood's
past. As we pored over the menus, Addison held forth on his
proposed museum dedicated to motion pictures.

'I'm flummoxed that one doesn't already exist,' he said. 'It's a
natural with all the tourists who come here to see their favorite
stars. It's a guaranteed moneymaker.'

'Any progress with the Academy?' Bill asked.

'Still jousting. I'm afraid Freddy Sewell, my right hand on this
project, was right. Too many egos involved. Everyone wants a
museum, all right, but they're squabbling over particulars. It's
maddening.'

'That's because you're used to getting your own way,' I teased.

'True.' Addison reeled in a sardine of his own. 'But I'm an
optimist. They'll break ground on a museum by next year at the
latest. They'd be crazy to wait any longer.'

'How is Mr Sewell working out?' Edith inquired.

'My best hire since Lillian. He's putting his journalism skills
to work on a series of what he calls "oral histories." Talking to
people about the dawn of the picture business. Starting with Mr
Reynolds, other warhorses like him.'

'Warhorses?' Bill lowered his cutlery. 'Am I one of those? I
did work with him.'

'Of course you are,' Edith said. 'So am I. But some of us
warhorses are still in the race.'

As Bill and Addison chatted, Edith leaned closer to me. 'And
how are you faring with Mr Sewell?'

'He's insufferable. I can hear him on the telephone constantly,
he monopolizes Addison's time, and he was a smash at the Labor
Day cookout because he wouldn't stop saying "Howdy, ma'am"
and "rootin' tootin'" in that accent of his.'

'You'll get used to him, I have no doubt.'

'I'll say this for Freddy, he was right about the tea. He makes
his own with leaves he brought over from England, and it's
ambrosia. So much better than any I've ever had. The only problem
is I have to talk to him if I want any.'

'A small price to pay for quality. Have you heard from Detective
Morrow?'

'One or two brief updates. You already know how he is, seeing he's been all over the newspapers. He solved Glenn Hoyle's murder and tracked down the notorious Heshie Rieger.'

'All practically singlehanded,' Edith noted.

'That's the papers for you. Captain Frady's just busting at how his protégé has performed. The sky's the limit for Gene.'

'Good for him.' Edith extracted something from her salad and placed it at the edge of her plate with a coroner's care. 'Did I mention I received a lovely postcard from Lorna the other day?'

'Really? I didn't get one.' The oversight didn't surprise me. Lorna Whitcomb had lived her entire life on the basis of billing order. Retirement in the desert would do nothing to break that habit.

Reynolds returned to oversee our dinner orders. He complimented Edith's choice of risotto à la Milanaise ('the kitchen has wonderful truffles this week') while advising it would take twenty-five minutes to prepare. I asked for tagliarini with mushroom sauce so that Edith wouldn't be alone in waiting for her entrée. Bill had been sufficiently impressed with the sardines to request the brook trout, prompting Addison to do likewise. 'Maude will be proud of my restraint,' he said.

Edith then introduced herself to Reynolds, who confessed that he had known both her and Bill on sight. 'A delicate business, reminding people of past acquaintances,' Reynolds said, 'so I seldom do it.' After a brief exchange about mutual friends, Reynolds left with more steam in his stride.

'You two have known each other for some time,' Addison said to Bill and Edith.

'Nearly eight years now,' Bill replied.

'Though it seems longer.' Again, Edith flashed her teeth. Twice in one night. A new record.

'We met on *Cradle Song*.' Bill's eyes gleamed, and the candle-light wasn't to blame. 'Bonded over our love of all things Mexican.'

'Like that dinner we're not having,' Edith put in.

'We've been through epic productions, petty feuds, and one bad marriage.'

'Not to mention a host of girlfriends,' Edith shot back. Bill raised his wineglass to her.

'You two should get married,' I said, letting my own *vino* voice the *veritas*. Addison clanged his glass in agreement.

'Lillian, that is a marvelous suggestion.' Bill pivoted on his seat to face Edith squarely. 'What do you say, Edo?'

'What do I say to what?'

'To the notion of us getting married after eight years.'

Edith's hand flew to the silver pendant in the shape of a seashell that dangled around her neck. 'I say I know when I'm being had.'

'And you're not now.' He gazed at her with a radiant warmth. 'I mean it, Edith. Let's get married.'

'I believe he's serious,' Addison cried, and the tone of his voice set my heart racing.

Edith tried a laugh, but it refused to take. She took off her spectacles, then put them back on. Never had I seen her so flustered. 'You're not . . . are you—'

'I am. I'll marry you tomorrow if you'll have me.'

'I'll fly you to Las Vegas in the morning if that's of any help,' Addison said. 'I'll fly all of us there.'

For the first time since I'd met her, Edith blushed. 'I hardly think that's necessary.'

'Oh, I think it is.' Now Bill's voice had me blubbering.

Edith sputtered, feeling herself backed into a corner. 'If we go to Las Vegas, we won't get married. You'll wander off to gamble, or go fishing, and leave me looking the fool.'

'There's only one way to find out.' Bill's rejoinder had the quality of a dare.

Something in his steadfast manner convinced her, because Edith simply sat back and said, 'When do we leave?'

'We fly at dawn!' Addison thumped the table as Bill and Edith shared a kiss. 'I'll make the arrangements tonight. Or rather, Lillian will. Provided she doesn't mind putting in a little overtime.'

'For this, gladly.' I rose to my feet. 'But first, I have to powder my nose. I must look a fright.'

Edith and Bill hadn't heard a word we'd said. But Reynolds had rushed back over, his elbow at the ready. 'May I have the honor, Miss Frost?' At least someone was paying attention to me.

As he whisked me across the floor, he said, 'Good news, I trust? A happy occasion?'

'The happiest.'

I came to an abrupt halt, Reynolds briefly tugging my arm

before applying the brakes. If we were hieing ourselves to Las Vegas in the morning, that meant I'd be missing Kay and Ready's equally impromptu nuptials, also slated for the next day. Hardly the way to curry favor with the new queen of Hollywood. Kay would never forgive me. And I couldn't bring myself to care.

'Sorry,' I told Reynolds. 'Drive on.'

Edith and Bill, Kay and Ready. Every knot in sight being tied while I stayed at a loose end, facing the world solo. I checked my watch. Perhaps we had time to visit Club Bali for a nightcap and a number by Bruz Fletcher. I could request 'Drunk with Love' or something maudlin about soldiering on alone.

I opened the ladies' room door, set on my course of action. It might not be ideal given the joyous circumstances, but a sad song would definitely cheer me up.

AUTHOR'S NOTE

F irst, our heartfelt thanks to the usual suspects, namely Edith
Head's biographers, Paddy Calistro, the late David Chierichetti,
and Jay Jorgensen.

The inspiration for *Idle Gossip* was a casual purchase made
many years ago at Powell's City of Books in Portland, Oregon.
(Let that be a lesson: always browse in bookstores.) We have
no way of knowing how accurate *Hollywood Leg Man* (1950)
by Jaik Rosenstein is. But Rosenstein, who held the title position for Hedda Hopper, tells a good tale, and opened our eyes
to the machinery behind a successful gossip column. Hopper
and Louella Parsons each wrote their own books about their
careers, and George Eells's dual 1972 biography, *Hedda &
Louella*, remains informative. But the best way to appreciate the
signature style of each scribe is to read their columns. Lorna
Whitcomb's stage show is based on one Louella took on the
road in 1939, which really did feature Susan Hayward and
Ronald Reagan.

The saga of Heshie Rieger is drawn from a favorite piece of
Hollywood history. In July 1937, Irving 'Big Gangi' Cohen was
one of several men alleged to have murdered Cohen's longtime
friend Walter Sage, believed to be skimming money from a Mafia
operation in the Catskills. A mishap during the hit led Cohen to
suspect he too would be killed, and he fled New York, disappearing
from sight. Flash-forward to 1939, when two of Cohen's Murder,
Inc. cohorts took in the silver screen adaptation of the Clifford
Odets play, *Golden Boy*. The film starred William Holden and
Barbara Stanwyck, she of the flat backside and the best legs in
the business. Appearing as a ringside extra during one of the
film's fight scenes: Gangi Cohen, or as he was then known, Jack
Gordon. *Golden Boy* wasn't even Cohen's first movie appearance.
Murder, Inc. decided now they *did* have to bump off Cohen. But
before they could do the job, the New York DA's office caught
wind of his new racket. The happily married Gangi was arrested

at his apartment, a stone's throw from the Paramount lot. He proudly told the men who apprehended him that he'd played a police officer in the 1939 film *Streets of New York*. Cohen was acquitted of Sage's murder in a 1940 trial and returned to Los Angeles, his wife, and his film career. Over the next thirty-plus years he worked as an extra in dozens of movies and TV shows, including *It's a Wonderful Life* and *Some Like It Hot*, directed by Billy Wilder.

Bruz Fletcher held court at Club Bali on the Sunset Strip throughout the late 1930s, drawing many famous fans and appearing regularly in gossip columns. Sadly, Fletcher took his own life in February 1941 at age thirty-four. His song 'Drunk with Love' became an anthem in gay bars and clubs throughout Los Angeles. Writer Tyler Alpern has done much to keep Bruz's legacy alive, and Bruz's songs have been reimagined and recorded for future generations to enjoy.

Oleg Cassini – sorry, *Count* Oleg Cassini – did not remain at Paramount long; according to Cassini, he was fired in 1941 when he eloped with actress Gene Tierney against the wishes of Tierney's family and her bosses at 20th Century-Fox. He would continue to work as a costume designer, often on films starring Tierney, and became personal couturier to First Lady Jacqueline Kennedy as he created his own fashion empire. He lived quite a life, and *In My Own Fashion* is the autobiography to prove it.

Preston Sturges cut the ribbon on The Players in 1940, and it drained far too much of his money and energy before he finally shuttered the joint in 1953. (And yes, his helicopter scheme sounds a lot like the one hatched by Joel McCrea in Sturges's 1942 film *The Palm Beach Story*.) The Academy of Motion Picture Arts and Sciences made several attempts to create a museum over the decades, including the ill-fated attempt to take over the Trocadero; the Academy Museum of Motion Pictures finally opened its doors in September 2021. Rumors regarding Joan Crawford's, ahem, uncredited early screen appearances have long dogged the actress, even appearing in several biographies. No copies of these alleged films have ever surfaced.

The proposal that takes place at the end of *Idle Gossip* is consistent with how the actual one occurred: on the spur of the moment, in the company of a friend who chartered a plane to ferry

the happy couple to Las Vegas the following day. We trust that
Bill and Edith wouldn't object to us altering a few of the particulars. The surprise wedding, it should be noted, rated a tumble in
many gossip columns.

Cent 23.02.22